I0822644

Wish

a novel

Written by
Troy Wayne O'Neill
2001

Published Posthumously by
Lori Christmas Fagan O'Neill
2008

O'Neill, Troy Wayne, 1966-2007
Wish, a novel
ISBN 978-0-6152-3510-3

dedication

This first book is dedicated to my mother. Not just because she is my mother, but because she is my mom, always this wonderful amazing mom. And for that, I thank her for everything that was, is, and always will be. Also, for not killing us both as a field mouse pattered over her bare foot, a foot deep in the gas peddle of a black Corvette on a long tempting stretch of farm road...filled with the potholes that eventually led to this story.

Troy O'Neill,
Proud son of *Sharon Lee (Kemnitz) Tschetter*

forward

A young mother crossed the hardwood floor of her mid-western home with the gliding stride of any other set out to finish the simple task of brownies. Passing the hutch, she glanced to the black-and-white photograph of her seven-year-old son, laughingly pretending to be driving his father's red International pick-up, his string of teeth beaming between the half-moon of the steering wheel and the dashboard.

Humming, 'I see skies of blue, and trees of green,' she began pulling sugar and flour from the kitchen cupboards with her kinked yellow hair drawn back in a spotted bandana like lassoed heat lightening. Cautiously proud of her favorite dress, patterned with tiny bears exchanging Christmas gifts neatly wrapped in red and green, she tied on a protective apron and stood at the double sink waiting for the summoned water to warm, one finger trolling in its flow.

Her eyes were a pretty iceberg blue and capable of a transparent warmth when she unknowingly reminded her son of summer mornings, no matter the season, as she wrapped her arms around him each day before he stepped both on and off the school bus. But there was a problem. An enigma bigger than most can ever solve, and that very problem began its tricky trek across her retreating mind as the water began to steam over her reddening pink finger. It was then she heard the first reaping breath of a close whisper, giggling softly words in her brain. Her eyes floated up the kitchen window filled with the reflecting forest of willows that stood guard around her two-story home at the river's edge. Coming to her tiptoes, she craned her neck and leaned nearly against the glass, peering to the tip-tops of the trees where their twisted limbs spread seemingly wider as they eerily became her mind's puppeteer.

Unable to pull herself away, she clung to the sink's stainless edge, her jaw muscles wrinkling back as their mighty rain of words began hurling to her ears like axes.

"I am too pretty!" she fought back, "And it's not too early for my Christmas dress to be out of the trunk!" Mesmerized by the bark-armored beasts swaying in sync to the beat of the breeze, she balled her hands into tight fists at the end of her raising arms. "You all act so la-de-da, like you're conducting some wizard orchestra when these little winds wind you up in the afternoons! And you, Madge!" she pieced together from the last of her guts, poking the glass like a drill sergeant. "I'm sick of watching life pucker up year after year, crowning you with a new green do right on cue! Well I want a new do too!" she demanded, glaring at the seasoning willows as she tore free a lock of golden hair with a squall of hate bellowing from her throat. Between the thumb and forefinger of her extended arm, the uprooted hair spiraled free to the floor. Then with one backhanded swat, the oval tin of brownie mix slung end over end in the air, spattering across the oak floors like mud that took impressions of her stamping soles with a squish.

A wedge of light stabbed deep into the dank garage with the outline of a housewife plagued with bursts of uncontrollable screaming. Dragging power tools and paint from their appointed shelves, she kicked her way to an oil-stained crate the size of a child's coffin and flung it open. There was the tool. The screaming stopped.

The garage door chattered up with a knocking wobble and the braided cord was jerked from the guts of a green chainsaw. It first choked to life with a rattling howl, then exploded to one harmonic war-cry under the rule of her trigger finger. Marching half sideways, toting the weight of the gas-powered switchblade, she cried war to the willows and cupped one ear as if an out-voted part of her couldn't bear to listen. "Too early for Christmas, huh, Mulch? Well then, I guess the holidays will just have to come a little early!"

She squeezed the trigger and lunged. The saw's serrated tongue kicked back wild from Madge's waist with a high pitched zing showering tree's blood against tiny bears exchanging gifts neatly wrapped in red and green. She swung again. The saw stuck and bogged down, digging through the timber that began pleading by popping and cracking as its trunk narrowed. When her triceps began to quiver she cocked one foot out for leverage and let her mouth fall agape in a saw-muted scream as she tore into the tree that surrendered with a final spinal snap. The wavering tip of the willow leaned to the west then gained speed as it disappeared from the forest's canopy.

One by one, huddling high above the echo of a rampaging chainsaw, the willows that had offered shelter and shade to her family's humble home, fell. Some into the spider web of branch arms seemingly offered by their neighbors like trust lessons. Others lay strewn about the backyard with their crooked limbs naturally grown up and away from their torsos as if they'd died screaming.

Starved of its two-part purple juice, the saw's piercing bawl stuttered to a stop deep in the belly of a wounded willow. The mother shrieked to the dying machine, pumping the trigger, begging it. With one defeated swoop, the bandana was yanked free and her yellow hair slumped free to her shoulders like a nest of frayed wiring. Offering her arms to the sky, she spun in the backyard mud before falling to her knees. One hand covered her eyes as the other pressed into the smeared soil where her panting body began to sob in slight heaves.

As new light warmed the once shaded strips of earth, a twig snapped under the weight of size five tennis shoes. The near hysterical mother peeked through the envelope of her trembling fingers, realizing that she had not heard the school bus downshifting to her mailbox, nor its doors folding open and her son jumping free the way kids do. She did not see him lofting his baseball high in the air as he walked, picturing it never falling back to earth, the imagined crowd of seven-year-olds go crazy with cheer, their hero.

Avoiding eye contact, the plagued mother hinged a broken-down smile on her teared face and failed to catch a gasp as the onset of shame unfurled in her wintery eyes. Tighter and tighter the laced jaw of the mitt eclipsed the ball, as the boy's expression helplessly unraveled under a ripple of blond hair. He stood with his own limbs dangling, knowing immediately this to be far worse than the time the ceiling fan had threatened to fly their house to hell and back in August, or when all their laundry turned up some four miles down river and Mrs. Roberts ran flailing into her own kitchen wall thinking the entire town had drowned at her pump house.

Watching a blue jay fluttering over its cracked eggs, the mother winced and drained one arm into her apron producing a cigarette. Her son stared as she hinged it between her lips and lit it with the same hand in one awkward swoop. Still denying himself of breath, the boy stood fast as the first drag of cigarette crawled down his mother's throat, into the cave of horrors, then blasted from the barrels of her nose like a rocket launching to a planet where the trees don't whisper.

"Mom," the boy said hugging his mitt… "I wish I could make you better."

one

Despite their huge age difference, Cole Caffy and the Alaskan mornings have become close friends over the past twenty-six years. This, the morning of his sixty-fifth birthday, his knees remind him of the growing toll six-and-a-half decades collect without so much as asking, as do the deep and struggling breaths he draws now jogging down Patch Road. This special road leads back to his special house where he thankfully slows to a walk in its circular driveway. The garage is part of this circle and bends with it in perfect silhouette with white slatted doors at either end allowing him simply to drive in one and continue through the other when leaving.

Cole designed this brake-light-illuminating house with classically rich pole-vaulting lines creating an imaginative reach for its steel torso. He has indeed built much in his life, a life well spent as a structural engineer for what seems to him as long as there have, in fact, been mornings in Alaska. Bridges, big beautiful bridges, carefully drawn and patiently constructed for trains, people, cars and even cattle at one point. But by far one of the most locally talked about was this, his own home. Built to span the mighty Spring Creek, all of about sixty feet from shore to shore, the home was constructed of steel and rivets like any other single span bridge. Its floor, made of thick glass, allowed Cole to easily keep tabs on the mountain's sweat in the spring, spawning salmon in fall, and the occasional lost log from the mill up stream. The boys up there got sloppy every so often and lost one, cheaper to let it go than use the men and machines to retrieve its brown spiraled meat. This always pissed Cole off, the lack of responsibility, not to mention the waste.

The main body of the bridge was dedicated to the living room, announced by white French doors standing open at each end. Pillow-soft furniture finished in leather rested on the transparent floors under vaulted ceilings that left fat beams of well-varnished Douglas fir shooting overhead. The rest of the home completed in red brick spilt neatly out either side of the bridge as its split-level legs. The oval kitchen, dining room and circular garage, being on the north side of the river, left two mahogany paneled bedrooms below a den filled with photos and a classic James Bond poster showing a pistol wheeling Sean Connery at his best.

The eight dining room chairs were each very different, reflecting their individual time period. At the head of the table sat a brass framed high back from the turn of the century farmlands of upstate New York. To its left a teak captain's chair used aboard the tug boat *Hallelujah* during the late eighteen hundreds working mainly from the port of Halifax distributing southern tobacco and English bourbon to men who knew the sea. Opposite, his latest, a box seat taken from the Seattle King Dome before its destruction early in the year two-thousand. Famous people cheered from this seat spilling expensive champagne and their naughty little secrets behind sudden financial windfalls. All were equally interesting to the unique tables' guests and made for fine conversation. Bordering the two longest walls of the dining room were gray ash wood pews rescued from a Russian Orthodox Church before being flooded in lieu of the Flariken Hydroelectric Dam's construction in nineteen sixty six. Two months after their removal the church was only a painted spire stabbing through the water like a drowning unicorn.

As he would freely tell others, Cole had always harbored a great respect for water. But truth be told it damn well scared him. When he was nine years old he and a few other local kids were swinging on an already tattered rope over the Chimney River just upstream from Provo, Utah. They had decided to take a quick detour after Sunday school, done on a dare basis as they were dressed in their best. One of the dumber of the clan decided to cut through the braided line with a freshly stolen pocketknife. The rope failed, leaving Cole and Mary plunging helplessly into the muddy water winding toward the Great Salt Lake.

The frayed rope made short order of looping its way around Mary Pearson's legs and finally, her neck. Unable to swim any longer she started down river with its smothering flow. Under now, Cole dove between air sucking retreats to find her but could see nothing through the whirl of red murk. He yelled for the others to grab the far end of the rope and pull. Sunday ties on fine young lads submerged, screams from pretty red and yellow dresses with matching muddy shoes at the river's edge.

Mary Pearson died that day. The official cause of death was drowning. But a well-kept secret between Mary's parents, the town coroner and Cole's father was the fact that she had been strangled by the pulling of the rope. Cole's father never found the heart to tell this to his son.

Some twenty years later a bridge was constructed just up stream. It was christened Mary's Bridge by its young designer, a safe way to cross the Chimney River.

Showered and looking for the truck keys after his morning run, Cole crossed the bridge or his 'living room,' found them hiding in plain sight atop one of the copper countertops in the kitchen and headed for the garage. Along his way, a mirror told him his tie needed to go left then he'd look right. He saw the map of wrinkles around his eyes revealing sixty-five years of life like the age rings of a downed spruce. He then decided all mirrors were useless as he checked his rear view to see the garage door closing behind him.

The Range Rover should have known the way to downtown Anchorage by now, though it still needed its five, and at swervish times, ten fingered hints. To Cole, Patch Road was more of an obstacle course than a road really, basic training for those with sway bar hips and die-cast hearts. Potholes, littering the dying pavement like shuddering minefields, pounded Cole's lengthy body six days a week weaving a course through this maze of "shit holes" as he fondly referred to them. First left, then far left, right, more right, then over to the oncoming lane the black Rover swung wide, stirring the ditch, trying to avoid the Great Bastard Hole of Them All. More of a trench really, slithering deep side to side as if a dinosaur's tail had been resurrected by those with tiny fine brushes and an eye for the past. Cole saw it, and braced for the impact. Impossible to avoid it entirely, he tried to strike the least damaging part of the great fatherless void. The Rover took it with a pounding and then another as the rear tires were scolded. Cole's leather gloves ground at the steering wheel, "Fix the son of a bitches!" But no one heard…again.

As the Rover struggled to find smooth road, Cole saw the real enemy. One of the Aurora logging trucks bearing down Patch Road ahead of him was the uncaring cause of the "pots" as the handful of locals called them. Cole managed a mute yet loud finger for its driver.

His anger simmered to a boil when he thought of Clark Owens, the self-justifying runt of a man who owned the Aurora Logging Company. Left with only his lamb-chop sideburns and the grumbling hate for those who hated Elvis, Owens would only dare spend his cold cash on hot weeklong getaways, caring little about crumbling Patch Road or anything else but Marlin fishing for that matter.

Refusing to shout the tickertape of four letter words crossing his mind, Cole watched as the focus of his anger disappeared from the vibrating horizon of his rearview mirror.

A fading bumper sticker - *Engineers do it right the first time* - crookedly guarded Cole's parking space.

Expecting a short subdued last day, the elevator craned him to the fourteenth floor. A familiar mundane tone signaled its arrival at the offices of *Here to There Engineering* as the stainless steel doors rolled away from one another on ball bearings slippery with a haze of fine grease. Expecting his forest green carpet dotted with salmon flake to be stretched out quietly sleeping across the office floor, Cole's face reeled back, finding instead a circus rink of bodies twirling with books and boxes about the reception area, the squeal of tape guns and ruffle of wrapping paper crackling in his ears like a spring storm. Anna, his loyal, yet ever dyslexic secretary of nine years, spun center stream of the heaping incoming and outgoing office goods. Over Cole's grief for his personally hand picked carpet being suffocated by cardboard, mounding books, and the occasional piece of office furniture, came the alluring halo of a foreign perfume that drove him to realize how Leonardo DaVinci's mind must have seen the nape of a woman's neck. With his nose gently drinking the air, Cole recognized some of the more sloppily packed boxes as his own, but seeing the name "Poland" smeared across the bubble wrap snuggling a small bronze statue of a woman, answered any and all of his questions immediately.

"Behind you sir."

Cole turned to see a man passing with an armload of draftings swallowed by cardboard cylinders with chrome caps as he read *Mountain Movers* embroidered under a group of snow topped peaks from the man's blue denim shirt. Cole looked to Anna, allowing his thatch eyebrows to bend in the form of a question.

"She's here early, Cole," she noted, her cinnamon voice floating in the direction of his office.

"That's apparent. How 'bout Philip?"

"Yes. He's been growling on the phone, but he's in."

With a soft knock, he entered his partner's office of over twenty-five years as the last traces of perfume were regrettably replaced by the rich smell of leather-bound books and the cherry bookcases they resided in. Philip Norran, who discovered hair in his shower drain some six years ago, now sat in his chair, one hand atop his shiny head, the other holding the telephone's receiver to an ear ironically filled with hair. He aimed a stumpy finger to the red leather wing chair in front of his cluttered desk. Cole sat crossing his legs, straightening the handsome black pleats. He trained his gray-blue eyes on the metal-framed picture atop Philip's desk taken nearly a quarter-century earlier. Two men holding shovels alongside the Battle River, smiled with their ties loosened...Ground Breaking Day. Cole remembered that day, remembered them all. Posing beside it was an identical photo captured in the same stylish aluminum frame. The only difference between the two photos was the completed red steel bridge rising in the air behind them in the second. Looking at the photographs one might think they were magicians just pulling bridges out of thin air.

His thoughts of those days flashed away as Philip said, "Yes, thank you, you'll have the aerial photos in the morning. Anna will get them to you...okay...you bet." The phone bounced back in its cradle.

"Cole! How the hell did twenty-six years get by us?" Philip asked in a boisterous voice.

"Twenty-six? Hell, I'm looking around for sixty-five, must've dropped the damn things somewhere. There's a bottle of Scotch older than the both of us in it for you though if you happen across them." Cole said, forcing a grin from a long strong face the color of desert.

"You never lie, Caffy, but two weeks ago you tried your hand at it." Philip scowled, peering over his thin wire-framed glasses like an all-knowing owl.

"Oh, was I telling you about a girl from Alabama and a tube of hand lotion?" Cole joked. "Because I swear it's true, she really did! God only knows how, but it didn't even get in those pretty crossed eyes of hers. You really gotta' wonder what she's doing nowadays don't ya?"

"Uh, no, Cole, we really don't," Phillip said grinning as he pieced the image. "It was when we were driving to Seward to inspect the city bridge after that little tremor that shook everybody up down there. The conversation led to retirement. You said you were looking forward to what it might bring. 'An overdue change of seasons,' I believe were the words you so carefully chose," Philip recalled, resting his case.

Cole leaned back in the leather chair and put his hands behind his head, remembering. "I don't think I was lying to you then, Philip. But if I repeated those words now, maybe," he admitted.

"Do you remember when we discovered that bad foundation on the Canadian Pass Bridge, Cole? I said quit. Quit now and pass that son-of-a-bitch to another firm before it sinks clear to China. You said get excited about it! Well, Cole…get excited about retirement! Hell, you're not dying on us, are you? Keep building your bridges. Not just another stretch of steel that some trucker weaves across trying to get a peek at the river below, but personal bridges, bridges in your own life. Cole, I know how much of yourself you've poured into this work. Hell, it was near all of it. And that's only the time that I can account for you sitting here glued to the drawing board. God only knows how many more hours you've spent scratching your head over projects on your own time. And what was that little Seattle computer company you started investing in a couple of decades ago? Micro something or other? Oh, yeah, MicroHard. In other words, poor ol' Caffy, I know just how rich you really are," Philip said lowering his voice but raising a brow, shaking his round head as he leaned forward intertwining his fingers atop his desk. "Listen. What I'm trying to tell you, Cole, is…live. Unwind yourself from your drafting table, and see what else is out there. Toss Alka

Seltzer to the seagulls. Go to a drive-in with a carload of hookers. Fall in love. Jog on the Great Wall of China, or drive a motorcycle across India. Whatever blows your hair back…but live, Cole. You, far more than most, have earned it."

Inhaling, Cole waited to let it out and looked back to the men with shovels standing on Philip's desk. Without making eye contact he stood, started for the door and politely said, "Certainly I could have done without the hurry of the place today."

"Poland's anxious, Crazy Man Who Lives On a Bridge, so were you."

Cole turned to find the remains of his own office, stopping to say, "You've been a good friend for these years, Philip. Thank you."

With a humbled smile, Philip replied, "The Canadian Pass Bridge, Cole…it's beautiful."

Trekking the reception area, Cole spotted an unsmothered patch of his hand-picked carpet. For a moment, he was tempted to scurry and claim it with a victorious pose, fists curled high about the humming florescent skies, neck craned, steel eyes distantly fixed as if judging the mighty leap to the next land he would soon conquer. But the *Mountain Movers* came and went heaving their goods in and out like uncaring thieves with an idle whistle under their growing breath. Clearing his throat for a raspy doorbell, Cole awkwardly peeked through his own partially opened door. Peeking right back at him was Bridget Poland, the new partner, producing a smile that Cole was convinced had been chosen just for him. His mouth went dry as if someone pulled the plug under his speechless tongue and his brows pushed back and off to the side. She was beautiful.

Bridget Poland stood, making her way from behind Cole's mahogany desk without saying a word. Cole said nothing as well but for different reasons, he'd forgotten English. She WAS beautiful, and coming closer with that unwavering smile, approaching. She leaned in close and softly took his hand. A little on her toes now, she leaned up his long six foot-two-inch frame, placing her other hand on his arm to steady herself. The halo of perfume reached him an instant before she did. Caught off guard, his eyes widened and reflexed to the window. Her lips reached his cheek, wet with red. Time stopped, but only for a second or two, ironic. For that moment all the shit in the world strewn about the office wouldn't have mattered. Hell, she could have flung his desk out the window and burned his handmade drafting table for all he could have cared.

As Bridget's suede high heels sank lightly in the carpet accepting their curvy cargo, she paused long enough to poke at Cole's golden tiepin. "My, what a handsome little bridge." Unknowingly leaving Cole stammering for words, she strolled a few paces back towards his desk and leisurely turned to say, "Happy Birthday, Mr. Caffy."

Still under siege by her breathtaking perfume, Cole's cheeks felt flush as he fumbled for a response. It had been some time since he had felt any affection from the opposite sex. (Brij'-et) the opposite sex - Woman possessing all that is needed to lure male species into tee-pee, cave, or across active minefield with wild leap and bound motion. See also: magnificent, desirable, seductive…want. Those words fell short the true meaning of her hourglass hips wrapped tightly in a gray dress suit oh so innocently brushed open to one side, letting her long tan legs escape unsheathed to the floor. Healthy black hair falling well beyond her firm shoulders, her amber skin from a Swiss commercial, needing to be touched. Cole, pissed with himself for not being a younger man.

"Respond, Cole! Respond now!" his racing mind warned, as he tried to compose himself by nervously tapping his thumb and forefinger together at his side, creating a laughing upside down 'ok' sign. "Yes…yes, thank you. I was born on this day, but many days ago. It's so nice to place a figure with the lovely voice I know from the phone, and might I say they're perfect for each other."

"What a wonderful thing to say," Bridget said sliding her placid eyes to the window. "You'll surely miss this, won't you? My god, you can see around the world from here. I'm surprised you've managed to work with a distraction like this lurking over your shoulder all day."

With a subtle grin, Cole realized that if she had been part of this view his entire career would have been a flop! Her left hip rested against the cherry window ledge as she rolled her completely blue eyes over the powerful mountain landscape, her silhouette perfect against the great Alaskan Range. Like a ten year old finding a Playboy, a surge of lust rushed through Cole for the first time in years, tickling just under his flat belly as his thoughts raced.

Since she greeted me with a Happy Birthday kiss, maybe I should welcome her to the new job by throwing her on what's left of my desk and make passionate love to her for hours and hours. Then shake hands and wish her good fortune in her career. Cole thought probably not. Maybe at the next meeting.

"Cole, this is wonderful," she said turning to a glass case, housing a bridge made of toothpicks. The now fragile toothpicks, stuck together with yellowing glue, formed a crossing designed by Cole in the eleventh grade. He'd received an "A" for his work and a grown-ups handshake. A real atta boy considering the short-fused teacher was Mr. Williams whose handlebar mustache spiraled like split dandelion stems in warm water. That had been the final straw for his decision to enter engineering school so he had well guarded this first bridge and its glass case that prevented dust and curious fingers from reaching it, precisely made by his father while Cole was busy scattering from class to class down at Berkley. This had become all the more meaningful after his father, with a stiff upper lip, one day told Cole carefully chosen bits and pieces of what his doctor's thoughts were. The bridge in its prime withstood the weight of three high school architecture books. As it was tested, the straining toothpicks gave way with a spine-snapping crack as the fourth was slowly added. Cole's face lit with pride as Mr. Williams pronounced between the dandelion stems to the entire class that there just might be a future bridge builder amongst them after all.

"This bridge was my first, and my best in some ways, Bridget," said Cole.

Brilliantly smiling, she displayed straight white teeth like a string of tapered pearls. "Call me Bridge."

For Cole, that was the book that broke the bridge's back. Far from being a stupid man, he lived in reality. Although knowing he would stand a better chance of surviving a screaming plummet from fourteen floors, surprising the living shit out of his Rover, than her being attracted to him, he found himself hopelessly slipping from character and feeling like he was back in the eleventh grade all over again. He realized he was about to flirt for the first time in nearly ten years, his tie salmon colored with the dark green spots, a little to the left. Searching for the perfect words he said, "It's a perfect name. And if I were a hundred years younger, 'Bridge,' this would be where I'd say you were perfect for me!"

Without ever knowing it, Bridget kicked Cole in the feelings by dismissing his comment with a youthful laugh. She turned for the desk, with no hint of interest in any way. Not even a band-aid for his 'hundred years younger' remark to make him feel he was still worth the breath he was holding. As Cole humbly turned to leave, he realized the eleventh grade had been left well behind, forcing him back to reality, that reality he lived in so well. Too well.

A knock from the door spared him further self-pity and he turned to see a confused *Mountain Mover* looking to Bridget for directions with an antique floor lamp that had bugs all over it. Wearing a loose tank top and faded jeans, the mover looked to Bridget with a grin carving back in his brawny cheeks, long blond hair splitting over his lean shoulders that said he'd been in the moving biz for some time. Appearing as though he had been moonlighting as some sort of male dancer, Cole already hated him and the hint of tanning-bed glowing along his muscular arms. As any sane man would, the mover was taken by the sight of Bridget and offered a bit of a pose, holding the lamp as though he'd designed the damn thing for her.

"Oh, just behind the desk for now is fine," said Bridget smoothly.

Cole noticed the smoothly part and began to speak just to speak. The mover set the lamp behind the desk and Bridget's eyes followed the tan shoulders. Cole clumsily asked if she had chosen a home yet or if she would be renting for a time. There was no reply. "Would you plug the lamp in for me?" she asked the chiseled mover. As he knelt to search for the outlet, her eyes followed this too, inspecting the work. Cole noticing her noticing the mover and being aware of himself still noticing Bridget was all too much. He suddenly felt all of that one-hundred-years old, and being ignored thrown in with it made his shoulders sag.

"Well, Bridge," said Cole briskly, "think I'll take my 'bridge' and head back out to the south thirty. Out to pasture you might say."

With her eyes unknowingly taunting him she said, "Oh yes, I've heard so much about your home, and of course saw it in the article. I can't lie to you, Mr. Caffy. I only took this job in hopes of getting a tour," she said, highlighting those blue eyes with an illuminating smile.

"Yes, yes, of course, but after you've had time to settle in here."

Cole watched as the Mover God went for the door. Bridget's cool eyes helped the man get there. Anxious to be out of the office, Cole picked up the glass-encased bridge and glanced from the corners of his eyes at the elevated view of Alaska for the last time. Passing Bridget on the way to the door, he reminded her she had his home number for any future questions and it would never be a bother.

Again, Cole felt the warmth of her hand as they shook, but this time refused any youthful daydreams to leak into his old mind. Fumbling for words, he quickly said, "Good luck in your career, and I'm certain we'll run into one another again."

"Well, yes, as a matter of fact and soon! Have you forgotten your own party tonight?" she asked, hinging her black hair behind the cuff of an ear with a row of manicured nails.

"Nooo, Nooo, and you'll be there I assume?"

Tilting her head with another smile he thought was made just for him she said, "Of course, a chance to drink with a mentor? Who would miss that?"

She escorted Cole from no longer his office to the busy reception area. Making his way to the elevator doors, he poked at the round white button "G" and winked at Anna, buried up to her long nails in cardboard. Waiting, he overheard Bridget ask the muscular longhaired fella if he'd be so kind as to start moving Cole's desk out of 'her' office. Furiously, he punched at the button and listened with satisfaction as it dinged open. Another mover rolled out a new desk on a flatbed dolly. The squat-heavy mover eyed Cole and playfully said, "Out with the old and in with the new, huh?" He meant nothing personal by this, however it was not the last words Cole had hoped to hear in this place of twenty-six years.

Finding his Rover patiently waiting right where he'd left it, Cole retired the tattered bumper sticker from the cement wall with one quick ceremonial jerk. 'Out with the old, my ass!' He placed the toothpick bridge carefully in the passenger seat of the Rover and snugged its belt for the bouncy ride home.

After rattling the last Tic-Tac from its see-through cage, Cole headed north of Anchorage for twelve flat valley miles, then right on to Patch Road for another six winding mountain miles. As there were only a handful of scarce residences, and the majority of those being summer dwellers, Cole was rarely given the chance to use his perfected one-handed driving wave, aside from his one fingered salute reserved for the logging trucks. Landmarks told Cole and the Rover where the worst of the black potholes lay, such as here at the Temple's turnoff. Again the Rover won the battle, but not without telling Cole all about it.

Swearing under his wintergreen breath, he reached his own drive on the left. The mailman, with a casual wave, signaled with a free arm that the mail had arrived. "No shit, and all this time I thought you were the plumber," Cole muttered, flashing his perfected one hand wave, backing it up with a hollow smile.

The mail van pulled away and Cole collected the contents from the one-armed box, then coasted down the gravel driveway across the south thirty. The 'south thirty' was actually thirty-four acres of open range following the valley's hinting slope to Spring Creek where the home spanned over it as if a giant cowgirl with brick boots were straddling the river, lifting her girdered garter so as not to dunk its pretty red lace while she peed. Gravel turned to cement at the circular driveway, where Cole heard the bubbling sounds of river filling the background as he stepped from the Rover.

He managed today's mail atop the glass case through the kitchen door. Cradling the bridge, he rested it at its new home atop the long copper top dining table. His eyes pinched shut as he discovered the first real casualty from the ruthless potholes. The center of Cole's toothpick bridge lay fallen in an M to the Chimney River below as if it were sipping from the airbrushed water.

Too upset to be anymore upset, he just remained quiet for a moment, looking to the floor with his fists resting on the back of an antique warden's chair from Utah's State Penitentiary. Struggling to remind himself it could be repaired, Cole feared he'd discovered his first puttering job.

Soaking it all in, he reached for the mail and took it with him to the living room while he shed the tie that had miraculously gone to the left again. He dropped into the huge leather chair he'd found in a magazine ad for a Colorado ski resort; advertising an attractive young woman with steaming cup, snuggled up close to a fireplace after a bright sunny day on the hill, her life obviously perfect.

Detailed mechanical drawings of bridges hung in teak and alder frames throughout the living room, including the very bridge he'd chosen to hang them in, a collection of Cole's work. He was a little uneasy about showing them in such an egotistical manner, but then realized he was the one who lived there and rarely entertained, so to hell with it. He simply liked to sit over the river and admire his past work. Even when the occasional guests visited, they paid the draftings little attention due to the immediate shock of seeing a river flowing under their toes. Their eyes would float with Spring Creek some five-hundred feet to see it swallowed up by a stony-edged waterfall, signaling the end of his property. Tall stands of spruce kept a seasonal eye on the cold mountain run-off which instinctively searched for lower ground, where it surrendered to thirsty clouds in the shape of whatever your mind's eye might see them as, just to start all over again…nature's ski lift.

In May of ninety-four the water swelled dramatically under Cole's home from unseasonably warm temperatures needling at the mountain's icy helmets. Philip and a nervous Cole spent an afternoon sipping Scotch and making half-drunken bets as to just how high the water would rise. The following morning, severely hung over, Philip won the bet as the river peaked where he predicted before quickly receding that night due to a heavy frost.

Cole exhaled and began the task of sorting junk mail from really junky mail. It seemed that anything he actually cared about came by way of the office. Home mail was simply a task. First a catalogue of some crap or other, bills, then a letter wanting to know if he would like to renew something he never had in the first place. He thought to keep digging in hopes of finding a career renewal flyer, but only a handsome little envelope with a colorful rainbow dashing in a customary arch like a day-glow barbell weighted with pots of gold came last. He opened it to discover a new form of junk mail, one that actually expected him to take time out of his life before discovering it was junk mail. But for the effort of the delightful rainbow, he began to read.

CONGRATULATIONS

You have been chosen for the ability to WISH.
Go on give it a try, but let's be careful.
One doesn't want to hurt anyone.

Don't get excited about saving the world, curing cancer,
or flying over small villages to make yourself a legend.
This is not that.
Go on about your life as you see fit.
The reason you were chosen is because you're you.
Do not abuse this, as it is intended for you only.
Some tolerances will be made while you get
your wishing legs.
You'll see in the long run that...

Cole trailed off; somebody was always out for a buck somewhere, somehow. He didn't see the somehow, but felt it coming. Far from the mood to waste time, he lost interest with it all and stood hovering over the river in his untucked Levi's shirt. His legs opened and closed as he turned and crossed the glass floor, watching red steel beams pass under him to the kitchen. Two pieces of mail passed muster: a bill and a flyer excited about winter snow removal equipment. He slid them across the copper counter top stopping at the antique phone, the rest a treasure for the garbage men.

The long warm days of summer to the bite of winter normally took only two weeks, although Alaskans still affectionately called it fall. Spring was wonderful. All but winter ended reliably. Cole Caffy's life too was changing seasons he thought, as he stood at the window sipping hot coffee to warm his insides. This he knew and accepted. But what would it be? Spring to summer? Summer to fall? Today, especially, he saw his own leaves losing color, fading from a vibrant mixture of red and deep green, to a vein exposing frail brown. This told him fall to a bleak and permanent winter.

He didn't expect to, or want to, live forever. He had worked, and worked hard. This was how success happened, something drug dealers and inheritance folk just didn't seem to get. He was taught this at a young age and was smart enough to grasp that knowledge for everything it was worth. With a brief scan of the river, he realized he was his father, not an overly strong man, however he hoped he was a good man. Ben Caffy had seen to his only son growing up properly, and not the properly one might envision. Cole was immediately taught what money could do and was well tutored in its ugly side effects. Aside from buying a nice home, it could also destroy a person and others with the same unfortunate last name. "Cole, never wake up and notice your friends are shallow and empty, caring more about how they look than the color of the air they breathe, and God only knows what keeps their marriages together, whichever one they're on." The lesson was clear, be smart enough not just to know the difference, but to avoid these things all together. "You may have a wife one day, son, love her. If there are children, love them. Work, but don't lose sight, the love of money can be the root of evil. Work for more of a reason than just supporting yourself, Cole. Work at what you love if you are fortunate enough to. Make that happen or you'll just be another person sitting in traffic someday convincing yourself it's everyone else's fault."

Ben's son did succeed in his work, managing to never step on anyone, hurt their feelings, or even sell something to someone they didn't need just to make a buck. In nineteen seventy-seven Ben Caffy passed away after the doctors informed Cole his father was in no pain and would go peacefully sometime that evening…they were right about it being that evening anyway. Cole had never spoken of that thorny night to anyone. He also had never spoken of his mother. Anyone that ever really knew Cole understood if there was something to be said that mattered, he would say it. In the end, all that mattered was that Cole, like his father, never took life for something it was not. He was honest with others, but most importantly, he was honest with himself.

Cole's retirement party was set for seven o'clock. However, he secretly wasn't looking forward to it. All of this and that chatter over his career, reminding him that it was all behind him now instead of ahead, where he preferred it to be. Philip was indeed a good friend, so if not for any other reason, he would play the part for him. This was probably a good thing, the alternative to watching his leaf suck dry around its veins like fall on time-lapse.

From his bedroom closet, he found a friendlier tie to match a thin gray scarf that still carried cologne from the last time it stepped out and to keep the cold from getting in, he draped a long black trench coat around his lean frame.

His thick salt and pepper hair never failed him, staying on top of his head and not slipping into his ears or insulating his back. Although his interests never strayed from work much, he'd dated but in spurts. Women regrettably seemed to find other pastures, when his mistress 'work' sooner or later reared her flawlessly drafted head; home late, fingers smelling of charcoal, her rice paper picture rolled and tucked under his arm as if escorting.

Cole straightened his tie one last time as he thought about marriage. He had lived with a woman at one point for almost two years. She had straight yellow hair and small feet, liked Saturdays, and collected something from every restaurant table she and Cole had ever eaten at: spoons, salt shakers, Sweet and Low. Candles were the best. Sharon Kemnitz, who owned a floral shop in Berkley, California, called *Stop and Smell the Roses*, lived with Cole in the small two-room apartment above the shop. Cole commuted nearly thirty miles to work every day, dodging in and out of traffic on the torn black seat of his motorcycle. Sharon later told a friend he was the best thing she never had. On their last Saturday together, he admitted to being better at building bridges than relationships and apologized for his failure to treat a wonderful person wonderfully. Cole sold his orange Honda 350 and moved to Anchorage, Alaska four days later with a pasta fork from *Antonio's*, their first date.

Plucking a rose from his bedside stand, he smelled it, remembering Sharon. He tore off the stem and placed the rose in his lapel.

Six weeks had passed when Sharon received an order for a dozen of her best roses and was asked if she would be kind enough to pick the color. The person on the phone said to write only "I will miss you" on the card, paid for them, and said to have them sent to 111 East Connelly Avenue. By the time Sharon realized she was writing down her own address, the phone fell silent.

A regrettable thought had been slowly clawing up Cole's spine, using his toothy backbone for a ladder to look his conscience straight in the eye as he aimed the Rover for downtown. Will I be desperately alone now with the absence of work, or am I about to discover a huge error far too late? Is love for another what life is or *was* really about? Will I run from this problem back to the drug of work vowing never to retire, and die one late night while staring at the first of my bridges I'll never cross? Or shit, will ....

These thoughts, a monkey clinging to the back of Cole's aging skull, gave him a headache as he began the ritual dodging of the potholes. Bouncing first left, far left, right then far right, then way the hell over into the oncoming lane to everything but miss the final great gouge.

His eyes landed on one of the Aurora logging trucks racing straight at him from the smoking gates of hell, the dull red monster forcing the little black Rover to retreat wildly back to the right. Cole felt the gust of the semi blowing inches from his window. He clinched his buttocks and rose from the seat just as the Rover struck the great hole dead on, throwing the entire world up slapping his ass in mid air, hearing pieces of broken pavement from the pothole shooting into the Rover's own ass like a drug deal gone bad.

"DIE! DIE YOU WORTHLESS FUCKING POTHOLES!" Cole screamed, as he regained control over road and Rover. Left half shaken and full of rage, doing his best to collect himself, he slid back in the soft British leather. A childish embarrassment wrapped around him, finding that somehow through the ordeal he'd been given a wedgie, not just an unfortunate misplacing of underwear, but an honest to goodness rubber band tight, ass flossing wedgie. With one hand barely on the wheel and the other digging at his shorts, the Range Rover was left thinking they must be about to encounter another pothole field dodging right, then hard left, slightly back to the right, but the Rover saw nothing, remember, it's a car. Feeling the blood flow to his legs again, Cole managed both hands to the wheel. Now with a bit of a chuckle in his throat he patted the Rover's black dash and calmly said aloud, "I just *wish* the potholes would go away."

Cole pulled his Range Rover into a white-bordered slot in front of the Fifth Avenue Theater in downtown Anchor-town. He looked across the street and upward to see his office window where he knew the view oh so well. A dull shine of light still glowed in his old square pane of glass as though someone was reading Alaska's tallest building a bedtime story, then told to count supermen jumping over itself in a single bound to fall fast asleep. Assuming someone forgot to hit the switch, he frowned and walked away to the theater's entrance seeing his own breath. Preparing for the long evening, he chose a smile that might possibly last for the three or four hours looming ahead. Pulling the heavy door toward him, he tapped the snow from his dress shoes and saw the row of warm lights lining the mountain muraled walls of the lobby like a runway to the belly of the theater.

Expecting fifteen, he entered the theater's great room discovering more than fifty people who began standing as each discovered his arrival. A great applause mixed with cheers left him in a rare moment of awe. He found Philip's smiling eyes amongst the crowd and was certain to have found the guilty party for the echoing hoots and howls. Anna, doing her part, guided Cole, the retiring birthday boy, to his assigned seat center of it all. He surrendered his arms to the air with a shocked and thankful smile. Anna's arms shot around him and she squeezed. She has always liked her boss Mr. Caffy. And so does Brett, her now twenty-two year old son who attends forestry school down in Juneau. It was the profit sharing check that Cole left on Anna's desk after hours that paid for his tuition…to the penny. When Anna discovered it, she whispered to herself, "But there is no profit sharing." Brett was set to graduate in the spring.

Letting go any thoughts of this night being droll, Cole looked about the momentous room with its red velvet walls and mahogany pillars as a deafening silence suddenly replaced the loud cheering. A glass of cabernet was slid into his hand as busy bodies began moving cleverly about the theater's room, forming a pre-planned line some thirty feet long. Then, with a glass in every free hand, they were raised in unison constructing a spectacular crystal single span bridge with its two shining load towers high in the air half filled with a ballast of red wine. This bridge of Philip's design, a last gift for his friend and partner, was beautiful. Cole slowly raised his own glass as well, the wine within gently rippling under the wake of his pulse.

"It even has a glass bottom, Cole, just like yours," Anna proudly pointed out.

As Cole sat fixated, seeing the faces of the dear friends and coworkers from over two decades, Philip spoke.

"Cole, you have built bridges that will stand for many years, and friendships that will stand for an eternity. You have always had a purpose in this life, and you always will. That purpose you do well, it is just simply you being you. Happy Birthday, my friend!"

With a sharp, "HEAR, HEAR," from Anna, the bridge slowly rose in a salute and began to lose its form on the way to toasting lips. A dam upstream behind Cole's light blue eyes gave way as he again raised his own wine, drinking in the moment, knowing this would certainly never be forgotten. "I've been so fortunate," he whispered.

Anna strayed from the pack, quietly hugging him again. Her ear on his tie, she said, "This one is from Brett."

Caterers spilled in from side doors carrying everything from prime rib and sweet potatoes to sweet tarts and black forest cake. Glasses were never empty. The sound of laughter and back slaps echoed from the top of the thirty-foot ceilings as each person visiting Cole's table left their own traces of cologne and perfume triggering thoughts of Bridget and those red lips of hers slowly saying, "Who would miss that?" Inquiring, he found she was the culprit who left the office lights on and was still using them. Eager was one thing, but this seemed a bit much. *Maybe it's all part of the plan, Cole thought to himself. She'll be the last one here. Yes, she'll be wheeled in by the caterers crouched in a six-tiered birthday cake, leaping from it wearing her own birthday suit, just for me. Then he thought probably not, maybe at the next meeting.*

Cole had to snicker a little at himself, thinking it would be the greatest of all gifts and maybe he should have dropped a hint to Philip, but then pictured his balding fifty-six-year-old partner misinterpreting his over head roping motion to mean he'd always dreamed of being a cowboy, and instead getting him a pony.

The banging on a thin glass full of red port with a fork brought Cole back from the magical land of brunettes jumping from over-sized cakes, to Philip asking for everyone's attention.

"Please, Please, everybody, I think it may be time for a word from the old engineer himself, what do you think?" Ordered by cheer and applause, Cole hesitantly climbed to his feet and unfurled a pleasant smile as he searched for words. The room grew quiet again, all eyes on his and the hounds-tooth jacket he'd worn twice now. He swallowed, and looked to one of the few jealousies he was guilty of having in life, Philip and his wife of twenty-nine delightful years of marriage. Caroline, a woman who once captained her twenty-four foot sailboat, 'Woe-is-me,' from San Francisco through the Panama Canal then on to the Gulf of Mexico, alone.

Then Cole glanced to Morris Hays, a man who once carried him through three feet of snow for over a mile to get his broken wing to the emergency room after taking a nasty fall while surveying a remote creek in Denali National Park back in eighty-eight. This, with Anna simply beaming as she sat beside him, perched for his every word, gave Cole exactly the tools he'd been searching for to tune up his 'Please don't let me retire because I'm afraid to death of life after bridges' speech.

"First of all, thank you would never cover tonight. I want each of you here to know what this means to me, so I'll try to describe it for you. The things I'll miss about work are not what most of you might think. Do you all see Philip and Caroline there? We can't see this because of these long white tablecloths, but trust me, under there on Philip's leg, you'll find Caroline's hand. You see I know this because I know them. That's how they are, and always will be. I'll admit I've even been envious of what they have at times. You all see Morris hiding back there. Well, he'd give you the shirt off of his back, and tie it around you in the middle of a snowstorm to boot. I know this because he did it. He did it for me! And then there's Anna here," Cole said proudly stretching a grin at her, watching her dimples poke even deeper into their blushing cheeks. "You see, I happen to know she's the greatest mother I've ever met, or for that matter, ever will. I suspect her son Brett knows this as well. This, this right here is what I'll miss the most of all. I'll miss knowing all of you. Yes, it's true I'll miss putting lines on paper and watching them grow into cement and steel. But mostly, I'll simply miss being a part of all of you. So maybe now you'll understand why thank you just doesn't cover tonight, but I'll try it anyway. Thank you all so much my friends."

Cole gazed back to the sky, finding his office window had blended with the rest of the faceless black panes. Bridge must have given it up for the night, he assumed, then stabbed the Range Rover in the door's eye with its own steely key.

It was a laid-back drive this time of night, slipping out of the sleeping city. The Rover's brake lights took a break heading north on Highway 1 into the arctic air for a silent drive home, a talented Scottish lass on the radio singing *Here Comes the Rain Again.*

Eighteen miles from the wooden Anchorage city limits sign to home; one thing he wouldn't miss passing five or six days a week and neither would the Rover. Winding up river, his rectangular headlights reflected the ghostly groups of towering spruce standing at attention, as if Cole were inspecting their darkly brush-stroked ranks. A tin gray mailbox with the name Temple stuck to its side came and went, its red flag already lowered announcing to Cole the start of the infamous pothole run. He and the Rover knew just what to do. A turn of the wheel launched them for the ditch, another at just the right instant saved them, and the passenger side tires scattered gravel. Cole, now more aware of his underwear than ever, rested his left foot on the brake pedal and braced for the ramming jolt of the great black hole. But there was none. Even the dark shadowy gouges that usually raced under the truck had vanished. Patch Road was smooth. However, instinct still sent the Rover through its usual pattern, but for no reason. Low beam, "Where are ya bastards?" None. He came to a skidding stop, then swung the Rover back, driving slowly so as not to be fooled like an old fool. Again, just the long run of frozen gray pavement sparkling with frost as if mirroring the stars. With a final wide-eyed u-turn, the window hummed down, sucking icy air.

"Well son of a bitch…the holes are gone."

two

Cole's friend, the sun, awoke him by dawning its light through his window from ninety three million miles away, casting a shadow on the far wall of his bedroom that looked like a one-eared donkey smoking a cigar. He rolled his head from the pillow to see the snow-topped peak of a spruce swaying with the wind as if conducting an orchestra. Retreating in the window's corner was a thin sheen of frost, Mother Nature's autograph for yet another perfect painting.

The elastic doors of Cole's glacier-blue eyes squeegeed morning from his narrowing pupils. Blanketing him were the thoughts of pothole-less pots as he lay staring motionless from the single-man's trough of his cherry sleigh bed. How? Who? When? Surely not Clark Owens and his greedy logging company. My imagination? Maybe Philip did something about the bastards as another departing gift? No, foolish. Cole remembered he drove down Patch at six thirty, then home again by twelve thirty. Who would be filling holes at any of those hours? It couldn't even be done in that little of time. The machines needed and the men to run them, following behind with shovels, tamping the fresh asphalt level. He couldn't picture Teresa Temple, the closest neighbor, doing anything about it, especially in the middle of a two-degree night and bound to a wheelchair. "Well, all I know for sure is *I* damn well didn't fix them!"

He unburied himself from the down bedding. Then he crossed the living room, hunting the banks of Spring Creek for deer he would certainly never shoot, then down a few steps to the kitchen, his favorite socks on cold hardwood floors. He sucked cold orange juice straight from the container until it burned like swallowing dry ice. He looked through a dull reflection of himself in the kitchen window. Patch Road could barely be seen from across the south thirty. "Mailman's early this morning," he muttered. The mailman seemed to almost gaze into Cole's eyes from across the five-hundred yards of cleared valley. "Either I'm still asleep or he actually just waved at me." From habit, Cole started to return the gesture, even though he well knew it was impossible to be seen standing here from Patch Road. Cole and his reflection in the kitchen window frowned at one another in unison and tottered off to the bathroom.

Cole stood aside Patch Road looking at what he couldn't figure, as a blast of wind sent his eyes slamming shut. His silvery hair blowing crazy in the moment tried to leap from his head in waves as another of the eighteen-wheelers loaded with freshly cut timber exploded past.

He walked to the center of the road sliding his snow boot like a windshield wiper across the frozen ground in hopes of uncovering some great lie the gray pavement was telling. Even the absence of cigarette butts discarded by workmen bothered him. No matter the project, someone always left that little trail behind, but no butts.

With a long sniff to the breeze, Cole mumbled, "It's true, the holes are gone. Every damn one of them just gone. No black patches, no heavy machinery tracks or even the smell of fresh asphalt in the air."

Another eighteen-wheel ambulance full of dying trees rushed by in the opposite direction between the grieving black spruce. Cole could see that the driver recognized the parked Rover and was ready to receive the customary flipping-off. Not this time. Cole actually raised all of his fingers in a neat row, creating a small wave.

Eight-and-a-half miles beyond Cole's bend in Patch Road, six past the Aurora Logging Company, was the home of Laura M. Day. Widowed after twenty-two years of marriage to Cole's best friend,

Daniel, she closed the doors on their small airline that delivered fisherman, hunters, photographers, and even the occasional engineer to the bush. "*All Day Airlines,*" Daniel proudly told his Fairbanks banker back in the spring of seventy-one. "That's what I'm going to call it."

He'd been in the puddle jumping business for some three years when Cole Caffy made a reservation over the phone asking how much it would cost to have a peek at the Russian River for the better part of a day. Agreeing to the price, they lifted in the air by floatplane the next cloudless day, showing Cole the real Alaska for the first time. Mountains not hills, blue ice gouging the earth as if heaven were carving a smile across its frozen canvas. Cole counted seven black bear from the sky. Daniel told him they were bigger face to face. "Don't pet, they bite!" Pressing his nose against the cool plastic window, Cole watched a bull moose stand his ground as the tiny red Cessna pitched and yawed at the trickle of water below. The plane came to rest at a small slippery dock smelling like a forgotten greenhouse on the shaded side of the Russian River. The loud thumping bass from the motor stopped. Thoom..Thoom....Thoom..... Thoom........ Thoom............Thoom. Cole, so taken with the whole experience, decided then and there that he would never leave Alaska again. "I absolutely must learn to fly!" he shouted back to the sky, before anxiously asking Daniel if he could possibly teach him to do so. Laughing at Cole's excitement, Daniel agreed, as he released a common feather from between his thumb and forefinger, spiraling past the rim of his waterproof boots like a helicopter out of juice.

Over the following years they had flown together to some of the remotest parts of the state. They once circled Mt. McKinley in Denali National Park, whooshed over herds of caribou in the western tundra, and even took a frost-biting trip to Barrow where they communicated through a series of head nods and blinks with icy lashes. "Don't touch the aluminum skin of the plane, Cole, your hand will stick." Cole was not a hunter, but would tag along just to go. He did fly fish, however, and fished well, took to it like a fish to water some might say. Even to Daniel's envy, Cole always seemed to be trying to get his attention, hooing and haaing from some hollow on the river, holding up a string of trout, salmon, and even halibut from the occasional saltwater trip. Daniel would politely nod in his direction pretending to be thrilled at Cole swinging yet another damn fish at him. He would cast all day and well into the evenings, sometimes only to still find himself later that night carefully picking bones from Cole's mess of fish. But none of it mattered. They truly enjoyed one another's company, and Cole still missed his friend terribly. He once proudly said, "This is my best friend, Daniel," while introducing him to people from *Here to There Engineering.*

Three large photos always hung in unison in Cole's den beside the French barn door window. The first, showing Cole and Daniel standing and waving from behind the Cessna's open doors holding fishing gear and backpacks with outlines of nipping bottles. The second was the plane lofting from the runway, and the last just a small dot in the distance heading for Light House Lake. This was Cole's first flight after getting his license. He caught nine brown trout and Daniel two.

In late March of ninety-four, Cole worked on site up Colony Creek, stuck to his knees in sucking mud. The cell phone that he hated to hear ring did just that. Anna, silent for a moment on the other end, tried to sound professional but failed.

"Cole, my God, I am so sorry. Daniel and Laura were flying back from dropping some big-shot professor off in the sticks. There was a problem, Cole. Their plane went down about two miles from Talkeetna….Cole, Daniel was killed." Anna's voice broke, "Laura is hurt, but she's alive. She's being flown to Anchorage right now; whoever found them said she was asking for you. Cole, I'm so sorry. Please tell me if there's something, anything, I can do." Cole closed his eyes, and pressed the off button on the phone. He tried to hold his emotions long enough to tell his crew he had to go, but failed.

Four days later, Daniel Day's body was cremated. Laura's jaw quivered as she looked for words from her electric hospital bed. "He would want to be up at Light House Lake," she finally managed in a whisper. Cole and Daniel took their last flight together, the earth frozen below, clouds fat with ice crystals failing to claw over the mountains. The white Cessna broke the silence, rolling downward at the frozen lake. Cole drew the yoke back and the plane leveled out just off the ice, perfectly, as Daniel had taught him. Whirling blades screamed at the sleeping snow, scaring it from the flat lake in streaming hoops just behind. The plastic window opened,

"Good bye, my friend."

Cole pulled the Rover to a stop in the familiar graveled driveway. Laura Day's home sat curiously at the banks of Spring Creek as though it had found a quiet place to admire its own reflection. The house stood two stories tall, but inside were the best tall stories, or had been before Daniel died. Built facing due south, the front of the home was promised all the light Alaska could ever offer. "This house is square with the world," Laura had proclaimed, as the Days tucked themselves in for their first night's rest in their first new home. It was given a light gray siding and white carpets to compliment one another, arched ceilings cradling a balcony for the room where she now slept alone. Skylights and bulging bay windows washed the home in light. This was a welcoming place: thick clean blankets around every corner, lemon bars and Dutch cookies always on display in the kitchen, the smell of vanilla softly happening.

Cole ambled about Laura's deck peering through a ship's porthole beside the arctic entry, a gift from himself he presented with a card that said, *"I polished this for Days."* He thought it was a little funny.

The wrap-around deck was wide and had the fingerprint grain of Cedar. Not wanting to intrude, he sat with his leather gloves tugged on and passed time watching water that would flow from here to under his home in an hour and twenty minutes. He knew this from summertime inner-tube rides, dangling feet a-freeze, middle finger waving at the sheet-metal sheds of the Aurora Logging Company's spruce morgue as Clark Owens sat peering back, toying with thoughts of installing pop-up dams with teeth.

The thought of having a cigarette ran through Cole's mind, then he remembered he'd quit smoking thirty-four years ago, but what a perfect time this would have been.

Half asleep, he heard the sound of cold rubber tires on gravel coming to a stop, Laura's faded yellow Wagoneer. Metal on metal, the Jeep told anyone who would listen that its door was closing.

Pilot, a pug with far, far too much skin on a face kicked in by Satan himself, rounded the corner and tried desperately with his stick-like legs to jump in Cole's lap. Seconds later, Laura appeared and found Cole sitting bundled in his long winter coat carefully wrapped about the knees, only the tip of his nose poking over the sagging rim of a ratty red scarf. Instantly, she narrowed her pretty green eyes at him under waves of red hair lapping from the brim of her hand-knitted stocking hat, her slight frame tucked in a down coat twice her size, zipped to a fiery little mouth that was ready to explode. Squeezing Pilot, Cole could only sit idle as she came to a crunching halt in her snow-packed tracks.

"Cole! What in the *hell* are you doing sitting out here in this freeze? You know damn well which door is left open and pretty much left open just for you. In other words, get your frozen ass out of that deck chair and in the house! Now!"

Shots of breath steamed from his aging scarf in puffs of laughter. He liked this part of her; he liked everything about Laura for that matter. Even catching hell for sitting in the cold. Truth be known, there were times when he felt more at home here than anywhere else.

As the glass-filled door closed behind them, Cole immediately felt the warm home wrap around him as he undid his long coat after hanging his scarf on a loyal man made of oak with pegs sticking out of his head.

Laura added today's mail with yesterday's pile as she passed the kitchen table. She busied her hands with cupboard doors and silverware drawers. "Do you want a little coffee in your sugar this time you old half frozen shit? Not that you deserve any," she said playfully masking her joy for his visit.

Cole tossed a humbling smile from the living room that said, "yes please," Laura matching it with her own in reply.

Listening to the sounds of kitchen, Cole remembered back to the dark days when Laura Day was forced to go on with her own life after the death of her husband, as most do willingly or not, carrying the world on her back for the first few quiet years. She had never remarried, and never really gave it much thought. She'd admitted to Cole a few lemon bars back, that her only dip in the dating pool was a one-time effort with a tall man from Homer, but his teeth were too far apart to be trusted and he took to whistling John Denver tunes in the many lulls of their starving dinner conversation. Cole had never pressed upon the subject of why she'd shied from flying the remaining little red Cessna that could so wonderfully fill its plastic windows with Alaska. She had quickly sold the other two Cessnas after a lingering pause, and a small "yes" into the telephone's receiver, leaving Daniel's first plane to sit alone at Anchorage International Airport, the end of *All Day Airlines*.

Their plane that day was starved of fuel from a fitting worked loose by time and Alaskan runways. Gliding as far as possible, they came up two miles short of the closest strip of debearded soil. The Cessna's left wing caught the top of a high spruce throwing the plane into an unforgivable spin for earth. The first life to find them was a dairy cow, its bulbous pink nose blowing in under the wreckage. Daniel's body unknowingly pinned Laura to the floor that once was a ceiling. She lay unceremoniously buried at the end of her left arm which trailed off under twisted aluminum.

Suffering nearly losing her left hand in the accident that killed Daniel, she had perfected the many ways of hiding it, now deeply scarred and nearly useless. With her red hair sitting on her head just so, she managed to move on, favoring the winter months due to its call for gloves and stretched sweaters offering shelter to her left hand hiding just inside the understanding sleeve. Though at fifty-eight, the grocery boys down at Johnson's still scuffled about deciding who would get to carry diet Pepsi and brown sugar to her fish-eyed Wagoneer.

Breaking his stare at a model airplane lofting from the coffee table on a tiny plastic check-mark stand, Cole heard, "Happy belated birthday," pouring from Laura's small red mouth as she aimed a mug of Irish coffee at his mug. Politely, he closed his eyes in the first deep sip of spirited chocolate, secretly buying time for Laura's left hand to sneak beneath her sweater's stretched cuff as she sat squarely across from him in a favorite chair the color of her hair.

"Anna called me a few days back about some shindig for ya down at the Theater. Sorry. I thought it might be a bit, ya know, 'engineery' for me. That's just not the light I've painted our friendship with. I hope that somehow makes sense to you?"

Well understanding Laura, Cole stretched a smile across his warming face as he raised the Irish coffee in a forgiving salute and fired a friendly wink her way. She started to laugh saying, "You old son-of-a-bitch, if I ever catch you sittin' in the snow outside this house again, I will, Cole Caffy, I'll have your ass! Do you hear me?" A hard laugh came to both of them as Pilot the Pug stared fearlessly at an outlet.

Cole knew that on the many flights Daniel managed over his years as a pilot, he picked up the hobby, then later the habit, of collecting the feathers of nearly every species of migrating bird known to Alaska. His eyes were always stuck to the ground prospecting for another find between each and every leap the Cessna would make. Cole once gave him the rudder feather of a Gray Sea Eagle, a rare find under the crisp Alaskan sky. Daniel quickly mounted it with the many others on a piece of teak the size of a Twister mat that hung where it still did today high on the east living room wall in the arch of a modern ceiling. Cole would patiently watch at times, as once a month or so, Laura would carry an aging three-step folding ladder from the garage that allowed her to reach the feathers for dusting, ironically with a feather duster.

Daniel was short only one quill, the Ruddy Turnstone, which hunted mainly on ocean shores during low tide, doing what its name implies, turning over stones and shells in search of food with its probing bill and busy orange legs. Cole began as well to search high and low for the Turnstone's shedding feathers, usually found first by the incoming tide. A place for its feather still remained vacant, leaving the collection incomplete by this one elusive feather. Staring at the single void in the row of feathers like a hobo's smile, Cole again sipped his loaded coffee contemplating, thought it a shame, like being thrown to the lions the day before your hundredth birthday. Not wanting to think about it any longer, Cole turned his attention back to Laura, whose eyes were on him as though she'd read his thoughts and agreed with them.

"Where were you off to so early on this cold morning?" Cole asked, wincing from a pure bite of Irish that had settled deep in his mug.

"Oh just up to Jenny's. We - I - came up with this walking every other morning thing. We tromp from her mailbox up Patch Road to where we can see the top of Mount Bashful. Takes us about forty-five minutes unless Jenny starts on about how much she hates her kids, then it's an hour at least. Her mouth works like a giant damn wind scoop and slows us down a touch."

"Oh, Hell, Jenny Massey would rather be forced to spend a month strapped naked to a men's maximum security prison covered in glitter than see any of those overgrown tots of hers go without so much as lip balm," Cole said raising a bristly brow, picturing those fat carnivores of hers fighting over a jar of petroleum jelly with blistered lips.

As Pilot ran wild after his favorite blue-and-white beach ball from one end of the house to the other, bouncing it off of his foreskin face, Cole thought of a recovery van chasing its hot air balloon.

"And to what do I owe the pleasure of finding your carcass frozen to my porch this morning? I know you can't already be bored with retirement," Laura asked.

"Oh, no, just wanted to start my day with my best friend, Miss Day, that's all."

"Okay…I'm not mad at you anymore. But keep saying things like that, Pilot's been lonely ya know."

Pilot, back waiting for the outlet to do something shocking, unintentionally aimed his ass at Cole, who grimaced as if inhaling the flu, making him think of what a smoker's dying heart valve must look like.

"I do have a question for you, though," Cole rallied, scootching forward, giving up on his empty cup. "When was the last time you drove in to Anchorage?"

Laura's sea green eyes arched in mild surprise and rolled in the air, "Oh, I'd say four days ago I guess. I try to only go over the hill and through the woods about once a week anymore. Why?"

Cole paused, frowning, "Well the screwiest thing happened, Laura. You know that run of potholes down by Temples?"

"Yeah, I know them well…all too well in fact," Laura said, floating her pretty eyes in the air once again, resting them sadly on the displayed feathers.

"Well, they're gone!" Cole said, looking into those same eyes, hoping to take her mind off Daniel.

"How do you mean?" she said, returning her focus to him.

"The road, it's smooth, void of voids!"

He was relieved to see her face light up. "Ha! I'll be damned. I always figured they'd be around long after I was done with Patch Road. The ol' wagon'll love it."

"Yeah, my Rover does already." Cole pushed back in the overstuffed corduroy couch, exhaling a little. "Here's the funny part though, Laura. I drove down to the theater around six thirty. Those damn holes nearly killed me, and I'll spare you the misfortunate story of where they made my underwear swerve to! I drove back up Patch after the party, at say, twelve thirty, and the damn things were gone, just plain gone. Vamoose!" he said, surrendering his arms out wide in question.

Laura snorted in disbelief, and narrowed her eyes at him. "Your underwear swerved, Cole? Swerved where? …I'm not sure I'm following you. Don't tell me you want the pots back?"

"Sweet Jesus, no!" he shouted. "I haven't turned sixty-five and simply decided to lose my mind! And never mind my scooters, or the unbearable trench they dove into to hide from those damnable pots. Now, here's the thing," he said lowering his voice, "who, without losing their mind, would be out there after hours, in the dark, on a freezing Friday night, filling potholes?"

Laura leaned forward, resting her chin on her fist. "Are you certain, Cole? You're up and down Patch every day it seems, maybe you and your 'scooters' confused a couple of them?"

"Nope, I've gone over it and over it as many times as I've been over the road itself. They simply were there and then not there. And by not there I mean gone, Laura! I drove back this morning and did some walking of my own. This is where it gets weird, Red. GONE, not just fixed or filled, but GONE. No sign of there ever being a single pothole, road so smooth you actually notice the scenery now." As Cole drug four deep lines through his roof of silver hair, he exhaled, and watched questions bubbling up in Laura's eyes like champagne.

"Don't get mad at me for saying this, Cole, but you rarely drink, and you noticed this coming home, right?" she gestured with a loopy smile.

"Sober! I wouldn't have driven at all otherwise. Sober as you and I right this very moment."

"No offense, but you just drank a shot of Bailey's in your coffee. How many fingers ya seein' these days?" Laura's right hand flashing one, then two, then three fingers as if counting her steps to the kitchen to make him another.

"I'm not crazy, I just can't figure it out, that's all. And I wasn't drunk!"

"Oh, Cole, I know you weren't." Laura said, mocking him by swinging the bottle of Irish whiskey to her lips, pretending to suck madly at it, her left hand on a small gyrating hip.

"Oh, for the sweet love of Christ, Laura! I'm serious here!"

The sight of Cole's expression as he yelled from the living room, trying so hard to make his point, proved too much for Laura as she burst out laughing, sending her liquid chocolate spraying into the sink.

Pilot, still entranced by the outlet's spell, continued to moon Cole, whose eyes accidentally landed on the abyss and winced skyward with a shudder. "And what's wrong with your dog! When are you going to cover its ass with somethin'? Christ, that's just embarrassing! How can you get used to that sucking boil staring at you every time he's not? Twist a damn pencil in it I will! He'll never turn his backside to ol' Uncle Cole again, that much I can promise you."

Laura's laugh broke from a gallop to full run as she braced herself over the sink. Catching her breath, she wiped sweetened alcohol from her chin and said, "Cole, every time you're here we end up going through this. Face it, it's there to stay. He needs it. That dog loves you and you know it."

"Yeah, and I'd probably warm up a bit to him if someone would fix *his* little pothole." Cole chuckled, with a growing laugh of his own.

"Speaking of potholes, did you mention or bitch about the potholes to anyone lately, Cole?" Laura asked, clearing her throat and dabbing at her denim shirt with a kitchen towel.

"Nobody," he insisted. "I started complaining in the beginning, yes, but not for the last couple of years. With the handful of residents living on Patch, all my complaining fell on deaf ears. If I would have gotten a signature from every person living on the road, I could have given it to the State Department on the back of a match book, and believe me this isn't the work of the state."

"Maybe you just wished for so long that they'd go away they finally packed up and left," Laura said, muting her scars with a quick sleight of hand as she walked from the kitchen and sat neat as a pin across from Cole, pondering from the couch.

"Yeah, that's the sane answer," Cole said, slowly shaking a smile from his lips, eyes falling on the mail atop Laura's kitchen table. He thought of something then asked, "Hey, you haven't gotten any crap mail, like chain letters or anything lately, have you?"

"Nope, just the usual. You know, you just gotta have this and you just gotta have that sales stuff. Why?" she asked, looking at him curiously, her wavy red hair brilliant in the light.

"Oh, just wondering if all of us on Patch Road receive the same junk or not."

"Why, have you gotten something special lately, Cole? Because you know you're such a special guy," Laura poked.

"No…no, just crap. Ah hell, it's all crap," Cole mumbled, still in his favorite socks. "Well, I should be headed down the road, a busy day of retirement, ya know." He stood and walked across deep white carpet, looking up to the feather collection on his way out, his eyes drifting to the one vacant slip.

"Well if I could wish the potholes away, then certainly I could wish for Daniel's Turnstone feather to turn up. I do *wish* it was complete, damn shame," he said, shaking his head.

Cole slid the thick rubber boots on, not bothering to tie them, and took his long coat back from the stick person. Somehow the tattered red scarf had disappeared. Laura followed close behind to the door wrapping a new thick plaid scarf around his neck. She managed to make it herself even with a poor hand. Cole thought of this as she kissed his cheek and said, "Happy birthday, Crazy Man Who Lives On a Bridge."

As usual, Laura scuttled across the white carpet to watch the black Rover wind back to Patch Road, through a porthole that Cole shined for Days.

The drive back down Patch from Laura's house was eight-and-a-half miles, mailbox to mailbox.

The Rover's brake lights paled in the strong midday sun. The spruce trees tall and naturally formal, ending somewhere in the sky. Tire treads packed smooth with gray snow from the drive. Cole, a bit more eager than usual, stuck his arm down the white box's throat labeled *Caffy R.R.9.* His black leather fingers walked one by one over the tops of the mail.

The brake lights were brighter as the Rover stopped in the dim circular garage, the door following its track to the floor closed behind. Once in the home, Cole dropped the handful of today's mail beside yesterday's on the copper counter top. Inspecting it all again, he remembered throwing the crap mail away and doubled back to ransack the metal garbage can just outside the kitchen door. Finding the bundle of half-wadded paper, he walked his fingers over an advertisement for men's clothing and several other flyers decorated with pretty people insinuating how he should live, lastly he saw the creased envelope with a sharp little rainbow stretching across it. Grabbing it, he marched back into the kitchen allowing the door to slam behind him. God the house was quiet.

Cole found his oblong reading glasses beside the phone that was flashing to say someone called while he was at Laura's. He pressed one of the many buttons in his life, hearing Phillip.

"Yeah, Cole. Just wanted to let you know all of your office things are taken care of. The movers said it all made it safe and sound to your storage. Hey, let me know what you end up doing with it, might have a good place for the stuff to go. Anna's boy may need a desk and some other things after he throws his hat in the air. Of course, I didn't say anything to Anna, but if nothing else I thought I'd give you something to think about. Hell of a party, Cole. We all hope you liked it. Call me." Click.

Cole made it out of the kitchen aiming for his favorite white chair over the river carrying his glasses and the paper rainbow. Just then, someone else pushed one of his many buttons, ringing the doorbell that sifted through the silence like light between jail bars. Whisking the side-by-side maple doors open, Cole found a teenaged brunette girl in blue jeans and an REI baseball cap holding a single yellow tulip wrapped just so in transparent foil.

"Hi… Mr. Caffy?" she asked, brightening her eyes.

"…Yes." Cole said, squinting in the shower of bright light.

"I have a delivery for you!" Her small white four-wheel drive purred just behind. "If you'll just sign here for me please!" A clipboard and pen came at him chest high. Cole agreed to this with an impatient but polite smile.

“Your house is SO cool sir,” she complimented, taking the clipboard back, heavier with Cole’s scribbled signature. “I’ve heard about it before. It was in a magazine, wasn’t it?” Before Cole could answer her eyes narrowed and lit up at him. “You’re the bridge builder right?”

“Well I was yesterday, anyway,” he tittered from his failing smile.

“Well today you must be just as popular. The lady that called the order in said it had to be delivered today, no matter what, and paid extra to make it happen! Oops, maybe I said too much, huh?” she shrugged, slowly spinning the tulip between her thumb and forefinger.

“No…no…not at all, and thank you for the trouble. The roads are slippery today so be careful going back, okay?”

“Oh…geez, here, I about ran off with your flower, there’s a card taped to the side right there!” she said, pointing a cozy finger hidden in a blue mitten, her breath smelling of cinnamon toast. “Well, ok, then have a nice day, Mr. Caffy. I’ll drive careful, don’t worry!” she agreed, bouncing back to her patient pickup.

“Say, Miss, how was the drive up?”

“Sir…?”

“The road. You didn’t hit any potholes on the way up, did you?”

“No…didn’t see any, Mr. Caffy!” she answered youthfully, rolling her eyes as though trying to remember.

Cole brought the tulip shoulder height saying, “Thanks again now.”

Alone once more, he cast shut the doors and finished his trek to the living room, admiring the new yellow flower on the way with the bright day providing a view worth all his many years of work. A Sitka black-tailed deer stood just down river, pawing at the frost, then there were two; a third, and probably a fourth, poised just within the camouflaging spruce. “I’ll bet that spike buck is close at hand. Well, more time to keep tabs on them now,” he mumbled, remembering an oath he’d made to himself that the day he started naming each of the deer was the day he went back to work. Falling in the white stuffed wing chair, he stared at the attached card. Expecting to find Anna’s words even more colorful than her gift, he read instead:

Dear Cole, I am truly sorry to have missed the party. Forgive my eagerness, working late has already cost me that drink with a great mentor. Bridge.

He carefully positioned the single tulip in the center of the heavy glass coffee table in front of him. It was nice, but somehow its standing alone reminded him of himself. Bridget's perfume came strong to his memory. If the police force replaced their pepper gas with Bridget's perfume there would be people keying the president's car in broad daylight hoping to get dowsed with the alluring elixir. And if Bridget herself was pulling the trigger….Cole shook his head and forced himself back to the business of having another look under the rainbow.

CONGRATULATIONS

You have been chosen for the ability to WISH.
Go on give it a try, but do be careful.
One doesn't want to hurt anyone.
Don't get excited about saving the world, curing cancer,
or flying over small villages to make yourself a legend.
This is not that.
Go on about your life as you see fit.
The reason you were chosen is because you're you.
Do not abuse this as it is intended for you only.
Some tolerances will be made while you get
your wishing legs.
You'll see in the long run that simple and discreet is best.
Most importantly, remember how a wish may affect
those around you, in turn later affecting yourself.
Best Wishes.

Cole found no signature, no company's name promoting its gag. And the oddest thing, the envelope had no return address in the corner of its clever little sleeve. He was hoping for a lead to some prank, or something threatening he'd grow a tail unless fifteen copies were quickly mailed to his friends. But there was no such thing. Just simply the waste of somebody's time?

"WISH, WISH, WISH, MY ASS!" Cole dismissed, stuffing the guts back in the envelope for a second time. His eyes aimed back to the lonely yellow tulip as he planned to call someone at the State Department first thing Monday in any hopes of getting to the bottom of this pothole mystery.

One of the braver mule deer downstream waded into the water with her front legs, craning its soft neck to investigate something uneatable floating by with its snout. The third and fourth were close by after all, lured from the spruce as though thinking the brave one was on to some great treasure of food not covered by ice cream headache frost. Cole pictured deer pressing their tiny hooves to their temples, waiting for the dull paralyzing pain to stop when the cordless phone pulsing beside him broke his thoughts. He crossed one leg over the other and cleared his throat as he picked it up.

"Yellow," he answered, looking at the tulip.

"Cole…the feather's here…how did you…."

"What? What feather, Laura?"

"Daniel's collection, you old shit! How did you reach it? When did you have time? I saw the empty space on the board when you were here. Hell, I saw it when you were leaving, Cole! You were rattling on about it for some reason or other."

"Laura I didn't do any…." Cole's heart began to hammer in his chest with each of her words as he felt himself sink deeper into the white stuffed cushions of the chair.

"I looked it up in one of Daniel's damn bird books! It's the right one, near as I can tell, Cole!"

"Laura, wait. I don't…know how…." he stammered, coming to his feet, plowing his silver mop with his fingers. "You're telling me that the feather, the right feather, is just somehow there?"

"Are you going to try and tell me you had nothing to do with this?" she asked, barking into the phone.

"Don't you ironically use a feather duster to dust that thing, Red? Go and get your duster and look at the feathers, I'll bet they're a match. Some sort of funny accident."

"I'm holding the frigin' duster in my hand, Caffy!" she growled through clenched teeth. "The feathers are big and black like a Raven got robbed. The feather on the plaque is small and red with just a touch of black on the end, exactly like the book shows!"

Cole stood staring blankly downriver, then his eyes lowered to the little bent rainbow envelope on the coffee table. For a moment no words came.

"…Are you there, Cole?" Laura asked with silence as her reply. "The only time I lost sight of you was for the second or two it took me to switch that, if I may say so, lovely, lovely handmade scarf, with that pest-infected red rag of yours. I don't see how you could have had…."

Cole interrupted, saying, "I'll have to call you back," then poked the off button. Laura's voice was gone.

His ringless hands trembled as he lifted the envelope again. For the third time, he read its contents. One phrase caught him, the most simple of them all. *"Go on and give it a try."*

He gave the letter back to the table, looking at the single yellow flower, laughing a little at himself for what he was about to do. Elbows on his knees, he looked past his feet to the river below, the home still, putting a spotlight on his every move. He closed his eyes, allowing his lips to move, letting a wish slip free.

Cole's eyes unhinged open to the trickling water below, the way the moon peeks over the tail end of a storm, seeing the usual flow as he'd expected so. Exhaling, he sat back in the winged chair feeling a fool with his snickering eyes slowly lofting above to the exposed ceiling beams.

Beneath him a single yellow tulip floated past unseen, then another and another going by at the speed of mountain water. Suddenly, thousands of vibrant yellow tulips exploding from their rich green stems, filled Spring Creek bank to bank, slugging quietly beneath the bridge. The bright Alaskan sun reflected the dazzling color through the glass floor, splashing the living room in pale brilliance. Noticing a shining tint crawling on the varnished beams, Cole's eyes lowered inch by inch down the glowing walls, and then below him.

"OH MY GOD…! OH MY GOD!" He leapt from the glass floor to the overstuffed couch. "OH MY…GOD!" Bracing himself there with one hand, slapping the other to his forehead with a thwap. He flailed over the back of the couch, and with a whoosh swung open the French barn-door windows center of the bridge. Instantly, the fragrance rolled over his face in thick waves as though he'd walked into a hundred floral shops at once.

The Sitka deer stood downstream, all suddenly brave, chest high in the icy water, the tulips their treasure.

Cole's breathless mouth hung agape, his trembling fingers wrapped around it, casting a shadow over his tongue like light across a jail cell floor, he uttered, "Oh my God…it's real."

three

Laura stood gazing at the spread of feathers above. How did Cole do it, and why had he just hung up on her? There hadn't been another guest in the Day home for a week, and certainly not Mrs. Kope, whose lack of imagination immediately ruled her out.

Daniel's bird book lay open on the coffee table, turned to a page full of feathers grouped in straight lines like windrowed wheat. "If Daniel didn't happen across one, how in the hell did Cole suddenly pop up with this rare little quill?" she asked herself, arms crossed, feet together. "And what's all this crazy crap about potholes, or lack thereof?"

Laura, double bundled, climbed into her Jeep, calling Pilot to come along. Twenty minutes later, she was following the Rover's tracks it had left earlier that morning along Patch Road near the Temple's box. The metallic squeal from the closing door told Pilot he was staying behind, his face as flat as the window he pressed it against. The Alaskan sky a pearl white, sanded smooth by high clouds as if painted in one passing stroke by an impatient artist. Laura stood, her petite body hiding deep in Daniel's brown denim overalls that were bleeding white insulation from its neck as though blowing a smoke ring from its severed collar.

She turned away, cupping her green eyes as one of the Aurora logging trucks thundered past, starting a squall on top of her red head. Realizing the giant ogre wasn't about to slow for her, Laura cringed, awaiting the charging smash of all eighteen wheels pounding over the rash of potholes festering in Patch Road's decaying hide. But there was none, only the echoing sound of steel-belted tires howling away on smooth black pavement.

Laura opened her hands from her face as if playing peek-a-boo with the road, then turned to watch the logging truck power over a knoll and out of sight like a breaching whale in a sea of trees. Shuffling her way to the center of the road, Laura eyed the asphalt for fault, but anything short of making snow angels in the gray freezing slush revealed nothing of there ever being so much as a dent in this pleasant little stretch of road, much less potholes. "Well shit! The Crazy Man Who Lives On a Bridge is right, they are gone," she said aloud, staring between her feet like the first time she'd stood in Cole's living room.

Pilot's stump tail thrashed fiercely from side to side as Mama fired the Wagoneer to life, her left hand resting limply in her lap.

She continued down Patch, headed for Johnson's Grocery, explaining this to Pilot in a well-honed Hillbilly imitation, "Wellza, I'za spozin we adda justin weal bu gone on inta town fer serplies, boay." And they did just that, while keeping a sharp eye out for a gang of fast-footed potholes hiding on some new unsuspecting corner with their mouths crocked open to the same pearl white sky.

"So, what's Cole gonna' bring on his next visit?" she wondered aloud to Pilot who stood watching the road ahead for the occasional deer. "This whole thing must be his idea of what retirement's about. Stump his friends with mystery and solve a few problems doing it, I guess." But as she continued daydreaming down Patch she realized there was a hole in her theory. Cole would never lie. If he told you he had a beautiful little piece of swampland for sale, you better rub on your skeeter lotion and go have a lookie!

The itch of leaking insulation that brushed against Laura's earlobes made her laugh and remember back to Daniel saying, "Black bear," to Cole over the phone, selling him on the idea of a hunting trip. "They're always the best trips, Caffy, and your ass is goin'!"

Cole pressed deep in his office chair, gazing south to the Chugach Mountain Range where Daniel was promising this alluring back wooded adventure. "I suppose I could wear my snowmobile suit, huh?" This was Cole's way of accepting.

A month later, the boys and the Rover were officially hunting after putting a slippery two hundred mile drive behind them. The clouds were friendly straight lines minding their own business as Daniel and Cole walked for the better part of each day, pitching camp in the evenings was all in good fun, the part of Alaska that made it Alaska. There had been no killing yet, and this is what made the trip so far so good for Cole. He never really understood the whole 'let's find some amazing animal and then kill it' idea.

There was another little issue for Daniel however. Cole laughed so hard when he learned what it was that he had to cradle his rifle with both arms so as not to drop it, possibly killing the both of them. Daniel just couldn't find the humor and that only added to Cole's screaming laugh, the same laugh that Daniel later blamed for never seeing one of those amazing animals the entire damn trip.

It seemed Daniel just could no way, no how, bring himself to shit in the woods. He would hover behind groups of unfortunate trees in these twenty minute stints, neck full of veins, eyes pinching like a hound that went and ate a plastic garbage bag the day before, but nothing…nothing for five days and four nights, nothing. The only thing Cole had to force was keeping these little jokes in that sometimes accidentally flopped out from time to time at Daniel's expense. "Hey Dan, you wanta' pass the bratwurst?"

They awoke the last day of the trip buried in over two feet of new snow smothering their small four-season tent. It left only brush strokes of blue and yellow leaking through the flurry. Daniel hurried into his one-piece denim overalls with a built-in, fur-lined hood. Cole proudly donned his racing-striped snowmobile suit as though he were about to sign autographs, Cole really did fancy the stripes but never let on to it.

By the time they had squeezed the camp back into the Rover, the sky had turned to a bruised gray with an impulsive wind. The Range Rover enjoyed the challenge of the small rutty logging road, as did Cole streamlined by his racing stripes. Daniel, quiet and fixated, suddenly grabbed Cole's right arm, begging him to stop.

The passenger door filled with blow, pressing it open as Daniel desperately shot across the forest floor, searching for privacy. Cole, gasping for breath between waves of laughter, saw Daniel finally working at his overalls like they were on fire. Cole's jolting body fell against the wheel accidentally blaring the horn through the blizzard. Between gusting sheets of white, he saw Daniel's figure ambling back to the Rover, cinching his hood tight as he hid his relieved stubbly face in a tunnel of fur.

"Oh thank God, Cole!" Daniel shouted as he slammed the Rover's door shut. "Thank God." Managing a laugh at himself, he said, "I'm sorry I haven't been myself, Cole, but you have no idea! Some poor bear's gonna find what I just left behind and it'll blow their whole 'top of the food chain' theory to hell!"

Cole, sleekly traced by his dull orange racing stripes, tended to the drifting road, over steering when possible to fan snow from the wheel wells. Cole liked the little blue indicator light, 4x4. A few over-steered turns later, something came over Daniel again. From the fur tunnel came silence.

"Hey, Dan, got a question. You told me the other morning to keep my eyes glued for bear shit, or what did you call it?"

"Scat," he mumbled from the cave.

"Okay, so what if you could actually smell it?" Cole asked, darting his eyes about the forest, slowing a bit. Daniel had no reply.

"You know I think it's getting stronger! Do you smell that?" Again nothing from the mute. "Christ, we must have run over one of the poor bastards and he's got us by the tailpipe!"

"Just let it go, Cole," Daniel snapped.

"Let it go? It smells like we're at the zoo, what do you mean let it go? Isn't this where you hop out and spray the forest with lead?"

"Christ, Cole, it's nothing. Just keep going!"

"What the hell, Dan, you can't smell that?"

"Yes, Cole, I can smell it! Just drive!"

"Hey, there's no reason to be so…Daniel...what's…what's happened to you? You were happy as shit a minute ago, pardon the pun," Cole said chuckling.

Well, what had happened here is it seemed due to Daniel's anxiousness in the blizzard, he was unaware that when he lowered his overalls in such a shit-happy tizzy, he'd forgotten about the connected hood and unknowingly filled it with his relief. The overalls were zipped back on and the hood, yes, cinched tight! By the time he had realized his terrible, terrible error, Cole was slowing the Rover looking for the posse of bears that were certainly surrounding them.

"Cole…I shit on my head…back there in the storm…my hood…I didn't look, usually yes, but with all the damned snow blowin' up my ass and everything, I was in a hurry, ok!"

Cole's eyelids sucked back in his head, exposing just how big eyeballs really are. Laughter starting at his spine worked north to the back of his throat and exploded in a paralyzing gasp like a two year old's inhaling silence between screams. Daniel knew two hundred miles of this 'shit' lie between him and his shower.

Laura, treasuring the same grin, remembered the Rover as it pulled in the drive that afternoon, every window down and the boys' hoods up tight. Daniel bum rushed past her through the front door nearly overshooting the circular staircase leading to his scalding shower. Pilot, suddenly huffing at the air, snapped to a defensive bull-legged stance, sensing certain death nearby. Quietly, he suspected the outlet.

Daniel tugged back the heavy denim hood revealing a semi-hard plaster-of-paris mold of his skull. "OH…GOD!" In the mirror's reflection sat a perfectly good toilet.

Cole, at the door, speaking between jolts of laughter, could hardly manage a sentence. Laura's left hand slapped around her small chin as she decoded the story. "Oh Bull shit, you're making this up…." She paused bringing her other hand to her chest…. "In his hood, Cole?"

A dull wedge of light grew across the vaulted ceiling bringing with it the sound of running water from the bathroom. "You tell another living soul and I'll fuckin' kill you, Caffy!"

Cole's eyes slammed shut, his left hand reached in the thin air searching for anything to lean against as the laughter came again like dry heaves.

After'n getting her and Pilot's supplies, Laura wound the yellow eggbeater back up Patch clinging to its frosty corners, a glass bottle rolling somewhere in the back on each turn. She snickered hearing Pilot snort desperately trying to stop it, realized there's only so much you can do without thumbs.

"Well, well, well. What do we have here, Pilot?" Laura said, craning her chin and shushing Garrison Keillor's story-telling voice from the radio as she spotted her favorite bridge builder sprinting up the center of Patch Road. "There's Uncle Cole, dealing with retirement about like I thought he would."

Running for all he was worth, Cole never looked back as Laura's Jeep crept up behind him. She watched as his knees charged high in the air like patella pistons, silver hair streaking back in the wind, fists swinging eye level, the faint sound of blue jeans rubbing wild at the crotch, packed snow rooster tailing from the thick tread of his snow boots. She pulled beside him, lowering the window, a whistle of Alaskan air spinning in the curls of her red hair.

"Hey you, crazy old bastard, somebody been shootin' at ya?" she barked, through a ring of white insulation orbiting her cheeks as if her halo had slipped.

"No ma'am! Just out for a run." His possessed eyes fixed to the road.

"Ma'am?" Laura echoed, hating the way the word perched on the rim of her ears to whisper "old." Even the boys in matching brown vests down at Johnson's hadn't gotten that brave. Shrugging it off, she arched her brows high about her forehead and hung her elbow out the window. "Well I'm sorry for the bother, kind sir, but you see I'm with the Alaskan Prostitute Organization and we work for firewood and whale sandwiches, so I was hoping I might interest you in…."

"No thank you, ma'am. Just out for a…."

Stomping her foot to the floor, Laura's body sank deep in the bench seat, thudding the Wagoneer past with a wild swerve before slamming on the brakes. She looked in the rear view mirror, but only caught a glimpse of Cole's running body going flat against the murky back window, Pilot forgetting to suck in his rat tongue before the tumbling blizzard of strawberry Pop Tarts and other life essentials exploded forward from brown paper bags embossed with a smiling J written in rope.

Laura squealed the driver's side door wide as Cole lay with the tailpipe threatening mouth-to-mouth. His eyes shot open to her hovering face full of panic as if a mouse had wiggled up her overalls. "Good a' mighty crap! I haven't killed ya have I?" she pled, poking at his chest with her pointer finger.

"Red?" he sputtered, bits of snow blowing from the corners of his mouth, his right ear packed smooth with slush the color of rain clouds, a faint outline of Edvard Munch's "The Scream" smeared down the Jeep's rear window. "No. Not at all. In fact, if I dare to say so, I'm…great!"

"Well, in that case," Laura announced, twisting her face into a playful sneer and giving her mitted hands to the notch of her hips, "the next time I solicit you for sex you better show a little enthusiasm, or I'll throw Old Yeller here in reverse and finish the job!…Are you sure you're alright Cole?" she asked, looking away to mask her chuckle as he lifted his silver mop from the near frozen slop.

She offered a good right hand. Cole, with an odd and distant little smile, accepted it to his feet. "What the hell are you doing out here running like damn Forest Gump anyway? Your place must be four miles upriver!" she said spinning him in a motherly circle and brushing snow from his backside.

"Oh, just a great day for a run…just a great day!" he readily answered, seeming to be inspired by a happy wonder.

"Yeah, well, there for a minute I thought maybe you might be out here looking for feathers!"

"Oh…feathers…no…no," Cole said, vaguely rolling his eyes to the forest.

"Ya know, you're not even out of breath, and there's not so much as a bead of sweat coming from under that mop of yours, Caffy. How long you been runnin'?" she asked, trying to corner him with her suspicious eyes the color of sea grass.

"Oh, just been takin' it easy, sightseeing mostly," he said, dodging the real answer, and the color of sea grass.

"Cole, you were running like you saw a group of spray paint pack'n teenagers headed for one of your precious damn bridges, and I just went down Patch to Johnson's and I never saw your baggy hide doin' any sight seein'. You must have been haulin' that old ass of yours pretty fast."

"Well, one gets anxious when you're out looking for a member of the Alaskan Prostitute Organization you know."

Laura pressed her full lips flat and squinted her eyes, pondering his colorful answer. "I bought a load of those stupid lemon bars you like so much. You want a ride back up to the house?"

"Nue thank you ma'am, joost out for a rune," Cole answered in a destroyed imitation of Sean Connery, the only star that ever shined for him.

Laura added a "mmmmmm" to her expression then said, "Well I hate to hit and run, but it's cold. You'll come up and see me? I can't wait to watch you try and flap your way around this whole feather conspiracy thing ya know! You'll probably try telling me it was the pothole God, huh?"

Laura pecked his cheek as always and made for the Jeep. She shuffled away, deep in her overalls when Cole stopped her with, "I was with Daniel at Morty's Plumbing. I remember when ol' Morty asked him why he went and cut the hood off of those overalls. He told him he was welding and caught the damn thing on fire! I guess he thought it might also answer why he just decided to up and shave his head out of the blue. Funny thing was, every living soul down at Morty's knew Daniel couldn't weld."

"Yeah, he told me that story before we went to sleep one night. I thought I was going to wet the bed for the first time in forty five years," Laura said staring into the chrome shine of the door handle, her reflection horribly distorted, reminding her of how she felt when the doctor answered her one word question, "Daniel?" The doctor answered only, "I'm sorry" as he clipped free the wedding ring from her widowed hand.

"I guess what I'm trying to say, Laura, is I miss him too."

With a sad smile, she hopped in the yellow Jeep and disappeared into the cold as Pilot pressed his face against the rear window, watching his friend get smaller.

Anxiously awaiting the Wagoneer's raspy whine to fade away into the many curves of Patch Road, Cole started his stride, and before he knew it, he was running crazy like an Olympian, running like only a sixty-five-year-old man could *wish* to run.

After a scalding shower, Cole reached for a sweatshirt he'd received as a token after giving a lecture eleven years ago. *Boston University* arched across its gray chest plate in bold blue lettering.

Daylight was fast and fleeting in the long northern winters like a sluggish lightning strike. The glutinous night worked around the clock, consuming its precious light by spilling dark over the mountains to the east towards Cole's heavy eyes drunk with sleep. Standing in socks that he really didn't think much of, he looked down river, unable to shake the new habit of letting his jaw go slack with every racing thought.

He turned to the inviting couch, admiring its subtle modern curves and double-stitched leather cool to the touch, his white taxidermed friend. First he sat, pulling one leg up just so on a fat cushion, then slowly the other followed, a soft accent pillow for the crook of his neck, the sound of blind water feeling its way around the smooth black rocks of Spring Creek sparkling just below. The dark bullied its way over the south thirty.

The morning woke Cole with a brilliant light that it fired at him eight minutes ago. The black-tailed deer inspected the river below with a bit more hope than usual, their bony hooves dotting the frost on their side of Spring Creek. Sitting up on the couch, Cole counted each of their furry necks. "Six," he said aloud, and then a seventh cautiously peeked from the spruce with his spike rack.

Yesterday's ten-mile marathon crept to Cole's waking mind as he swung his stiff legs to the glass floor. "Nope, I wasn't dreaming." Slow to his feet, he stretched his mouth in a yawn then watched the young buck find his courage looking side to side from the line of trees as if he was about to dodge across a busy Manhattan street full of cabs. The doe's attention focused on something across the water. Soon, Cole noticed it too. A frozen yellow tulip pinned to the shore between two stones, and another just upstream, waving in the cold breeze as if for help.

Flipping on the lights in the garage, Cole reached for his flannel coat and buttoned it on while simultaneously fighting the ends of his legs into clumsy snow boots. As he swung the side door shut behind him, his warm breath revealed itself in the sharp air like smoke signals wafted by a tongue blanket. Carefully eyeing the herd of black-tails with his peripheral vision, he began a gentle whistle and trekked down the bank of the east shore. The stomp from a two-legged animal wearing black boots brought the deer's snouts from the ground, putting them on standby. "Morning ladies," Cole offered to the paralyzed group of does loosely huddled on the opposite shore. Warily, they watched him bend down for a tulip through their blank eyes. Cole's boot slid from a featureless stone layered with thin ice, splashing creek over its furry top. Instantly, the does turned and pranced for the spruce, only glancing back to make sure Two Legs wasn't in pursuit as they wove into the woods.

Corrigibly slipping the tulip's stem through the buttonhole of his flannel pocket, Cole went on to collect dozens more scattered about the east shoreline, his fingertips numb from the ones that needed an off-shore rescue. He could feel the doe's frightened eyes lurking from the tree line as another struggling tulip appeared, one the ladies must have missed it over on their side of the river. Seeing it there, abandoned with its limp yellow petals peddling in the current, resurrected a chilling memory that leaked into his mind and raised his pulse the way cold seeps between gaps and triggers the heater.

Bringing his round palm to his square jaw, he stared into the coursing water, where, for the first time in months, he thought of Mary Pearson. Briefly he saw her father cradling her motionless body that lay draped in a yellow Sunday dress baptized by the muddy shores of the Chimney River, Mary's mother howling, being led away by Ben Caffy, leaving Cole alone to stare into the river at its edge, into the life stealing water, just as he did now. Slowly, he looked just upstream to his house hurdling the river with its span of red steel necklaced with rivets, finally admitting to himself what had first drawn him to the drawing board dedicated to dodging water. With a bitter blow from reality, Cole saw his own home as a suture in earth's skin, a suture in his own fears, his monument to escaping over what had drowned his little friend in her yellow dress so long ago.

Turning to face a kin to Mary's killer, he looked across Spring Creek, to the opposite shore, then back to the frozen ground where he stood. Breath from his warm mouth escaped in tapered puffs as he closed his eyes to build his finest of bridges, his monument of monuments.

"I *wish* to be on the other side of this river."

With the faintest whisper of wind combing the tulips, Cole opened his awaiting eyes to what appeared to be the same hibernating soil, except, there were deer tracks, pressed here and there in the frost around the soles of his boots, and the sound of the river in his ears. It was no longer in front of him, but coming from behind! Cole spun on his cloddy rubber heels, discovering Spring Creek had somehow snuck past him.

“SWEET…JESUS!” he bellowed as his chest ballooned, vacuuming an inhale that sucked back even his eyelids. Cole’s footing gave in the spin, throwing his legs out from under him with a “guh” from his blue lips. His left hand went to his chest riding out the triggered deep gasp. Quick to recover, he rolled onto his butt with small patches of snow packed to his sweat pants. First a little smile inched across his stunned face then exploded to a laugh as he realized he was staring at the same river, but from the other side.

Back to his feet, still holding the tulips, the rustle of life came from above in the spruce. Cole’s beaming smile first flattened, but then was reborn three-fold as the next wish came to his mind as naturally and freely as caramel pouring over ice cream.

“I *wish* the deer didn’t fear me.”

Dropping to one knee, Cole held the bouquet of frozen yellow before him. “Come on ladies, I even brought you flowers!”

A small doe was the first to gracefully poke its head from the trees, then another with its brown glass eyes. A third, that couldn’t seem to control its excited black tail, advanced down the bank spirited by a new found courage. Even more broke from the spruce followed by the spike buck appearing as though he’d jealously heard a rumor.

A sharp snort blew from behind, scaring Cole. He turned his head to find a doe with a thick blue-gray coat and white underbody curiously staring him down with oval eyes the color of what boogie men thrive in. “Well, where did you come from, girl?”

With a nibbling tug on the bouquet, Cole flinched back around to see the tulips being devoured not by one, but by two does, and then another, using its long pink tongue to corral the prized flowers. Quickly Cole found himself surrounded by a baker’s dozen of snooping Sitka black-tailed deer squeezing in and out of the huddle, looking at him as though he was made of pure honey. Giggling, he reached for each of the doe’s faces, scratching at their coarse cheeks as they rubbed their sleek coats along him, butting one another for the chance.

The spike buck prodded his way forward to have a look see at his competition. Cole stayed still for a moment, then offered all he could. Extending his arm, he revealed a fist full of stunted stems. The buck declined with a vane snort full of anger and left the circle of does with his black tipped tail waving goodbye and good riddance.

Watching this, Cole was suddenly blindsided by a foot long wet tongue shooting deep into his ear. “Oh…Gaawwd that’s…horrible!” he cringed, as another politely fired snot in his face with a welcoming huff.

With his yearling spirals of horn aiming up the bank, the spike made his way back to the dense line of spruce, hearing Cole’s amazed laughter echo from the valley as the rest of the herd introduced themselves to Two Legs.

After setting in motion her plan to discover the truth behind potholes suddenly going belly-up and feathers turning up, Laura neatly arranged lemon bars in a fanning circle about the edge of a plate painted with blue and yellow sailboats going nowhere in particular. She expected Cole to be winding down her drive, slinging slush from Rover’s wheel wells at any moment, but somehow the road seemed to grow even more barren with each impatient glance through the porthole.

After finally hearing his raspy voice agree through his antique phone, he claimed, “I should be there in about an hour or so,” about an hour or so ago, but Cole had never been the tardy type. Another glance, more barren.

Pilot stood at the nose of Laura’s white tennis shoes with lemon on his breath, daydreaming of what it might be like to figure something out, but then couldn’t figure that out, so he contemplated a go at his beach ball. Suddenly, Cole’s tapping on the porthole beside the glass door broke his delicate concentration, sending him into this ‘thing’ he went through every time the tall man with silver hair came to call. Pilot did truly dig his Uncle Cole.

In a swoosh the front door swung open with Cole filling its void, a little outside sliding inside with him. “Pilot…Pilot…Pilot!” he announced, raising his bare hands over his head like antlers. The bags of skin surrounding Pilot’s bug eyes drew back and his jaw dropped open in a dog’s smile. As Cole aimed a steady grin in return, he pushed the door closed with his pointer finger and proudly hung his new plaid scarf on the oak guy that was always hanging around.

Laura's left hand fled from the busy countertop, hanging to her side. The right went on alone, tending to the business of making Irish coffee.

"Hey there sweet stuff!" Cole called out to the kitchen, plucking Pilot from the tiled runway, raising him high in the air with one hand.

"Pilot to co-pilot…Pilot to co-pilot" he radioed, in a rough and ready ground control voice.

Flying a map of the living room, Cole tried to blow the pink tongue out of his own mouth imitating an airplane. Pilot's tongue always looked like that.

As the two of them spun about the living room skies, Laura closed in each lap toting the plate of lemon bars weighted with two steaming cups to the coffee table while Pilot's face slipped deeper in his baggy skin from the G's he was pullin.' This was Cole's favorite part, just like Daniel's, coming in for the landing. But as Cole noticed Laura's left hand off hiding on the far side of her body, he was reminded of her landing of landings and thought to cancel this part of the flight.

The coffee made its landing on a table of the same name. Cole's whirling buzz sat him down sideways, laughing on the corduroy couch. Laura snorted through a smile at Pilot's drunken stagger for the kitchen, or staircase, no, the kitchen, as she sat directly across from Cole in an ironwood rocker she'd refinished herself,

"I swear he knows when you're coming," said Laura.

"I'd bet it has something to do with you accidentally spilling a few of my lemon bars on the tiled tarmac?"

"Speaking of spilling," Laura said, motioning her good hand in the air below the feather board like a game show queen selling some wonderful new product. "How's about spilling the truth behind my new little feather here."

"Oh…yes, I'd somehow forgotten," Cole realized, feeling a climber's axe bury in his stomach as he squirmed a little on the olive colored couch. "So, any luck with the mystery yet?"

"Not until you tell me!" she said, cornering him. "Because I know damn well you put it there, Cole, there's just no other way!"

"Well…I didn't really…you know," he stammered, "Why are you so certain my hands are in this?" His wide-eyed innocence fooling no one, especially Laura, she'd known him far too long and far too well.

"Oh horse feathers, Caffy, you look like you just remembered you left your house on fire!" Laura shot back, determined to break him. "Now shall we start this conversation over again, my fair feathered friend? Good, I'll start. Spill it, Caffy!"

Cole drew a deep breath before he let the lie come, the concentration on his face threatening to reveal he was about to. "Well you always told me the door was left open just for me, Laura, so I thought I'd be sneaky and see how long it would take you to find it," he answered, picturing two large birds arguing over their sprawling collection of human fingers.

Laura tried to swallow this while Cole swallowed hot coffee.

"You know, you're not really the sneakish type, though, Cole," she said, narrowing her eyes. "You've never been alone in this house, and if you say different you're the damn liar that I know you're not! In fact, we both know you'd rather sit out in the freeze and wait for someone to let your Forest Gump runnin' ass in than lie."

"I was jogging," Cole let slip from his lip, staring into his coffee mug as if awaiting all the right murky words to turn belly up in the magic eight balls window.

"You were runnin' and damn silly at that. Like an escaped P.O.W headed for the motherland, and don't change the subject. So now just where did you find this ever elusive feather anyway?" she demanded, leaning in close as if about to close a deal.

"Well…I called a friend in the Forestry Department and they led me to someone who they thought could help."

"I'm listening," Laura replied, tapping her bright red pinky nail against her coffee mug.

"I told them the story and leaned on their hearts a bit, it wasn't easy but there it is," he lied, rolling his palms upright to the collection. "I'm sorry it's been such a bother. We should have just put it there together." But with each word, his eyes shifted further from Laura's.

Finding too many holes in this touching story, Laura went for the throat by asking, "So, where do I keep the only ladder I have?"

"I'm sorry, I don't understand the question," Cole said, understanding the question.

"Well, unless you and your tiny feather flapped your happy asses up the wall, I don't see any other way you could have reached the display, so either you start flappin,' or tell me where the big wooden ladder is."

Hopefully seeing through the trick question, Cole gambled back with, "I didn't see any big wooden ladder, all I found was a small metal one in the garage, and oh, as long as we're on the subject, I just love my new scarf!"

"Hmmmm...dandy of an answer you've got there, Caffy, but there's still something funny in the air about you this weekend, must be lack of sleep from filling potholes all hours of the night, huh?"

"Oh…let's solve one mystery at a time," he said, unable to take giving another lie, forced to swerve the potholes in a new way he never could've imagined.

"Laura, would you mind if I asked you something personal?"

"You're not going to ask me about my boobies again, or anything, are ya?"

Cole closed his eyes with a jolt of laughter. "I guess I just got my answer."

Pilot sniffed the air about Uncle Cole, catching a whiff of black-tail, smelling as if someone had been hunting again. His buggy rat eyes shot to Cole's head, searching for a hood.

"Do you ever find yourself…a bit lonely?" asked Cole, his voice growing serious.

"Well, lonely as anybody would be at times I guess, why?"

"Let me approach this another way. If you had three wishes, Laura, what would they be?"

"Three you say?" Pursing her lips together, she looked at him carefully, trying to catch this ball that had come wild out of left field. "Well off the top of my red head I guess I'd go for that tan Moroccan houseboy with a terrible fear of clothing, my freezer could use a good defrosting, ya know!" She laughed, batting her eyelashes as if she'd just purposely dropped her hanky. But seeing that Cole wasn't in the market for a good joke, she sat up straight, letting go any thoughts of shirt-shy island boys to ask, "So, what's so personal about asking me that?"

"Because I'm after the truth, the real answer, three wishes that might come to you, say, laying awake at three in the morning on a winter night."

Slowly, Laura gave her coffee mug back to the table with her good hand, deflating her smile. After ensuring with a quick tuck that her crippled hand was buried away at her side, she lightly cleared her throat to make room for truth. "Okay…I think I understand. Well…yes, I do of course get lonely rattling around with only Pilot to look forward to in a house that my deceased husband built for me, if that's what you mean. And I assume you want to know if I would wish for a little company?"

"Maybe this is a bit too personal," Cole softly said, offering her an out.

"No, no, now I've been given three wishes here, and that doesn't happen every day."

Cole watched as her shy hand was revealed when she leaned back in the mauve-colored cushion of her rocker. Two purple scars, like railroad tracks, began at her bowed fingers and crawled away under the cuff of her turquoise sweater. She did not look at Cole as she spoke. Instead she looked for the courage to keep her scarred hand resting in the open, before her best friend.

"As you probably suspect, I miss using both of my hands around the kitchen. My handwriting looks like Morse Code, and then there's driving. I think one hand at the wheel scares Pilot sometimes. But most of all, Cole, I'm always afraid of having to tell someone the damn story of how it happened, that's the hardest part of it for me." Gulping, she turned away, and her hand began to retreat behind the moon of her thigh, but Cole's strong hand came from his lap, trying to rescue hers. She tried subtly pulling it away, but years of friendship wouldn't let it go.

"Well, okay now, two more right?" she sighed, uncertain if she wanted to continue. Pressing on, she cleared her throat and said, "I have enough money for three people and aside from what you're holding, I'm in good health. I do have another thought, but if you laugh I'll scratch your eyes out with my good hand and personally see to every last one of your lemon bars 'accidentally' hittin' the linoleum from now to eternity!" she warned through a tight row of white teeth, her right hand hovering over the plate of pastries. As her next wish came to mind, she glanced up at him, then away, embarrassed. “So…I guess I’ve always wished to have a beautiful voice. A voice that could light up these dark winters, but I couldn’t carry a tune if you put it in a backpack for me. I’ve always been a little envious of those breathtaking voices in the world, mine just isn’t one of them.”

“I’ve never heard your voice over anything more than a holler and it’s usually my ass you’re chewin’,” Cole scoffed playfully, squeezing her hand, confirming to himself that this was exactly what he had always liked about Laura, the fact she could consistently impress him with the simplest of things without even realizing it. “I assume you’ve given singing a solid effort?”

She half smiled a smile in Pilot’s direction and said, “Cole, it’s true, even Pilot won’t tolerate it for longer than it takes him to leave the room, and he’s tone deaf.”

“I don’t suppose your third wish could be for me to have a quick listen?” Cole asked, realizing a touch too late that he knew better than to ask.

“Cole Caffy! Do you want me to start droppin’ your silly lemon bars left and right, here and now?” she fired, daring him to ask again. “Pilot get your wiggly butt in here, three lemons in a row boy, you just hit the jackpot!”

“Here now, there’s no reason to lose our minds! I think it’s a lovely wish from a lovely woman,” Cole said bending an honest smile from cheek to cheek as his arm leapt to save one of the jeopardized pastries. “And your third and final wish would be?”

“I know what it would be, Cole. I think of it often…and fear that only a wish could ever make it come true.” Laura let her eyes roam from Cole to the view offered through the glossy porthole. He encouraged her with a gentle squeeze to her hand.

“I’m sorry, Cole, but it’s just too personal for me to talk about right now. Maybe someday.”

The warm home took on a comfortable silence. This was one of the many things Cole felt a person could judge a best friend by, the ability to just shut the hell up and sit with each other sharing a good ‘Day’ dream.

Cole collected his new scarf and went into the cold. Laura heard the crunch of his boots cross the deck as she gathered coffee cups and a plate, loosely arranged with lemon bars. Then she hurried to the porthole aside the main door, as always, with ample time to watch Cole's black Rover pulling him back up her long lumpy drive to Patch Road, her least favorite part of these visits. However, Laura's eyes searched side to side, finding no sign of any black Rover, no sign of an engineer…just a yellow Wagoneer.

Bridget Poland started life thirty-six years ago in the quiet town of Pelican Rapids, Minnesota. Her mother and father separated just after Christmas during her first year of junior high school. Her bedroom door opened earlier than usual one morning, her mother asking for an answer to a life-changing question from her daughter. Bridget answered with a hug, and two days later, she was throwing her arms around her father who was already talking about seeing her on Christmas, nine months away. She waved wildly at him, trying to wipe his tears away as their loaded Toyota pickup backed down the driveway.

During the long warming drive south, Bridget stumbled onto some pretty big questions. "Why Texas, Mom? Isn't it flat and hot there?" Then crossing Kansas, "Why don't you think you'll come back for Christmas with me?" And finally the hardest question passing the Brownsville city limits sign that her mother could find no answer for, "Why would two people that wanted to be away from each other so bad like you and Dad, hug and cry so much when they have to say goodbye, Mom?"

Life would be the one to give Bridget the answer seven years later when saying goodbye to Kevin Stoller. A high school love had been crushed when Bridget opened the big white envelope from Boston University. Three weeks later Bridget was throwing her arms around Kevin talking about seeing him on Christmas, nine months away. Her mother silently watching this from the living room window, one hand to her mouth trying not to add the tears, knowing her turn was next.

Bridget had gone on to do very well in Boston. Those long legs of hers carried her long dark hair class to class, picking up A's along the way. Her striking looks could change conversations when she entered a room, but she wasn't egotistical, not in the way others might assume from afar. She was indeed very bright and carried herself so. Bridget knew that one and one were two by the time she was two. Never once did she call mommy or daddy for money and couldn't tolerate those who did. "Get off your ass and get a job," was her usual reply. "If you can't do it on your own, then don't!"

Bridget dated a handful of times during her sophomore year at the University. More or less just for the company. Later, she stopped altogether, focusing on her growing studies. One anxious fellow that had taken a shine didn't seem to want to go away. He passed right by her walking on Davis Street missing her by only a few feet; months after it had been made very clear to him she wasn't interested. Bridget saw him first and managed to duck into Beck's Antique Shop. While hiding in the corner she found a lamp with stained glass butterflies welded to its rich dome shade.

During her final year at B.U., she attended a lecture. "A guest speaker from Alaska, someone out there doing it, a Mr. Caffy," she told her boss at *Sky Scrapers,* a window washing company, while hanging over three hundred feet above downtown Bean Town. Waiting tables never appealed much.

In front of no less than fifteen hundred people with note pads and November sweaters, Mr. Caffy began with "Engineering…is art dictated through physics." Bridget never let a word slip past for the next hour and a half.

She worked weekends, summers and after school for several hours before returning to her piling books. During the warmer months, when she was able to work full time, Bridget would peer in huge office windows, hanging from her wooden platform suspended sometimes forty stories from earth, smiling from within as the North Eastern sun tinted her body. Businessmen appearing eager at their desks would peek up to find this gorgeous brunette sliding up their window as though she was an angel climbing back to Heaven.

Bridget was asked to dinner thirty-four times, given three marriage proposals, and even offered a weekend in Martha's Vineyard, twice. She would always find that certain smile that could tell them "No, thank you" and still leave them even more taken with her than before.

She knew one day she'd be looking out of those bulging windows rather than in, determined to change the view, however, with less people and more mountains. Texas took the flat out of her in more ways than one.

After graduating, she accepted a position with the New York State Department working as an inspector for some thirty-five local bridges and two small agricultural dams. Her office was more often than not a white minivan with studded tires and tax-exempt license plates. She did, however, enjoy the solitude. Soon after, she progressed to the drawing room where she spent the next two years working under the calculative eyes of structural engineers. Bridget's talent quickly became evident through her exquisite lines and measurements, proving she was more than just a lovely woman with exquisite lines and measurements.

She was later given control of her own project. The Little River Pass Bridge was completed ahead of schedule and under budget. Constructed of concrete and steel, it spanned over eighty feet of slippery clay and very little water. It was the first time Bridget had ever felt truly proud of herself.

The very afternoon of its completion her glistening resume was sent to the offices of *Here to There Engineering* in Anchorage, Alaska. The location, the work, and the future she wanted. Two weeks slowly passed before she got word from the firm. "There's a message for you on your desk, Miss Poland, a Mr. Caffy from Alaska," the office secretary said, envious of blue eyes and brains.

The driving wind from Turnagain Arm south of Anchorage racked its clear cool fingers through Bridget's come hither hair as a cell phone chirped from the passenger seat of her new white Subaru parked slanted aside Highway 1.

"Hello. This is Bridge," she quietly answered, cautiously returning to the front of her car where she leaned against it, feeling her pulse speed as a bull moose hoisted his head from the saltwater of the inlet.

"Yes, hi. This is Cole Caffy. I hope I haven't caught you at a bad time?"

"Cole, no…" she stammered. "It's just that there's a moose, this giant moose, not fifty yards away from me!"

"God, I hope you're not at the office!"

"He's so huge, Cole! His shoulder blades are like peaks on his mountainous back. I had to pull over, this is amazing!"

"Hey, you want to keep an eye on those critters though! They only seem slow until they're not," Cole warned.

"And I just stopped not more than four or five miles back to watch these beautiful mountain goats climbing right beside the highway. I spotted them through my sun roof."

"Not goats, Dall sheep, doll, and it was all a ploy…they're thieves."

"What?"

"Did you get out of your car at any time?"

"Well, yes, to watch them but…."

"Your purse, tell me you took your purse with you."

"No, Cole, I didn't take my purse with me," Bridget said, showing the moose a smile he could have easily thought was chosen just for him.

"Oh sweet, sweet, naive Bridge. They look for out-of-state plates, you know," Cole warned, hearing Bridget's laugh crackle in and out over the cell phone. "It's true. They once left a husband and wife from Texas, I think it was, naked, without a dime in the ditch. Oh sure they got what was left of their car back eventually, but most of it was spread out in pawnshops across the lower forty-eight, the poor souls."

"Cole, what are you up to today?" Bridget laughed, picturing the Texas couple filling out a lengthy knee-slapping police report.

As Cole sat peering into the James Bond poster hanging directly in front of his desk, he searched for that same self-confidence that Sean Connery's steely eyes conveyed without question. At first he hesitated, spinning his legs out from under the desk and reclining his leather chair to its limits. As he gripped both temples with one hand, he couldn't help glancing between his fingers back to Connery's suave and speechless reply instilled in his reassuring eye. Anxiously clearing his throat, Cole sat up straight, biding time as he squared himself behind the desk before using his northerly voice to say, "Well, I was hoping you might consider having dinner with an old engineer like myself tonight?"

Cole's words ricocheted off a satellite into Bridget's ear, triggering loose her stare at a moose. Thinking of reasons she shouldn't…couldn't, she stepped heel to toe from the front of the Subaru following in the ribbed impression of a snow-packed tire track. “Oh what a great invitation, Cole,” she said at last, “but I don’t know if I can make it tonight.”

“Oh…I *wish* you could.”

four

A sleek train bound for Edinburgh, Scotland, fired across the English countryside like a pissed-off snake wearing sunglasses, scaring dairy cattle to the boundaries of fish bowl pastures. They bawled back to their curious calves with sticky pink tongues arching center their bullhorn mouths, warning them of the thundering machine that had already disappeared down the great shiny cow path in a controlled scream.

Winter green scenery flashed through the train's tall tinted windows onto a subdued crowd of commuters. A quiet man with a loud family minded his own business by burying his nose in a magazine about other people's business.

"DEAR…GOD!" shouted the silvery-haired man sitting across the aisle who had somehow gone unnoticed until now. The quiet man, recognizing the western accent, said "Crazy Americans," under his breath as he went back to reading about crazy Americans. A pleasantly dressed fat woman with tricky eyes the color of November offered a smile saying, "Yes, it is quite amazing," pointing to the ruins of an eleventh century castle anciently rolling past on a hilltop.

Cole Caffy sat stunned, his wide eyes circumnavigating the train's beige interior to discover where his wish had taken him. Seeing the castle his mouth formed a small 'o,' the charcoal English sky pacing overhead through partially transparent ceilings.

Gathering himself, he made his way down the center of the speeding train, dragging his fingers over the backs of each olive-green commercial seat, three deep and facing each another throughout so parties of six could effectively argue about the world. A young British boy, poking into his teens, answered Cole's question with a hitchhiker's thumb aiming to the next car where the private booths segregated the richer commuters. As he meandered gazing out the windows a farm neat as a pin, with black-and-white cows and an orange tractor, came and went by at eighty miles per hour.

Cole peered discreetly into each of the private rooms divided by metal and glass. A woman with a fancy pillbox hat, nursing, seemed to know Cole was a foreigner before he did with never a word spoken. Then with a rake of curtains she was gone. Turning his eyes to the next booth, three men in tight suits and loose ties calmly spoke in accents he couldn't hear but imagined. A fourth, studying the northbound view, wore a white fisherman's sweater high about the neck that grazed the back of his salt-colored hair.

Gently, Cole slid the compartment doors open, bringing the suits to a seated attention. "I'm afraid you have the wrong booth, Sir," the lead suit said over a muscular jaw that drew lines deep in his cheeks with each word.

As Cole quickly surveyed the booth clockwise, his mouth dropped open and his arms went limp at his side. "Forgive me, I…"

The calm man in a turtleneck turned from the thick British countryside draping one eye a bit in a question. "I think what my good man here meant to say was, can we help you, sir?" The man spoke through a traveled Scottish accent that made Cole realize just how bad his Sean Connery impressions really had been all along.

Nervously Cole spoke, "Well, you see, I just wished for a few minutes of your time, if it were possible?…You are Sean Connery…I believe?"

"Well, I certainly believe I am, I've been under that impression now for some time anyway." Connery, ever the gentleman, answered in a friendly note. "Usually I'm up to my ears in busy, but something's telling me it's time for a short break. Gentlemen, would you please excuse us?" he asked to the suits with a smile, a picture perfect smile that Cole instantly recognized from the poster hanging in his den, a poster he'd just been standing in front of only moments ago.

One, two, three, the writer, the editor, and finally the bodyguard got up and departed the coach like the beginning to a bad joke in search of whiskey; whiskey named after the country the train was entering. The last man out ran his trained hands over Cole's torso with a thousand-yard stare, then down his legs as if getting the last drop of toothpaste from a tube. He trusted the finale crotch grabbing was the usual procedure. Cole nearly turned and coughed.

"Sean Connery…I believe," Connery said, offering his hand.

"Caffy…Cole Caffy, and thank you for your time."

"Please," Connery said, motioning to the opposing bench seat, shrink wrapped with the hide of those that live in fishbowl pastures. "May I ask, friend or foe?" Connery asked, with a slight hesitation in his strolling voice.

"Well…friends take time, but certainly not foe, Mr. Connery. At the risk of sounding like so many others, I guess I would say I was a fan, although longer than most."

"I'm guessing you're on holiday, Mr. Caffy?"

"Only one holiday, just today, but then I have recently retired so maybe it's one big holiday from here on in."

"What did you retire from?"

"I am…was, a structural engineer, Mr. Connery."

"Oh, I would imagine you will always be an engineer. I'm certain the occupation has been more than just a job, has it not? And please, this is hardly a place for formalities, call me Sean…Cole, is it?"

Cole hadn't realized just how nervous he was until now. Taking a deep breath, he forced his body to relax, smelling Connery's expensive cologne that made him think of white wine in winter. "Yes, Cole."

"Cole, if I retired today, I would still consider myself an actor tomorrow," Connery said, completely at ease as he crossed one leg over the other, his shoes putting off a brilliant shine. "Tell me, what did you engineer?"

Feeling that his years spent idling at the drafting table paled in the light of the present company, Cole shifted in his seat, entwining his fingers in his lap. "Well, mainly bridges. I worked on a handful of dams, and dug a few tunnels for a short time, but bridges were what kept crossing my mind ever since I was a boy," he humbly answered, noticing the gray sleeve of the bodyguard resting just outside the butted coach doors.

“Bridges, I’ve always been impressed with them, and speak of the Devil, here comes one now,” Connery said, nodding his chin to the glass ceiling. As the blind train brailed its way across a clever steel bridge its black beams flashed past overhead as though a high school film had jumped the tracks of its projector’s wheels.

Smiling at Cole’s enthusiasm for the passing bridge, Connery slowly raised only one thick brow and asked, “Moight I ask where a western-tongued stranger like yourself calls home?”

“Alaska. Just north of Anchorage, in the foothills of the Chugach Mountain Range,” he answered, firing the question back at Connery.

“Edinburgh. Born and raised. Although, I never seem to be able to spend as much time there as I would wish to.”

“It seems I’ve heard somewhere that you drive a Range Rover?” Cole asked, maturely as he could.

“Yes, in fact I do, black as a coal mine, Cole. It’s one of those things I look forward to on these trips home,” Connery admitted, inspecting Cole as though realizing how this silver-haired character greatly resembled himself, right down to the wire-cropped eyebrows unfurled over a slight map of crows feet as if a tender-footed bird had been hunting bushy caterpillars at the rim of a gelatinous blue puddle.

“I, too, drive a Rover, black as a coal mine to boot,” Cole said, proudly arching up the corners of his lips.

Inching forward, Connery lowered his tone a bit to ask, “Don’t you joost love the little blue 4x4 indicator light?”

“Well yes…of course!” Cole answered, as if the question even needed to be asked.

Letting an easy smile drift to the corner of his lips, Connery asked, “Tell me, Cole, is there anything in particular you wish to ask me?”

“Actually, yes,” Cole said pressing up straight, his palms denting the seat’s leather cushion, “That’s sort of the question in itself. Bear with me if you will…but if you had three wishes, Mr. Connery, Sean, any three wishes, aside from say, saving the planet or wishing for gold, what might they be? These are, let’s say, personal wishes just for you.”

Crossing one leg over the other as he relaxed back, Connery glanced out the window and spoke through a play-along grin.

"Wishes? Well my friend, are you familiar with the term, 'Wish in one hand and shit in the other to see which one fills first?'"

Cole gently captured his bottom lip between his teeth and let it pop free, twice. "Yes. But I'm still curious. Let's say, just this once, the wishful hand fills. And please remember you're not talking to the media, and there are no prying ears here waiting for a politically correct answer."

Hearing the seriousness conveyed in Cole's voice, Connery genuinely matched it with, "Well, as I mentioned before, I would like to be able to spend more time at home, with my family. Another would probably be along the lines of being able to be the best person I possibly could be at all times, and that would be without exception," Connery said, aiming his pointer finger to the ceiling while keeping a cool eye on a carload of British teenagers hanging out the windows, waving and screaming as they raced the train. "And the last I should think, would be to never have a need for a bodyguard…there's a lot to that one if you think about it, Cole." Steel and glass prevented hurting anyone's feelings.

Remaining silent for a moment in thought, Cole overlapped his hands in his lap and crossed one leg over the other before answering. "I believe I'm a good person. However, I couldn't swear to the always part. I do have a great deal of time to spend at home, but no family, and certainly no need for a bodyguard. But let me tell you, it's not all that thrilling," he said, remembering all the late night meals alone, in a house filled with silence. No family, or wife, to brighten the quiet of his life.

"Tell me, Cole, and what might a few of your dreams be?" Connery asked, in a natural way that surprised Cole with its directness.

"Well…I guess one of them was to simply meet with you."

Connery, taken aback by this stirring answer, nodded with an appreciative smile, noticing that Cole's stainless steel wristwatch was nine hours early.

The city of Edinburgh came into view, swept with rain, as the rushing train began to relax, nearing its destination. Connery's thick jawed bodyguard slid the compartment doors open and stated the obvious, that they were arriving. "I would like to make a quick low profile exit from the station sir, and your Range Rover is waiting for you."

"Wow," Cole whispered, witnessing the undeniable dedication offered by the hard-lined man taking control. Crossing his arms, he pictured Ray Bans sheltering Anna's steely eyes as they militantly scanned *Here to There's* parking lot, discreet wire coiling from collar to ear, patiently awaiting her chance to catch a bullet. "So, this is what it's like being rich and famous?"

Connery answered with only a humble chuckle, as Cole watched the real deal go back to standing his post just outside the compartment doors. Cole recognized the tricky-eyed woman through the compartment window, making her way up the corridor. He remembered her pointing out the ancient castle rolling past on a distant hilltop. The bodyguard studied the length of her coat without smiling. "Ma'am."

Politely turning to one side, she draped an arm just behind to skirt past the solidly framed man in the corridor's narrow throat. Connery's speechless mouth raced to find words as only he had time to see what was gripped in that hand of hers. What the bodyguard did not, and could not see, was the sweeping stun gun as it was rammed to his ribcage, its surging venom of purple lightning ricocheted from the bodyguard's extremities to his arcing heart. Tricky Eyes watched the pupils of her target jump, then limply fade in their sockets, his electrified arms frozen wide against the coach's window amidst a muted scream that would shine the envy of mimes.

"John!" shouted Connery, seeing the snickering face of a jilted fan slowly inch over the brim of gray suit. Her sickly smile grew, then flattened as her thumb hopped from the jolting devise. The actor and engineer could only watch as the guard's limp body slid to the train's floor, dreaming of static.

"What? What is it you want?" Connery demanded through the glass doors as if aliens had just destroyed the Capital. Then coming to his feet he sternly narrowed his eyes and said, "I warn you should calm yourself as I'm armed, and prepared to give you the proof."

Again, a grin twisted across her pitted face, her finger wagging side to side implied she knew it to be a cornered man's bluff. Her attention darted to the door handle. So did Cole's. No lock, only the slump of bodyguard to hurdle as if it were his last defense. With one clean swoop, her shocking right hand drained away into her trench coat's pocket. Before any sigh of relief could surface, Cole and Connery lowered their chins to a naughty little knock at the base of the window twinkling with the dull sheen of revolver. No electric jaws spitting lightning, no paralyzing rush of blackout, just plain old dead man's lead. Cole actually started to miss that tooth-bleeding sneer of hers as he hopelessly watched a far greater evil push back Tricky Eye's dimples as if about to film a recruiting commercial for Hell.

Cole did not turn to Connery when he spoke from the side of his mouth. "So, this is what it's like being rich and famous?"

"Well, I guess you moight say it's not all Ritz and Range Rovers."

The gun rose, and with it the hot flashing note of fear the mind inevitably sends to the stomach when it expects holes to be torn through itself at any instant. "Wait," Connery said, far more calmly than Cole could have mustered. "Joost wait long enough for us to say goodbye to this wonderful Scottish country side."

"Yes. Oh yes, and if I could call on your wonderful patience as well madam, I'm from Alaska. So if it's all the same to you, I'll just be back in two shakes of a lamb's tail."

Again she tapped the six-shooter on the glass, "If I were you, I'd just settle for shaking that fancy booger's hand beside you. Although don't write him, he'll never mail you a single word in return. No matter how many letters you stay up at all hours pouring your heart into!"

The hammer was drawn back and her eyes squinted in aim. Raw fear lunged to all corners of Cole's body, desperately missing the tranquility of his own den mundanely hovering over Spring Creek, so far away. He stood frozen center of the booth, watching as Connery prepared for his next and possibly last move by digging up the courage to rush the doors. In doing so he coolly turned to Cole, raising an infamous brow, "I'm betting you would joost love to have one of your wishes along about now?"

Cole's face lifted from the trenches, his lips unable to keep up with the words stumbling over his tongue. "Yes! Yes, oh yes. I would indeed my good man, I would indeed!"

Connery, squinting sideways at Cole's stammering remark, quickly realized he was on his own, and raised his square chin preparing to charge the bull.

“Now, Mr. Connery, Sean, I think we should shake hands like the kind lady suggested. I think it’s a good ‘plan’,” Cole said, staring deep into Connery’s eyes until they met his.

With his heart leaping in his chest, Connery answered, “Don’t think of me as rude, Cole, but I’m a little busy. You moight say my mind is racing, racing at the door for all I’m worth, as a matter a fact. That is if you can read ‘my’ plan?” His voice was low and smooth as possible, spoken from the side of his acted smile as if pleased to be at gunpoint.

“Shake it!” Cole blurted, plunging the air with his offered hand, his gambling eyes never leaving the revolver. Connery exhaled and reluctantly grabbed the hand as if he’d just surrendered. The doors began to part, and a pistol leaked in. Connery attempted to pull away, but Cole hung on, pinching his eyes shut as if about to step from the rail of a bridge.

“I *wish* Sean Connery and I were off this train!”

As she burst in with the pistol aiming wildly about the abandoned compartment, her tricky eyes reeled open with stun. An enraged and defeated shot was fired through the glass ceiling. Before she could realize it, the awoken bodyguard had wrapped his iron fists around her ankles and yanked her to the floor. One quick move followed, and the pistol was shoved between her not so tricky eyes. “Where is he?” the bodyguard growled with a flat and deadly voice. As Tricky Eyes flinched for the stun gun, her arm was broken and the question was repeated.

As though in a dream, the train sucked away down its shiny cow path, leaving behind the two men holding hands in its whirling tailwind. Hair the color of salt and pepper danced wild on their wondering minds, as Cole watched the train disappear with a crazy woman who no doubt was searching for impossible answers herself. Connery’s eyes opened to the ground covered with treated timbers smothered with steel rails that still moaned from the charging iron wheels. Floating his arms away from his side and feet spread wide, he stood gawking at Cole. “My God man, what in the hell of hells has just happened? Who, who are you?”

Nearly as shaken, Cole slowly turned to Connery at the speed of a second hand. “I’m just a retired bridge builder.”

Connery's palms went to his temples as he approached. "I heard something. I heard something just then. If I said what it was, I'd sound crazier than all the Jello toppings in the world mixed together."

"This thing you heard, was it…color?" Cole asked, as if he were asking himself.

"Yes…yes it was," Connery stammered. Patting and rubbing his own body with his shaking hands, his thoughts raced to one simple conclusion. "I've died. She pulled the trigger and I've died. This is what it's like to die?"

"No, Mr. Connery…Sean. This is what it's like to live. You're very much alive," Cole answered through a growing smile as the sky spat rain.

"You took my hand. Then you…wished something?"

"Wish in one hand, and shit in the other," Cole quoted, completing his smile.

"Retired engineer my arse!" Connery scoffed in perfect Scottish note.

"It's true, Mr. Connery."

"Why here? Why am I standing here?"

"I was just as afraid of that six-shooter as you were. I'm certain I would have been next on her ludicrous list. I didn't know what else to wish for except just getting us the hell out of there, so here we are," Cole tried to explain, shaking his head at the tracks, struggling himself to believe his own seemingly ludicrous words.

"Wishing? No, no, no!" Connery shouted to the rolling green hills. "This is some elaborate prank put together by an American studio having a laugh. Special effects and all. And you're the key player, aren't you? The wish master that leads me through it? Keeps me playing along? How much?"

"I'm sorry?" Cole said frowning.

"How much are they paying you? Have they promised you a commercial or two?" Connery turned away, to further convince himself, then spun in place to show his sly grin once again. "It was Eddie! Wasn't it? That bloody rascal is getting me back for constantly having my bodyguard hide his cars!"

Cole watched as 007 shook his head and laughed under the drizzle. "You might want to ask your bodyguard just how much fun this prank was," Cole said, hoping the guard had awoken from his electric nap.

"John?" Connery sputtered, tipping his chin at the tracks. "Neva. Sure he seems far too serious to play along with a gag, but let me tell you, all that straight faced stuff is just part of the job, a job he does very well I'll remind you."

"I should get you to the train station."

"Why certainly. And along the way let's joost pop up at Paramount to say boo!" Connery said this confidently enough as if he were delivering lines, but Cole could see something still scrambling for answers behind his eyes to fill the gaping holes in his Hollywood theory. They both turned to the sound of a car swerving up the gravel road that followed the tracks into Edinburgh. Connery no doubt expected to find a limo streamlining the horizon with the entire special effects department crammed inside, waiting to leap out giggling with scantily dressed blonds wielding champagne bottles. Instead, Cole quickly recognized the rust bucket as the same carload of British teenagers he'd seen earlier failing to keep stride with the train. And the bottles wielded were not expensive champagne, but bottles just the same.

"Tell me, Cole, if that's your real name," Connery said, doubting with his brows. "How long is this joke to continue?"

"Like I said, Mr. Connery, I should get you to the station," Cole said, eyeing the car as it rattled to a stop no more than a football's throw away. From across a ditch of wild alfalfa, the curious teens leaned out the windows, finding themselves staring at a star who stood squinting back at them.

Not liking the sneering nod coming from the only girl, Cole stepped three rail ties to Connery and asked, "Color, can you explain how your movie folks made you hear color? I don't think I'd make much of an actor. I'd see it as lying and blow my character by apologizing to the audience for what I was about to say. In other words, Mr. Connery, I don't lie, and I'm not lying now. You were wished to where you stand."

Connery didn't make eye contact, but turned his head in Cole's direction just the same. "Your watch. I don't think even ol' Eddie would have caught that little touch. Alaska, you say. And joost how long ago were you there?"

"Half an hour."

Connery's eyes made contact. He held them there directly on Cole's long enough to learn that this man, indeed crazy or not, wasn't telling any elaborate lies, or at the very least believed what he was saying. Simultaneously the teenagers' four doors cried open with two beer cans and an empty bottle of vodka falling to the gravel with a clank. "It's him I'm tellin' ya. It's him! Lives around here he does."

They approached the trench of alfalfa, curious as alley cats, and appeared to be judging the distance between just another day and one that could make history in their juvenile lives. Cole faintly heard the raspy voice of the only girl carry to them on the breeze. "Fetch a fortune he would. We'd be rich before that worthless pecker of yours was ready again!"

Cole, and especially Connery, didn't care for what the breeze had to say, or the seemingly agreeable nods of the scratchy-throated gal's four big boys weaving into the alfalfa as if the shot was fired and the bird lay fallen.

"Good Lord. Was it something I said today?" Connery mumbled, turning to Cole who had his hand stuck out before him once again. "Oh no. The last time I latched on to that bugger the world turned inside out and upside down."

The first of the side-winding juveniles slunk to the tracks with worn Nikes just fifty ties away. Another, draped in a black leather jacket laced with zippers, joined him with a devilish look that Connery had perfected for the screen when cast as the bad guy. The others, fanning out on the girl's command, inched up the grade slowly but surely. "Don't run away now you handsome bloke."…"Yeah, be a good rich sort and give us an autograph!" hissed the leathered one.

"Yes. I certainly believe they want your John Hancock all right, but in blood, and spilt across the bottom of a ransom note to boot," Cole said grabbing Connery's shoulder. "It's time to catch the next train!"

The gangliest of the lot inched forward tie by tie until Cole could smell the shoplifted spirits. Connery pushed Cole's hand from the rim of his shoulder, flattening his eyes to the drunken teenager who over-handed an emptied beer bottle in the air, shattering on the tracks just behind. With one swaggering step, Connery approached face to face, the others began to smile, yet kept their distance. "It's you alright. Swore to my partners in crime here that I saw your famous mug on the train just before. Now, what's a fancy fellow like yourself doing here on the wrong side of the tracks?"

"Well. First might I ask, friend or foe?" Connery quizzed, eye-to-eye, toe-to-toe, knowing the answer to be foe. The leather-bound one didn't answer. He only turned away long enough to gleam a hyena's sneer back to his pack. Cole stepped to Connery's side, balling his fingers into fists as he watched the flock's circle tighten. As the sneering one's face turned back. Crack! Connery's hand punched his soggy face, and another following jab sent the boy to the ground. As the girl screamed "Get him!" Cole drew back and let the next vulture have a taste of his whistling fist. Connery knocked another from his feet with his own sweeping leg and Cole flailed forth to pepper the goon with a left as the girl leapt to his back masking his face behind bony fingers and chewed nails. Spinning wildly in place, Cole rifled the air with punches as he tried to shake the monkey, randomly knocking one of the goons alongside the pierced ear, driving his gold stud to blood. Ducking a swat, Connery popped up and delivered a fireball right to the nose ring of another scrapper reaching for something pointy just inside his jean jacket. With a final twirling heave, the girl was tossed to the tracks where she lay draped over the rails as if a victim of Snidely Whiplash. The last of the bunch threw a weak-handed left at Connery's curled grin, but as quickly as it was blocked, the teen felt the fire of Connery's stiff uppercut burn into his jawbone. Lights out.

"Run!" Cole hollered, standing center the tracks littered with foe. As if the only weapon brandished were a starter's pistol, the actor and engineer high tailed down the slope of flowering alfalfa just as the wiry girl uncoiled to her feet with the others.

"The car!" Connery shouted.

"The car?" Cole howled, wanting to just shake hands and appear at the station.

"Yes! That is unless you prefer to race this wild bunch to town on foot!"

Neither of them glanced behind as they scrambled to the gravel and sprang for the tattered four-door. Windows down, doors left open, keys in the ignition were the only thing shining. As Cole rounded the trunk, he heard the scrape of gravel in hot pursuit. Connery threw himself behind the wheel and slammed the door while cranking the key. Cole, with a little less cool in his family tree, nose-dived headlong across the forward bench seat and cried, "FLOOOOR IT!"

The car pleaded through a backfire then lunged forward as Connery nearly tore the gearshift from the steering column. Fishtailing between ditches the car sprayed earth and the back doors swung shut. Hearing a raspy scream, Cole spun around to find the girl's body smeared across the rear window. "My God, they're vampires!" Connery flashed his eyes to the rearview and jerked the wheel. The vampire was gone, rolling to the ditch with a fading squeal.

Connery held the pedal to the floor and the car thudded on. Refusing to let go the dash with his white knuckled grip, Cole finally managed to close his mouth as he scanned the battlefield behind. He could see nothing but gravel bordered by the violet flowers of alfalfa. With a smile reaching deep in his cheeks, he looked to Connery, who was the first to burst out laughing, then Cole joined in perfectly, pinching his eyes shut in the roar as 007 and the retired engineer raced for Edinburgh.

The train arrived seven minutes late right on schedule at the Waverly Rail Station. Modern doors opened in to let people out. First to hit the red bricks running was the bodyguard who searched the entire length of train, window by window, for his unguarded body. The writer and his editor soon emerged with the tricky-eyed woman cradling her arm as she continued to spout crazy talk of people vanishing into thin air. A car that looked as though it were powered only by voodoo came to a thankful rest choking on its own smoke at the brick's edge. Connery, laughing uncontrollably again, wrapped his palms over the wheel as his body jolted in the torn seat. "You…you should have seen yourself bucking in circles with that young jackal strapped to you like a straight jacket!"

"Yeah, and when you hollered 'The car!' all I could think was, 'the car?' What the hell do you want with that pile of crap at a time like this!"

Connery's laugh held strong, but weakened to a powerful smile as he again happened to glance at Cole's inaccurate wristwatch.

"I'm grateful to you, Cole. I don't know how we got off that train, and away from that curse of a woman, but I'm grateful to you. Now…tell me retired bridge builder," Connery said pushing back in the knife-shredded seat, turning his face full view, noticing a small cut above Cole's right brow, "how, exactly, did you get on the train?"

Looking away, Cole swallowed and ran his finger along a deep crack in the sun-chapped dash that felt like the tear in a piñata's belly. "I was standing in front of a poster of you. It hangs in my den. I thought I might like to meet you after all the company you've offered me at all hours when I'm restless, or when my house falls asleep before I do and snores with a quiet that makes you wonder if you've done something wrong in life to be sitting there alone. Maybe I just wanted to say, thank you. Then…I heard color."

Connery remained silent, just looking at Cole for a long moment, resting his elbow out the window, not believing, nor disbelieving, just accepting, that this man, crazy or not, was indeed a good man. He leaned a little forward, aware that Cole was feeling uncomfortable with his own crazy, yet honest answer. "You're welcome."

With a somber face hinting with grin, Cole turned to Connery. "You know, I just pictured five outraged teenagers steaming our way with their zippers rubbing and beer bottles clanging. But with that mean uppercut of yours, I suspect we'd win round two as well."

"Yeah, so much for webs or laser beams shooting out of my wristwatch, huh?" Connery said, tilting his head, raising a brow, lowering his voice through a sloped grin, "But let's not go forgetting that flurry of swings you delivered while trying to buck that young gal. You were like a runaway gun turret spinning wild!" Connery and Cole, friends, shared in a roller coaster laugh with one another again on the ragged bench seat of a rusted car as it beaded with Scottish drizzle.

Cole's damp eyed laugh froze, when out of nowhere, with never a sound or warning, he felt the steely muzzle of the bodyguard's gun barrel press to his temple, "If you move, sir, you will die. If you have an itch, ask yourself first, is it really worth scratching? Now, one by one, place your hands on the dash. And Mr. Connery, will you please step from the vehicle and come round to stand directly behind me."

"John, no! He's a friend…not foe!"

The bodyguard followed closely behind as the writer and editor swung open the doors of Connery's black Range Rover. To their left, the station authorities passed with Tricky Eyes in tow to a wagon flashing blue. Cole could see the questions mixing in the bodyguard like oil and water, but gave him no time to start pouring. "I've never seen anything like it, John, if I can call you John? One minute there you were on the floor pretending to be all loaded with electricity, and the next, wow! Pow! Boom! She never stood a chance of keeping us locked in that glass cage, and we owe it all to you for getting us the hell out of there and off that train. I'll bet you're ex-C.I.A, aren't ya? Or at the very least some other letters that spell bad ass! Either way, I'm forever grateful to you, John."

The doors of the Rover closed as it was filled, leaving Cole to stand alone on the sea of red brick. "John, wait," Connery said, humming away the glass between him and Cole. "I hesitate to ask you this, but do you need a ride?"

"…No, no I don't. But thank you."

"Something told me you wouldn't," Connery said, arching a brow that tugged with it the corner of his lip. "Alaska you say? Well…I will then at least wish you a safe trip home."

"Me too."

An honest smile from his new friend and not foe, came at him through the closing window of a black Rover glistening with warm rain. A handful of western tourists stood staring at its famous passenger, wearing white hand-out rain ponchos as if someone had tried throwing them away. The Range Rover smoothly clicked into gear and wound out of sight down the wrong side of Market Street, a busy gothic puzzle of worn stones. Not knowing if anyone might be listening or not, Cole arched his face to the Scottish drizzle and said anyway, "Thank you."

Smiling to the sky, he closed his eyes and softly whispered to himself. There was color. He could hear it warmly surrounding him as his wristwatch leapt back to its correct time without ever realizing it by following Cole to his James Bond poster that would always proudly hang in his den.

Humans have claimed a difference between animal instinct and their own instincts ever since they traded in their damp dugout caves for fancy mobile homes with outlets and end tables to hold the latest TV Guide. This is another way of assuming a subconscious superiority, proving animals other than human endure yet another task in their daily lives that is a far greater accomplishment than we are worthy…they live only in reality, unable to hide behind a barrage of excuses for laziness or failure.

Wobbling from Pole to Pole, winter drags its frozen fingernails up and down the globe chasing animals, mammals, and bird life to its migratory ends searching north to South for something to compliment their short lives driven by this thing called instinct.

Some humans, too, make this migration, but for pleasure trips feeling the sun on their shoulders and bragging to others of their tropical adventures, and ironically, hunting trips. Can we even imagine the adventures taken on by those that lack voice boxes? Obviously not, it would show through a greater respect.

The northern timber wolf cries to its mate through bloody pain, rolling, painting the snow with burgundy death, only its own species will respond, unable to aid. Echoing across the white tundra, the Arctic musk oxen charge one another more than a dozen times like hulking gladiators dueling for the honor of sex. Frightened teenagers throw hate packed punches in high school parking lots after a glance at the others' potential mates. The polar bear rising on two legs before it strikes, one of them will carry the burden of defeat.

Alaskan mule deer crane their heads high before entering a meadow of does, like a drunken cowboy walking into a small town bar full of possibilities, a simple enigma really. We all have eyes, ears, mouths, and hearts beating for similar reasons in our bony chests, our fig leaf 501's seeming to make a difference that does not exist.

All breathing things also feel loss. The timber wolf that ran out of its burgundy paint leaves behind a devastated partner howling to the black night for answers, only cold mountains of silence reply. A shy wrinkled man screams through his violin blaming God and his cancerous tool for taking his wife.

Wounded animals return to dens less one, showing scars from the battle; Laura's left hand.

⊠

Cole entered the golf course restaurant, craning his neck a bit before entering the green carpeted meadow with its pine forest chopped and screwed into tables. This was a familiar place for him. He knew the yellow-haired waitress's name was Holly and she didn't like onions. On the occasions that Patch was buried knee deep in winter, he would stay in one of the Alaskan-fashioned resort cabins overlooking the snow-blanketed golf course where Spring Creek collided with the Matanuska River. He thought it was the perfect place for meeting Bridget with its high log ceilings and rich emerald green tones. Thick pine tables carved by chainsaw were surprisingly nice to the touch, as expanded windows allowed the golf course to join him for dinner, which was, more often than not, Cole's date. Tonight he would be cheating on her, however, with the lovely woman approaching him. Bridget Poland made her way to the table without giving a second thought to her shapely glide. A southwestern long sleeve tucked neatly into a pair of faded 501's seemed to do the trick, and it did. Cole's heart began to race as he corrigibly came to his feet.

Others began to slowly populate the sunbathed room chattering back and forth just out of earshot. Cole overheard a nearby group of businessey-looking fellows saying something about blue jeans while pointing their rich lazy fingers at his and Bridget's table.

"Cole, hello. Sorry for being a little late. Have you been waiting long?" Bridget asked, producing another one of those damn smiles that could end wars. "This is a wonderful place, I'm afraid I'm a bit simply dressed though."

"No, you're simply dressed wonderfully," Cole said, engineering simple words wonderfully.

As her smile widened, Cole nervously searched for words, patting his napkin. "Yes, I do like it here, though I'm afraid I'm starting to be considered a regular. I stay in one of their small cabins from time to time when home seems a bit boorish or when the road getting there goes missing for a few days after a storm."

The yellow-haired gal orbited their table and offered alcohol in any flavor they desired by nodding her clean face in the direction of the log bar guarded by a moose with his body hacked, quartered, and stuffed. "I'll go for a dark beer, any one you choose," Bridget answered, wiggling her tongue slightly to create the words.

"And Cole, I'm guessing you would like your Jack and Coke?" Yellow Hair said more than asked.

"Thank you, Holly, yes," Cole concurred, a little proud of knowing the place and its people.

Red, yellow, and black stripes circled Bridget by dying their colors deep in the fabric of her Arizonian shirt. Her long ringless fingers turned into smooth nails without so much as a speed bump separating them. "Something tells me you know your way around this place, Cole."

Feeling uncomfortable with sitting across from such a beautiful woman, Cole leapt behind what came naturally to him. Humor. "Well, Bridget," he said with a shrug, "Holly there and I were married for a short time. You wouldn't think it by looking at her now, but we managed to have nine children in two and a half years. Oh sure, there were some laughs going through it all, but I just started to feel a bit, you know, weighed down with seven of them being extremely mentally challenged. So, I just had to ask her to leave in the middle of the night. I guess she and the kids walked, those who could, down here where she took up work. I, of course, refused to pay any child support, but I do stop from time to time and tip her as much as thirty percent when I'm feeling a smidge guilty, that is, as long as she doesn't make any mistakes, then I just dine and dash. I'm sure it bothers her to see me with such a lovely woman as yourself, but she's just going to have to accept that I've moved on."

The businessey fellows heard Bridget's galloping snicker slip from her painted lips to the lucky bastard she was sitting with. "Cole…stop, she's coming," she said through a schoolgirl laugh that certainly broke many a schoolboy's heart.

Yellow Hair delivered the booze, describing yet another brilliant idea the chef had for salmon, something to do with a brown sugar cream sauce and orange juice.

"Sounds simply to die for," Bridget said, imagining brown sugar darkening as the juice crawled into it.

"I'll have that too, Holly, thank you," Cole nodded politely.

"It might be a little bit, so I'll be back to check on your drinks now and again," she said before leaving with their order scrolled in a mental notepad under a tuft of yellow hair.

Bridget brought her elbows to the pine tabletop and leaned in a bit to say, "Cole, I'm going to tip her too. I heard little Colleen went and got her leg stuck in the garbage disposal again."

The businessey fellows heard the lucky bastard's laugh slip from his lips to the black haired angel he was sitting with.

"Now that's not funny, Bridget, she's the slowest one of all. The poor thing once mistook the fireplace for her mama, had twenty-degree burns up the one good side she had left. By tracing the burn marks, you could actually see how she'd tried to hug the damn flames. Which reminds me, I think I'll shoot for the moon this year and get her that pretty little salve kit she's been wanting for Christmas. It's patterned with tiny pink hearts running on fire!"

Suddenly a jet-black snowmobile scarred with monster-green racing stripes exploded past in a rage in front of the restaurant's obese windows, tearing through the thin layer of snow hiding the golf course's precious imported Bermuda, its rider hiding under a matching decaled helmet.

"Jack ass!" shot from under the bartender's mustache, seeing the machine churn the rich frozen soil. "Holly!" the man cried across the frontierish room. "Watch the bar, I'm gonna' kill that little shit this time!"

"I can't imagine that would exactly make the greens keeper very happy," Bridget said, watching the huffy bartender burst through a side door into the cold, wearing only his red Alaskan Amber work vest for a jacket.

"No, however the rider of that thing looks pretty pleased with life...so far anyway," Cole said, curious of the result.

Wanting her full attention, Cole changed the subject. "Finding your way around here and there at *Here to There?"*

"Slowly. I feel a bit behind for now but Philip is really great about offering his time to help settle me in. He's always referring to you as the 'Crazy Man Who Lives On a Bridge,' and that reminds me, 'Bridge.'"

"...Sorry?"

"Call me, Bridge! My dad called me that the day I signed off on my first project."

"Oh yes, forgive me," Cole said, remembering the perfect balance of some things in life, like good news on a sunny day, her invisible perfume circled him.

"Thank you for the tulip, Bridge."

The jetting snow machine made its way digging across the manicured landscape with an angry bartender crazy in pursuit nearing the seventh hole, his black tennis shoes poor competition against the whirling knife tracks. The snowmobile's jockey whipped the throttle after stopping long enough for the mustached man to almost go in for his kill, a classic move. Fair patrons of the restaurant, caring less and less if their glasses were half full or half empty, began rooting for the vested man flailing his arms running wild from snowy knoll to snowy knoll nearing Spring Creek.

The businessey fellows began reaching for cash in their deep pockets. "I've got twenty on the Booze Baron!" Classical background music fit the scene with a woman tickling ivory keys spinning on recorded vinyl as Yellow Hair stood, hoping the excitement would prevent someone from ordering a drink with a long name.

"Care to place a small wager yourself, Cole?" Bridget asked with a hint of confidence.

"Well, what did you have in mind?" Cole curiously inquired, hoping the bet would be who had to pay for breakfast.

"I'll bet you once we lose sight of that snowmobile, we never see it again. That bartender stands a better chance of running past a winning Lotto ticket out there than catching that fish-tailing machine," Bridget grinned, fanning her eyes back to Cole. "And let's see, if I'm right, you have to stand and proudly sing the Star Spangled Banner, while saluting!"

Cole sat his drink down with a wink and chuckled without showing his teeth. "And for missing my party, Bridge, you will rise and sing Happy Birthday to me, Marilyn Monroe style, all pouty and such."

"Oh, ho! Now that's a wager, Crazy Man Who Lives On a Bridge, and I'll take that bet. Hope you're feelin' patriotic. Maybe your ex-wife there can scare up a sparkler for ya!"

The charging snowmobile roller-coasted from sight rooster tailing over the eighth tee, headed for the river's edge, with the determined bartender, sponsored by Alaskan Amber, cresting the tee in a breathless second place. Cole silently admired the machine's racing stripes, fighting the urge to describe his snowsuit to Bridget.

"Well there she goes, Cole! They say lemon juice is good for the vocal cords. Would you like Holly to bring you a shot glass of it with your sparkler?"

"It's not over till it's over, Marilyn!" Cole said, realizing how cool it would be to be President.

All fans of the Alaskan Amber Team could see for a moment was a creamy white desert run through with the occasional treaded scar. Cole slid a calm eye, James Bond style, to Bridget, receiving an equally confident wink in return that said the kid's long gone.

The crowd came to their feet with a cheer seeing the bouncing snow machine find its way back over the eighth tee, its mustached rider bearing no helmet and wearing a victorious red Alaskan Amber vest.

Cole banged the pine tabletop center of its age rings in winning fashion as Bridget's hands went to her polished red mouth in laughing defeat.

The bartender, now well worthy a name, Jerry, a twenty-two-year-old college student raised by good folks back in South Dakota, goosed the sled's throttle in a classic mocking of the stop-taunt-and-go game, toying with the enemy that followed out of instinct. Its thrown rider, seeming to have forgotten how the game was played, failed repeatedly to reclaim the machine, missing it by only inches just before each roar, bringing a howl from his yet unnoticed fans in the room with a dead moose. The businessey fellows settled bets with a roar of their own, passing dead presidents to the short suit that took a long shot.

Bridget, hiding, spread her pink fingers about her pretty face seeing Cole's smile spreading wide with them.

"Oh, there you are, Miss Monroe. I believe you were about to wish me something or other?"

Jerry's victory lap brought him front and center of the restaurant discovering his newfound fame from its waving patrons. Offering a grand wave about the sky in return, Jerry was burning up just enough time for.....GGUUHHH, a full body tackle from behind drug him off the long black seat to the buried Bermuda with the helmeted character taking a shot at the title.

“Fifty on the bar boy!” came from a spirited corner table and “I’ve got a table dance on this one!” shouted a retired engineer as spectators crowded across the restaurant’s floor to the bulging windows.

Attempting a wise move, Jerry tugged at the rider’s helmet in the heated wrestle. Hungry guests pressed to the glass, Holly looking for the baseball bat that hadn’t been seen since the resort’s last game, the recorded woman in a finale, Cole picturing Bridget’s Arizona shirt floating to the floor in slow motion.

Jerry’s hands sucked the helmet from the rider’s head, triggering an explosion of long fine red hair, also in slow motion, to reveal a beautiful Irish-looking lass. Jerry managed her wrists in his adrenaline, the fans’ mouths unhinged. The Irish girl ceased in the struggle, making eye contact with the crowd, her fiery hair floating to the shoulders of her snowsuit.

“Cole, she’s a she!” Bridget said, bringing a hand to her mouth.

Cole noticed the red head’s left earring had painfully stayed with the helmet, leaving behind a burgundy lobe. As she jumped to her feet, she wiped her face and said through an Irish accent, “Twoun’t be a need for the police now, wount be botherin’ you no mour.”

“I’ve seen you at school,” Jerry said, letting go of her small wrists, agreeing to the offer as her breath before her froze, escaping her exhausted body. All eyes watched her pick up the thrown black helmet that held a small gold cross earring her brother had given her as he hugged her goodbye in Cork. With the jerk of a braided cord, the machine screamed to life and the Irish girl disappeared into a stand of poplars on her Polaris, a humbled mane of red hair disappearing with it.

“Your attention, please?” Cole asked, turning to the room as he stood from his ringside seat, Bridget’s pretty face falling into her hands. “I, too, have placed a small wager on our fair bartender there! Surely you have all heard crazy rumors such as Elvis is alive and sleeping in a grocery cart, or happily standing in line at Burger King! Well, to my amazement, I’ve discovered that the lovely Marilyn Monroe is also alive and, furthermore, willing to sing for us!”

The crowd sparked with laughter and applause as they weaved back to their abandoned pine tables. Bridget, slowly floating to her feet in a bubbling sea of goodhearted cheers and whistling, let the color about her cheeks admit this was no hourly performance. Her sky-blue eyes flashing over pure white teeth trampled through the holler, leaving a silence, the businessmen forgetting their business and remembering their men.

"I think you're all about to put a little more faith in that whole Elvis-at-the-Laundromat rumor than any of that Marilyn-at-the-golf-course talk that's been going around," Bridget announced, warning the anxious through a stage-frightened laugh.

Holly pressed the long metal bar of a locking side door letting in the victorious bartender who found the lovely Bridget in a slow-noted, "Haaaaapppyyy Biiirrrrrtthhhdaaay toooo yooouuu." Jerry, afraid of someone discovering he was actually a Taurus, listened contently to the seductive woman slowly pushing warm breath through her voice box, smooth, like vanilla pudding coming to a boil. Bridget gently rolling her shoulders side-to-side using her rhythmic chest for ballast. A meek woman sitting in a quiet dress inflicted by Obsessive Compulsive Disorder momentarily wished to be her forever.

"Aaaand maaanyyy moorrrrre," Bridget finished, with her head tilted just so, lashes lashed. The room fell quiet, a dropped rolling pin in the kitchen the only sound. Cole tipped off a roaring round of applause as he playfully raised his arms high and rolled his eyes back with a robust exhale. Bridget sprayed the room gangster style with a humble smile as Jerry yelled, "Hell Yes!" announcing a round on the house.

Holly immediately paid the bar's debt in full by coming around with another round. "That was simply perfect! As we speak your phone number is going straight to the top of the charts in the men's bathroom. I just lent out three pens getting to your table, one was even a woman!" Holly joked.

"Could I borrow your note pad, Holly?" Cole asked, raising a finger. "Suddenly I need to trot off to the men's room and I'm terrible at remembering numbers."

"Very funny, Crazy Man Who Lives On a Bridge. You've already gotten me to do more wiggling than I do annually, and Cole Caffy forgetting anything to do with numbers would be as strange as Tina Turner on a camping trip," Bridget said, chuckling at the thought of Ms. Turner trying to use her colorful spike heels for tent pegs.

The order of salmon arrived at their table and was indeed brilliant as the orange moon peeked over the seventh fairway bearing its shadowy acne, the sleepy snowmobile's engine now cool to the touch somewhere behind a warm home.

"Cole, thank you, tonight has been so much fun and I needed to get out. Phillip invited me to his house for dinner and drinks but his wife hasn't exactly warmed up to me much. I think my skirt may have been a little short for her the first time we were introduced."

"Oh, she'll be fine, as long as you don't run out and sing happy birthday to Philip, that is. That could burn a bridge or two, Marilyn," Cole said, more aware than ever of just how many birthdays he'd had.

Bridget gave Holly her autograph plus thirty percent after making a crafty sleight of hand for the bill, Cole assuring through a grateful smile that that wouldn't happen again.

"Good show, old Man," Cole awarded to the bartender, while helping Bridget with her long wool coat dyed gray at its Oregon factory.

"Sorry you lost your bet there, gorgeous," Jerry said with an all-American grin. "Next time we should have that new subway vent installed, and I trust you'll be wearin' a lofty white skirt, right?"

A flattered Bridget fired back with one of her own all-American grins, putting Jerry's sickly attempt to quick shame.

"Ouch, you gotta' be careful shootin' a smile like that around a place like this," Jerry whooped, ringing an overhead brass bell the owner salvaged from his crappy sailboat before selling it to some poor unfortunate slob or other.

Cole pulled open the heavy doors, revealing the cold northern night like a country singer's reception to a heavy-metal stage. As each crunch from their treaded feet closed the gap to the new white Subaru, Bridget asked, "Hey, I don't know if you watch much TV or not, but did you hear about what happened to Sean Connery today?"

Bridget, a pace ahead, could not see Cole's eyes grow in his head. "Oh, is he that clever fella that played the spy in those double O something movies?"

"Yeah, and you know something, you look a lot like him. Anyway, I guess some wacko tried to take a shot at him on a train. The news lady said his bodyguard slipped him away somehow. Those guys must be good at what they do, huh? I guess they got the nut at the train station though. The cops said she wouldn't tell them anything and just kept babbling on about people vanishing, like ghosts."

"Yeah…seems I heard something on the radio," Cole said, denying his urge to gently brush the hair away from Bridget's ear to whisper 'boo.' "But back to this I look like Sean Connery thing. So you find this silver-haired devil to be, oh let's say, breathtakingly handsome do you?"

Shyly Bridget glanced away with a smile and rolled her eyes as if she'd been caught passing a note. "Yes, Cole, you're a very handsome man." Her dark hair perfectly bordered her angel face as she reached in the moonlight to gently touch the small cut above Cole's right eye. "Ouch. Don't tell me you've been shaving your forehead. I didn't want to ask over dinner, but that's a nasty scratch."

"That? No," Cole answered, folding the collar of his coat up. "I got that little beauty helping Sean Connery fight off all those bad guys today."

Bridget paused batting her eyes, then slapped his lapel laughing. "So that's why you retired, huh? Take up the life of crime fighting? Stick up for the stars?"

"Somebody has to do it. Why not me?" Cole said, wanting to grab her by the arms and wish them both away to Scotland. Settling for a run at his courage in the moment, he squared his shoulders and cracked the reins.

"Might I ask if you've found anyone interesting yet, Bridge?"

"No, Cole, you're just another average guy that lives on a bridge and fathered nine-and-a-half children in two years or whatever, and comes to the rescue of the rich and famous. Nope, you're just everyday Joe, ya know?" Bridget answered, forgetting to mention his fear of being overpowered by roadside gang animals.

"I think I've missed the target a bit. I was aiming the question at a little less professional level," Cole said, lowering his voice to a warm rumble.

"Oh…no," she said looking to the moon as it slowly orbited the earth. "I think that'll maybe all happen in good time, but for now I'm afraid the office building will have to be my tall, dark and handsome stranger," she answered, answering a tough one to answer. "Cole, I understand you've never married?"

"Well…I guess you could say the office building too was my tall, dark and handsome stranger for many years. It's free, however, to seduce whomever it wishes, and I think it fancies you, Bridge," Cole said, placing his black leather hand on her forearm. "Bridge, can I give you maybe the best advice I've ever been able to share with someone?"

"Yes…of course, Cole," she said, realizing he meant what he was about to say.

"Be careful you don't accept that office building for a mate, Bridge. Twenty-five years later here I am, looking into these remarkable eyes of yours knowing my time has long past. I've spent my life on things that I'm just discovering were not the most important. I have too many wrinkles to be going home alone, Bridge, far too rich to be poor, you might say. I think of the ones that got away," Cole recalled, finding the moon just over Bridget's shoulder. "They were far more than the simple lines on paper that I treated them as."

"I'll let you in on something, Cole, building bridges is easy compared to dealing with my love life. I think if you understood it all, you'd probably agree. However, advice from someone like you, is advice only a fool would ignore. Thank you, Cole," Bridget said, being more proud of her blue eyes than ever.

"It's cold," Cole said, walking her the last few feet to her Subaru. "Please drive home safe."

Bridget's kiss came from the dark frozen air like a search-and-rescue party breaking down the door of a starving man. His chameleon cheek changed to the color of her lipstick by fading red with blush. "Here's to a couple of bridge builders, huh? Tonight was perfect."

The new white Subaru disappeared out of the parking lot headed south to its rented garage. Slowly, Cole walked in the direction of a warm light glowing from the cabin left on by housekeeping, the crunch from under only two shoes promising a lonely night. Then the sound of four more feet suddenly shot from the tree line, gaining on him, then eight or a dozen. Glancing over his shoulder, Cole saw only the shaded outline of what seemed to be horned demons lowering their heads to break from the lower limbs of the spruce. Faster and faster to the cabin Cole built his stride seeing the door appearing to run away from him like in so many dreams. The chasing sound of now at least twenty feet grew, poking through the frozen crust just behind, weaving after him across the forest floor with seemingly great confidence. Cole fumbled with the cabin door, his heart racing as the beasts knocked him off his feet and threw themselves at him feverishly. Cole flailing in defense from the monsters certain deathly intent, cried out to the beasts for mercy. Silence followed. Flat on his back and terrified, Cole slowly pulled his leather hands from his frightened face, revealing the enemy huddled around. A familiar long pink SLAP of a tongue wetly crawled across Cole's face, another shooting in his snow-packed ear like gelatin sandpaper.

"Oh God! That's terrible!" he howled through a relieved laugh, finding himself deep in the huddle of his lady friends with black tails. "What are you doin' so far from home girls? You had me runnin' scared for my life, you know that?" he confessed, rubbing each shiny double-barreled snout that came at him from the pack. Then Cole realized something in the moment. "You're not the same deer at all are you?" Cole said, frowning. In a flash of realization, he understood that his wish for the deer not to fear him was complete, heard by all herds. Squeegeeing snow from his forehead with the back of his thumb, he pictured a jealous Grizzly Adams telling him to get the hell off his mountain.

"You girls must be pretty damn bored to want to bother with an old lonely sort like me tonight," he said with a deep exhale, not letting go the tail of a doe that was finished with inspecting him, her sleek body arching in the playful effort.

The wish that had been criss-crossing Cole's mind all evening finally managed to chase away all other racing thoughts and stood dangling its instant gratification before him, hopelessly jailing him in the moment. An endless night ahead looming with impossible reprieve, and want winning the battle over shouldn't, slayed Cole's questions of right and wrong. He looked into each of his new friends fearless blunt eyes, his own closing to make the instinctive wish. Hands to his side, the doe's aerodynamic heads raised, something else was there.

Sitting back with his hands on the snow, Cole looked again to the moon and spoke softly into the lonesome chill. "I *wish* Bridget were as attracted to me as I am to her."

With the muffled sound of hooves clicking through snow, the Sitka black-tails pranced back to the shadowing boarders of forest, looking for that 'something else' from the corners of cornerless eyes lined with lashes one could sew with. Coming to his feet and brushing snow from his pants, Cole watched them fade into the woods one by one, the clicking of their hoof beats the only sound.

Noticing that the moon too was snuggling into the wall of spruce that lined the golf course, Cole wrapped his hand, from pointer finger to thumb, around his forehead trying to come to terms with the wish he'd just freed. He remained ever so still in the cold, realizing just how long his day had been. Waking up seemed like a week ago, and he hoped that sleep would rescue him from stirring around in an empty bed, trying to convince himself that lying there alone was somehow justified by this solitary life he'd chosen.

The cabin was styled in an oxymoron of modern and old fashioned. False logs hung over drywall looked neat to the eye, as did the false logs in the gas fireplace, the smell of pine enhanced from a can. Cole hung his long black coat on the wooden butler with antlers of its own, trying to realize his wish. "Maybe she'll call tomorrow with that little extra-spicy undertone I sprinkle my words to her with, or maybe we'll just simply never see one another again."

Cole's shoulders slumped as his imagination carried away in the moment, scrolling over an endless menu of possibilities, his favorite socks the color of sky somewhere much warmer. The timber bed, beaten together with sixteen-penny nails, only one side of the sheets turned down as if to say even housekeeping knew he would be sleeping alone.

Flopping down on the bed, he heard the hollow sound of the springs reminding him that no one loved him. Clamping his eyes shut, he lay listening to his own heartbeat, wondering who would care, if it missed.

Slowly his eyes hinged open to the ceiling, his pupils expanded, bleeding into their surrounding light blue rings as he heard something more than just the fireplace hissing in the far corner. The pine door opened, allowing a miraculous perfume to fly sorties in the rush of cold air that washed over him.

Bridget Poland stood in the doorway, her eager body filled with a secret it was about to share. With her eyes only staring into his, she slowly advanced the pine bed where Cole was holding his breath. She paused, pushing back the Oregon trench coat from her shoulders until its collar gently fell across her back. Her lips lightly parted and from them she cast her words down to him. "Cole…I was on my way home…then I saw ribbons and smelled Christmas. It was somehow…you."

Cole gulped and rose to his elbows, hoping the need in his eyes could somehow remain hidden as the Arizona long sleeve continued to appear from under her gray cape like a magician revealing his shapely assistant in slow motion. With Cole's thumbs wrapped in his squeezing fists, she reached him. In her reflective eyes, he saw himself and how badly he had wanted her.

Crimson lips found his mouth, soft, safe, bending him to the rugged bed as the kinked ends of her hair rained across his chest like heat lightening tickles the desert, her palm running the length of his anxious torso. His trembling hands skated along her 501's, snake-charming his youth up from the deep reservoirs of his vigilance. Her mouth drug to his neck, drinking his skin, her rubbing palm stood like a Halloween cat driving her blue nails at his flat stomach. Bridget's arching body slid from the bed to her knees in front of a man to whom this was new. A short pause with long breaths told him what was about to happen, and he tensed, ready for her touch. Her tongue buried in his belly button painted a red ring around its bulls-eye with expensive lipstick, sending Cole's chin slowly back in the cooling air from the still open door. As she tugged at his pants, he opened his eyes, seeing the spackled ceiling washed in orange tickle from the hissing fire. Her warm hands, tongue…then mouth, eclipsed him. Cole gasped, plowing rows through her thick hair with his fingers. The sorcerer behind her perfume had been telling the truth all along.

Cole's eyes again flashed opened, this time squarely to Bridget and the brutal reality of just how wrong his wish had been. Suddenly he found himself tragically out of place, like a gun barrel waving out of sync with the rippling wheat field on opening day. Drunk on her perfume, feeling her softly draped around him, he found only a distant part of himself trying to fight it. But it, too, raised a white flag and the seductive battle was lost. His grip on her shoulders tightened and before he could stop his moment from coming, he heard wonderful bells clanging across endless pastures consumed with the concerned, telling the old a cure for death had been found, so please go on your way and play, play, play, before the ringing goes away.

Cole at the bed's edge, stomach reeling, the Arizona long sleeve floating to the planked floor in slow motion, only Bridget, before him, "Cole...."

"Bridget...we can't do this, it's wrong," he forced himself to say, remembering Sean Connery's wish to always be the best person possible. "I'm so very sorry."

As though unable to understand his words, Bridget disagreed through a speechless pose of body language. The heels of her small hands pressed hard at his legs, and unknowingly his guilt. Again Cole brought his trembling hands to her bare, confident shoulders, struggling to look past the spell in her eyes.

The Sitka black tails, bedding down near the cabin, raised a bit with another cautious glance to the surrounding woods, that 'something else' was charging through the invisible freeze again.

"I *wish* you felt the same way about me as when you were imitating Marilyn Monroe tonight."

Cole prayed the words more than spoke them. He watched her black pupils soak the spell from their retinas through a fading expression. "I'm so sorry," he whispered to Bridget, himself...to anyone who would listen.

Her hands came to his, trying to understand something, anything. "Cole...this can't be happening," she confessed in a soft, confused tone.

"Bridget, I know, please forgive me, it's entirely my fault...you're innocent." With an honest shame in his voice, he watched her wet eyes float to his.

"No, Cole...you don't understand....I'm gay."

Jerry, the faithful bartender, and his prey, the Irish snowmobiler, were married later the following spring. The ceremony was held on the shoulder of Spring Creek behind the eighth tee where they oddly first met.

Yellow tulips were proudly held by the Irish bride and red-vested groom, as well as each of the many guests spotting the day's bright shore. After all, it was the out-of-place tulips that had floated from somewhere upstream that caused her to pause the racing machine long enough for her future husband to wildly attack from behind.

They would have never met.

five

Like abandoned winter house pipes, Spring Creek was narrowing with each November night, ice growing to its center, nature creating its own winter bridge for furry critters that become more teeth than cute when played with under the quarreling northern lights. Polar pink, jogging sideways, mutely slammed into waves of chandelier blue. The enlightened parents giving birth to an elusive prancing green that immediately side winds away to mate with fire engine red. Human faces below cocked to the color, forgetting how much time and money they have to lose or gain in their fast elbowing lives, morning sadly bringing back the silent wishing for more.

Cole's face was expressionless as the shower's hard rain steamed over his skin, prying open the tight pores of his back. Last night's clothing was no more than a soulless pile of cotton and denim tossed atop his sleepless maple bed. The rain stopped, and he chose a crisp white shirt and stood tucking it deep into a pair of dark green cords while trying to avoid his own eyes in the full-length mirror. After summitting the spiral staircase from his bedroom, he crossed the glass floor of the bridge on his determined way to an answer, the little rainbow seeming to cower at his approach to the kitchen counter. "I want to talk to you."

His blue-gray eyes, filled with remorse, scoured the envelope like a paleontologist inspects the lifeless, nothing. He jerked the letter out, read it again and again. He paused in thought, reaching for the envelope. What caught his attention wasn't so much the lack of a stamp, but the absence of a postmark. Immediately, Cole's head spun to the kitchen window, where looking across the south thirty, up to Patch Road, he was shocked to find the mailman seeming to jovially meet him eye to eye with the same distant wave right on cue. Noticing how low the sun was still saddled in the morning sky, Cole turned to the brass kitchen clock that swore the mail shouldn't be there for another four hours. "Well son of a bitch!" he rumbled, reaching for the Range Rover's keys still setting where he'd left them two days ago.

The Range Rover waited anxiously for the garage door to hum open like a marooned salmon awaits an incoming tide. The English motor growled to life, barking its tires from the cement driveway. Sideways, the Rover skidded onto Patch. Forty, fifty, then sixty miles per hour, the spruce smeared past the crooked road. Cole squinted ahead, preparing to see the white breadbox shaped van that should have been just around the next blind corner, but was not. The Rover's determination took him past seventy. Finally a glimpse of the patriotic-striped van an instant before it rounded out of sight at the next sharp bend. Its darkened brake lights high about its self told Cole this just went from chase, to race. His foot pressed to the floor, his mind to its limits, wind squealing in through pin holes, eighty.

"Come on you son of a bitch, I know fuckin' Dale Earnhardt doesn't deliver my mail, so where the hell are ya?"

Another corner brought a slippery limp to the steering wheel. Cole corrected, bringing an o-shit look to his face as the Rover held true. Telephone poles sped past like fence posts as if he were racing conversations when the mail van appeared just ahead. Its brave brake lights brightly cried uncle as it careened from Patch onto a gravely snow packed side road.

"I got your ass now, Mail Boy!" Cole hissed through a sloped grin, pressing the button that brought the little blue 4x4 indicator light to life. The Rover shot through the corner tearing its tracks deep across the mail van's, leaving behind what appeared to be a knobby python stalking a garden snake. Cole knew this crumbling piece of abandoned road and that it lead to a small wooden bridge used by the forest service for a number of years before Patch followed Spring Creek on up the mountain.

All four of the Rover's tires spun wild in the air as it leapt over a rumbling line of washouts. Digging at the earth they gained on the racing van at every turn until the aging bridge came into sight. Cole pounded the brake pedal seeing the mail van stopped dead center the spruce wood crossing. Pellets of frozen road showering the truck's rear end said the race was over, Rover. An alert pair of eyes reflected back to Cole's through a tall gooseneck mirror.

"Crazy son'f a bitch," Cole mumbled, stepping from the riled Rover, realizing he'd forgotten to put on shoes. The alert eyes shook a little with a chuckle in the mirror seeing this too.

"Damn it," Cole growled to himself, walking toward the van on the balls of his feet.

"You there!" The mailman heard sliding his huge white door back, appearing like an excited Oz behind the curtain. Cole found a short sort with a round face and a matching half moon belly proudly hanging over his issued gray slacks. The official looking badge atop his winter hat was a blue and white postal eagle appearing to fly from the man's bald head using the built-in wool earflaps for wings in the breeze.

"Me here?" he answered to the tall angry man with silver hair and bluing feet. The mailman popped from his swiveling seat to the wood of the bridge. "Like my boots?" His stumpy fingers performing a perfect Vanna White wave over his lined black rubbers. "I hope you haven't chased me to hell and back in hopes of a trade, because I gotta tell ya, while yours will last a life time, mine are...."

Raising his hands, Cole interrupted in a tamed yell, "Whenever you're done selling yourself something, I've got a few questions that I want the answers to, and if you've got 'em, you're gonna give 'em. Starting with, why were you running crazy to get away from me? And before you say a word, I'll warn you not to waste any of your time trapped under the impression that you're speaking to an idiot!"

The mailman's pudgy eyes lowered over his matter of fact grin to the ground, taking a lengthy stare at Cole's bare feet and his naked toes straining upward from the freeze as though he'd just carefully painted each of their nails.

"Look," Cole demanded, rifling his coat pocket, "this letter was in my box! There's no postage or postmark! Yet it was delivered! How would you explain that, Mailman?"

“Simple…it wasn’t mailed. Someone slid it in your mailbox, that’s all. There’s a hundred scenarios. Why me?” the mailman answered in simple argument.

“Shit, shit, shit!” Cole cried, stomping his naked feet in frostbiting circles. “So you had nothing to do with this? You’ve never seen this letter before?”

The mailman’s pupils retreated at the sight of a little rainbow pushed to his face. “Now I gotta warn ya here, sir, I’m protected by ol’ Uncle Sam. And I think you’re going about this problem of yours all wrong, starting off on the wrong bare foot, ya might say.”

Cole’s shoulders lowered, taking on another load of anger. “So you know nothing about any of this that’s been happening to me?”

“Nothing of what, sir?” the mailman answered, watching the rainbow pull away from his chubby face.

Cole’s eyes went squint, away from the man and his van, back to the Rover. Over his shoulder, Cole offered, “I’m sorry for all of the trouble, sorry for scaring you half to death, I’m sure.”

Watching this tall drink of a man stomp back to his fancy truck on his purple toes was all too much for the mailman, who gave in with a loud chuckle from his windpipe that landed on poor spirited ears. Cole’s fist wrapped tighter and tighter around the British door handle as thoughts of kicking someone’s ass for the first time in years flashed in his adrenaline. As he was about to erupt, he heard from behind, “Oh, Cole…I *wish* you wouldn’t go away mad!”

Comprehending what was being said, Cole felt his grip loosen, his eyebrows floated up squeezing out a map of relaxed wrinkles about his forehead. Like pulling a miss-aimed safety pin from a baby’s bottom, his anger streamed away. Feeling the heartbeat slow in his chest, he turned to whoever this man was, letting out a small, “wow.”

“Yeah…wow, huh?” the postman agreed through a welcoming tone, backing it up with an all-knowing smile spilt across his round and beaming face.

With a new tranquility harbored in his voice, Cole calmly lifted one brow and began to ask, “How did you…?”

“Well Coole, I shood think the same way you met with new friend, Mr. Connery,” he answered, gutting an impression with a dull edged laugh, “That twouse a good woone Coole, a real clossic if yeeee arsk meeee!”

Cole approached him, center of the bridge. "Who are you?"

"Just a man standing here, *wishing* for your feet to be warm," the postman coolly replied.

Feeling the mailman's words as he spoke them, Cole looked to the shining frost of the spruce bridge. Without seeing it, he could feel warm white sand pressing between his purple toes. Another lack of words led him hopelessly back to, "wow!"

The moisture from some eight thousand feet above turned to ice, skydiving from the smoke white sky in the form of snow. The heavy flakes free fell in platoons of countless numbers using the freezing temperature for parachutes. Many saw two tiny men and two tiny trucks, on a miniature spruce bridge advancing at the speed of ground zero before landing on one of the giants hot melting noses.

"Winter is upon us, Cole," the mailman said, spreading his arms to the sky as if making an offer to the season, more flakes meeting their demise in the man's warm eyes. "How's those little piggies?"

"I could carry them to market on dry ice…thank you," Cole said, making his toes do the wave. In a sincere pause, he searched for the most important question he could find. Too many, all trying to jump from him at once like all the vibrant colors of the world mixed together makes black.

"Cole, you're standing in front of someone who has been in your shoes, pardon the pun. Take your time, keep your ground, everything is perfectly fine here, as it should be," the mailman said, knowing how everything could hit at once.

"Why me?" Cole managed through his dry mouth. "Why on earth has this happened to me?"

"Because…you're you!" he answered with a slap to Cole's shoulder. "I'll try to explain this in a way that might answer a lot of those questions you're beating yourself silly with," he said tapping his temple. "It's your payment, Cole, a payment for clean living, you might say, and for working true to your work, true to yourself, and everyone else for as long as you have been alive. True, true, true, that's you! From the beginning you've left behind a trail of deeds and care that few do. Well, what goes up must come down, Cole. Fair is fair. Peter pays Paul. The piper owes you, ya might say. Everything you've ever put aside to do what was best for others has been a savings account, of sorts. I understand you once waved your entire fee to allow your contractors to keep going in a financial pinch. Do you remember why you did it? I'll help you," the mailman said, billowing with admiration. "It was the only road into a small town. Cole, that bridge was finished on December twenty fourth! You spent the twenty fifth directing muddy cars full of presents over that new bridge didn't you?"

"It wasn't anything heroic," Cole said glancing away, "they had families, I didn't."

"Yes, yes. You see that's part of my point here. You'll never know what it's like to hold your own child, Cole, or spend your life with the same person you started out with when you had nothing. What family you did have didn't last long. Yes, your father knew you loved him when he died, as did your mother when she was taken away. You've grown and lived alone, and a fine job you've done building it, as well as other bridges in your life. While others were bragging about how much money they had, and slowly killing each other for it, you were quietly giving yours to the friends and considered family you love."

"So you're telling me this is making up for the things I've foregone?"

"Yes, in a way. The things, the time, and love. Above all, for putting your greed aside, Cole. You see, all things in life work on this wonderfully inescapable balance. In order for Alaska to experience its endless summer days, it must also endure the never-ending nights of winter. Fat people pay for their gluttonous appetites through a menu of side affects. One is their lives are generally cut short, much like the smoker who enjoys the sweet tranquility of nicotine. If you want to grow new hair on a shiny old head, well, miraculously, the side effects will be equal through money, time, and in some cases, the lack of sex drive, which for many was the shallow reason for the new do in the first place. It's how everything under the sun works. For better or worse, it's simply how it is. This is really a brilliant thing, Cole, how it naturally protects itself through good producing good. The weak will never share in this earned ability. Ironically those who spend their lives constantly wishing for more starve themselves of their own future possibilities, subconsciously aware. The people who do this don't realize that it's exactly that same mentality that prevents them from progressing to the places they wish to be in the first place. Unfortunately, this is where self-justification steps in, ruining so many things and so much potential. The insecure create an answer to their own weaknesses long enough to walk away from a reality that simply doesn't suit them. They do it for money, and attention. Without knowing it, Cole, you've been building quite a little nest egg for yourself over the years."

"If all of this is true, it's going to take some time for me to understand it all," Cole said, glancing away to the regretted memory of last night. "But I'm afraid…I've already made a wish, a poor wish that didn't come from good."

"Oh, yes. Well, if you're referring to Bridget, you'll have to trust me when I tell you she'll be just fine," the mailman said, turning his palms up. "She already understands, and has moved past it."

"How does someone just move past something like that?" Cole snapped, pulling his hands out of his pockets. "Why do you think I'm not jumping up and down here on my bare feet over this…this great, thing? I really am so sorry to say this, but maybe there's been a mistake."

"Cole, listen to yourself. This is exactly why you were chosen," the mailman said, leaning in close. "In the letter, it tells you that tolerances will be made until you get your wishing legs. Does it not? Well, I'm here to work on those tolerances. We're both here to work on them. So don't throw yourself off one of your bridges over this. You simply fell prey to a bit of honest instinct. I have every confidence in the world that you'll never allow yourself to be faced with that again. You meant her no harm. You've never meant anyone any harm, Cole," the mailman said looking to the ground, widening his smile. "Do you feel the warmth under your bare feet? Go there. Walk on those white beaches with a tan on your smiling face. Listen to jazz in the streets of brassy cities. Dance on those bridges throughout the world that you've only admired in pictures dog-eared around your office. You've earned it, Cole Caffy."

The thickening snowfall airbrushed away the distant scenery over the Matanuska Valley below with its natural ominous fade. A light northerly breeze blew the rudderless snowflakes miles from their intended landing zones. Some to their tropical deaths on the Rover's warm black engine hood, their clear blood dripping to the shoddy bridge, making Cole recall his reply to Philip, 'an overdue change of seasons.' Still looking away, he asked in his arctic voice with a happy nervousness, "So, what else do I need to know to do this thing right?"

"Now that's the spirit!" the mailman yahooed like a yahoo, his gray postal uniform loosing its form, earflaps flappin'. Pattering up closer, he took Cole by the arms to say, "Let's start with the simple dos and don'ts, huh!"

Unable to match the postman's thrill, Cole went silent just as he did in his college days before learning anything that mattered. Leading him to the edge of the bridge, the long ago dried Olsen Creek that once drained into Spring Creek appeared below only as a stony incision in the mountain's chest like a dredge mark left behind by rainbows out-running treasure hunters.

"First, Cole, for us to idly wish for water to run here again, would be a no-no! The water would run off and tell a secret for miles. You, of all people, understand physics, and the side affects that obey them. You can't have folks chasing one another upstream looking for the source. The water itself could offset nature in ways impossible to count. Maybe not as we speak, but over time the ripple affect could drive life in a way that it was never intended to be. Take this bridge," the mailman said matter-of-factly, resting his hands on his love-handles, "you could design it in your sleep. You probably have every confidence in what you're standing on, right? Tell me a little about this bridge, Cole. Tell me what you see and what makes its structure believable to you."

"Ah…well. See here," Cole said, tipping his chin to the ground as his furnaced foot swiped away the layer of frost glazing the treated timbers. "Her planks are 2x6's, individually nailed, not laminated." Then with growing enthusiasm, he craned his long frame over the bridge's side, describing what good condition the wing walls were in. Then drawing a line in the air with his experienced finger, he carefully pointed out the great thought its engineers had given to the upright support timbers. "No wheel guards though," Cole said, tracing a line near the bridge's edge with his big toe. "She was built before their time, and her spacer boards have seen better…."

As Cole was just getting warmed up, an immediate shock of black void swallowed him from inside. His arms and legs unconsciously fanned out in a paralyzing stance of balance as with one colossal moan, defying all that was mathematically correct and structurally sound, the bridge began to fail. Shaking both sides of earth that it clung to, the doomed bridge swayed just enough to send a horrifying groan through its wooden bones that collided under Cole's bare feet. The sound of mighty spruce logs crying for help like the giant falling from Jack's beanstalk, siphoned a scream from the bilge of Cole's windpipe. The sheer sag of the collapsing timber brought the mail van and Rover nose to ass like a couple of dogs seeing who's who. Cole spun in place, gasping as his eyes gained on the maze of cracks splitting down the center of the bridge's backbone like heat lightning. "NOOOO!" he cried at the top of his pink lungs, "Not the Rover!"

The mailman laughed, holding his half moon belly in the nirvana. High school architect books the size of entire libraries shot through Cole's ranting mind as his plan became an idea to having a thought of maybe making another plan to consider possibly coming up with a good idea for a plan. Chaos, the inability of reason…*run, Cole!*

His bare feet slung out from under him, rooster tailing the packed frost, throwing him to the separating planks. "I *wish* this wasn't happening!" Cole hollered to the laughing mailman, who suddenly shared in a slip to his ass, pounding yet a fatter laugh from his giggling chest, his short legs spread before him like he was ready to play pickup jacks in his favorite high water pants.

"Reword your words, Cole!" the postman shouted, hanging on to anything he could.

Cole's eyes slammed shut in the effort, his pale face shown to the dismantling bridge, the smell of his own fear washing away. "I *wish* this bridge would not fail!"

The hollow echo of tearing timber ended, the severed tail end of the sound bouncing off the steep walls of the dried creek bed and down the mountain like a bobsled course. All was still. Cole's mouth remained agape. The only words it could form were, "You son of a bitch!"

"Try one more time, Cole, and think of how you want things to be," the mailman said, with an encouraging calm.

Cole shot a grimacing look to the cracked and twisted planks beneath him awaiting their final pop. With all he could muster, his eyes closed. "I *wish* this bridge were as it was before asshole here trampled over it with his voodoo!"

With the words still puffing into the breeze, Cole could feel himself rise as the open wounds of the planks began healing themselves under his feet. The heavy timber moaned, cracking the spine of the bridge back into place. His eyes drove to the Rover, looking for so much as a scratch in its rich black lacquer as his sensation of balance stumbled back like the lab monkey's after a rocket test in the fifties.

He heard the frost giving in footsteps from behind. "Now, now, Cole, before you implode here, listen to what the lesson has to say," the mailman said bringing his hands together in a soft clap. "The physics you understand and the countless numbers you've added solving its solutions, are, yes, one side of things. But the math here too has its own answers. They're just different numbers working under the same laws. Think of looking at something from all sides. If you can't see them all at once, how do you know you've seen them all?"

Cole placed his hands on the bridge's mended guardrail, remembering his father's greatest lesson, 'Evaluate what has happened so you can apply what's learned'. "I'm certain you'll understand my not understanding this, not here and now anyway," Cole muttered, still trying to catch his breath.

"You will in good time, as all good things take, Cole."

"Is someone going to be there if I make a big mistake? For instance, what happens if I have a dream, say a nap jerk, and I accidentally wish for a thousand starving gorillas to be told the last piece of fruit on the planet is hiding deep in my ass?" Cole scowled, squeezing his hands into fists, picturing them leapfrogging over one another to have a look up his peach mine, bearing their long yellow teeth. The mailman wavered. His hands reaching the Rover's fender just before his bouncing half moon threw him to the ground. "Are you listening to me?" Cole demanded, flinging his arms open. "I mean what the fuck am I gonna' do? Pick up a stick? The son's of bitches can lift cars and tie knots with their feet. Only sweet Jesus himself could even guess how they'd go about it! The only chance I'd have is to go for it myself and lob the damn thing like a grenade! Oh my God, can you even ima…Oh God! Tell me this can't happen. Even if it can, please tell me it can't!"

The mailman nearly started banging on the Rover's engine hood before he remembered Cole's fondness for his baby. Through a barrage of loud sucking noises, he tried to control his barrel rolling laugh, his small right boot duplicating its waffle pattern in the frost over and over.

"I'm serious here! What are these new so-called laws I gotta' follow, and hey, you're getting saliva on my truck!"

"Ah…oh…." the mailman struggled. "They're pretty simple. And no, Cole, this gorilla conspiracy of yours…will never happen. But wait till I tell the others! They'll have to take turns slapping each other on the back to get their wind ba…. "

"…Others?" Cole interrupted, lifting his eyes. "Are there many?"

"Well, Cole, look around you. In the world today with modern influences like television and breast implants, I'm sorry, there aren't many. Remember, you gotta' be a thinker to be standing where you are in life, and not in the way most immediately assume they are because of one excuse or another. You're far above and beyond chasing after Ferraris and mansions to impress the Jones," the mailman said, coolly gesturing to his side and waving to the Jones as if behind the wheel of a four-hundred-horse power rocket with red fairings. "The most important lesson you can learn today is that self-justification is the real disease of the human race. But then somewhere you already knew that, didn't you?"

Sliding his chin to the valley and his mind away from life's brutal realities, Cole asked, "So, if I just went on wishing for everything that came to mind and imagination, wouldn't there be some sort of chaos? Or would I just wish that away too?"

"You are a fast learner aren't ya, Cole?" the mailman said, impressed by the question. "No, you're exactly right. Inevitably what would happen is you'd find yourself wishing in endless circles. An easy rule to remember is we can never wish would've, could've, or should've. The effects you cause are the ripples in the pond you have to tend. No, we cannot wish to live forever or cure our own illnesses. To change our natural destinies would not be a ripple in the pond, Cole, but a wave in the ocean, an ocean that is already well tended by reason."

The spruce forest leaned toward the north in the growing breeze as though it were drawing a deep breath before catapulting prickly cones over the mountains at whatever was chipping away at its natural borders. A gust of wind rippled through Cole's silver hair as he turned to the mailman who was rubbing his little hands together as if it were Christmas morning.

“Well, Cole, rain, sleet or snow, I gotta’ go,” the mailman quoted, ambling to his van, the eagle flapping on his head.

“So…that’s it?” Cole said, realizing he was on his own as the mailman began spinning the steering wheel back and forth while making engine noises with his tongue rattling around his mouth. “Why are you a mailman?” he asked standing center of the bridge on his warm bare feet.

The mailman offered his round head from the van with a quick wink and sincere gesture. “Because, it’s what I wished to be,” he said, aiming a proud smile through the growing mist of snow. “Oh, and one more thing before I go. It’s nice to hear that Brett will be graduating from forestry school about the time this stuff melts. Sounds like the kid has a future, Cole…and a friend.”

On a nearly forgotten bridge anchored in the foothills of the Chugach Mountain Range, a loud and laughing, “I *wish* I wasn’t late,” came from the mailman gripping the steering wheel for all he was worth as the white van silently vanished before Cole’s fascinated eyes.

The garage door lowered, capturing Cole’s Rover in its lukewarm bay. Golf clubs used twice and a red kayak yet to be were the 4x4’s roommates. The forward door had been left open in the morning’s hurry, a rattling overhead as Cole triggered it closed with the push of a button going into the kitchen. Red and black caution words on the inside of the door slowly lowered in front of the Rover as if it had just missed the early movie on its big screen. Apparently some guy by the name of Stand Clear was the star of the low budget film.

The chilly home’s thermostat was still set on sleep, right where Cole had left it. He felt his leg muscles stretch as he hoisted his dirty feet to the double sink. Like liquid floss, the steaming water flowed between his toes when the cordless phone yelled at him, pushing aside the thought that he’d ironically forgotten to check the mail on his way home. Three rings later, the machine took over.

“Hello there, Cole Caffy here. I’m probably at *Here to There*, so leave your message here and I’ll get it when I’m back from there, take care.” Ssssst beep.

“Yes…hi there. This is Bridge. I just wanted to say thank you for last night. You’re a real gentlemen, Cole. If things were different, they’d be different. By the way, when we first met at your office, you said if you were a hundred years younger, I’d be perfect for you. You probably don’t remember it but, Cole, even if you were two hundred, you’d still be turnin’ the heads of much younger women than you think. Well, I hope everything is okay for you today. It is for me, Cole. No burnt bridges. Thanks again.” ssssssst beep…click.

Cole threw a striped towel to the oak floor to catch his steaming feet. He kept looking to the answering machine thinking of how the day had gone from shit to shine like being found innocent of turning into your own worst enemy. He folded away his umbrella of self pity as his clean feet carried him center the bridge. Not seeing his new furry friends down river, he whispered more than sang a bar or two of an old song having something to do with where the deer and antelope had gone.

These were the only times when Cole truly felt lonely in his life, right after having his spirits lifted or at the end of a grand day of sorts, so much character to share, but no one there. His bare feet cooled on the clear floor as he stood gazing over Spring Creek, brought the mailman’s words warmly to mind as if each letter were carefully drawn in white sand, ‘go there.’

Inhaling through a slanted smile as his thoughts raced, Cole had to stop and think if he still owned a decent pair of summer shorts.

Laura’s Wagoneer sifted through the morning’s new snow on Jenny Massey’s gravel driveway. One, then two, fat juvenile faces drew back living room curtains to share in a stare as she squealed her mud yellow door shut. Pilot snorted and stealthily plowed his way toward the woodpile around back where he knew the occasional marmot to call home. Jenny’s home was a long red ranch style with customary white-framed windows. It wasn’t square to the world and far too close to Patch for Laura, but she did truly like the woman who lived there. Even more so after Jenny's hot headed husband went out for ice cream four years ago and never came back after telling Jenny he was going out for ice cream and never coming back. She was an outgoing woman at things that didn't involve going out, and it had been Laura's subtle encouragement that led to these morning rain or shine strolls up Patch. It wasn't so much that Jenny was overweight, Laura just wouldn't want to rely on her to carry her wounded body through a jungle taking fire.

"Come in, come in," she said, waving Laura through the commotion of circling kids and a narrow dog that was just happy to see someone else. Laura rose to her tiptoes, stepping back in the door's frame, as the fattest of the two fat kids clipped a half inhaled bowl of Captain Crunch, whirling it in an acrobatic three-sixty to the faded beige linoleum.

"Good Christ, Alicia! You act like you've never seen a skinny person before, now isn't that somethin'? You could've looked like that too if you'd of stopped eatin' about nine years ago!"

"But MoOOOom I'm only eight!"

"Clean it up and clean it up now!" Jenny yelled in her best we have company yell. "Oh, but feel free to take five if you start breakin' a sweat, pudgy!"

Through a why-did-I-have-to-be-so-damn-fertile smile, Jenny said, "I just tried calling you. There's a pretty good bite in this breeze this morning, don't you think?"

Laura answered, reminding her of their pact, "rain, sleet or snow, we go!"

As there were no skirts, the naughty northern wind had to settle for blowing up their pant legs, finding only a pair of long blue underwear and the other ones knee-high buckled boots weren't worth the effort. Rejected, the stiff breeze tumbled ahead, rolling over Pilot in a spoiled lashing out around his humpy shoulders and busy stick legs.

"Piiiillot, wait up for us now!" Laura hollered ahead, feeling the small pepper gas canister in her right pocket.

"Mind if I ask you something personal, Laura?"

"Not at all, what?"

"When's the last time you had sex?"

"Oh, let's see, about eleven hours ago. You?"

"Aaauu, day and a half or so."

"You mind if I ask you something else personal?"

"Not at all, what?"

"When's the last time you had sex with someone else?"

"Oh, let's see, about…forever. You?"

"Aaauu yeah, forever and a half or so, give or take a lifetime," Jenny answered, sharing in their laugh. "Well, at least one of us has a boyfriend," Jenny said, instigating.

"Oh good, you started dating again, I'm so proud of you!" Laura snorted. "Tell me all about this wonderful guy of yours," she said, knowing all too well where the conversation was leading to again, as it usually did about this turn in the road.

"Well he's tall, smart, rich, and funny. You know, sort of the knight in silvery hair type," Jenny said, hugging like a schoolgirl on Laura's arm. "But there's two problems, Laura. One, he's yoouuur boyfriend and two, he doesn't have a clue because you won't tell him!"

"Jenny, when are you going to let this go?" Laura said, not really wanting to let it go.

"Why on God's earth would you let this go, Laura? It's been over six years since Daniel died. Now I don't mean any disrespect for him but he's left behind a pretty good lesson don't you think? We don't live forever!" Jenny said bringing her hand to her chest as if pledging allegiance. "Do you really think that if there is a heaven Daniel wouldn't be happy to know that the two people he cared for the most in life were going to be there for each other?"

"Jenny, we've been over and over this. I won't risk losing Cole for a friend…a best friend!"

"That's my point here, Laura. Best friend! You can tell best friends anything! What do you think he's gonna' say? 'Oh God, Laura, you're gross and I'm gonna tell everybody you like me like, well, yoooou know?' Come on Laura, I've seen you two together. You're friends forever, no matter what."

Laura lowered her chin, watching Pilot's pockmark tracks pass under her stride. "You know, you're not the only person this week to ask if I minded them asking me something personal."

"Yeah? Who else is after your secrets?"

"Well…Cole, as a matter of fact."

"And do tell. Did he ask you about your boobies again?"

“No, Jenny,” Laura said snorting herself into a giggle. “I told you before, all he was asking me that time was if I, how’d he put it, ‘If I was regularly a gropin’ at myself to check for speed bumps that don’t just slow ya down, but stop you dead in your tracks altogether.’ It was just his funny way of caring that’s all,” Laura explained, pressing her cheek to Jenny’s, lowering her voice with a dash of spice. “I should have reminded him of my bad hand and told him he’d have to take over!” she laughed, remembering when her next mammogram was. “Three wishes.”

“Wishes?”

“Yeah, he wanted to know what my three wishes would be, but not from the hip kind, ya know? He was looking for real answers.”

“So did you tell him it was Laura and Cole sittin’ in a tree k-i-s-s-i-n-…”

“Nooo Jenny, I didn’t sing childhood songs. I told him what I felt they’d be. Except for the third one. I said I thought it was something only a wish could ever make come true.”

“Aaauughh God,” Jenny said spreading her arms. “You had a lead in like that and you just walked away from it?”

“Well…there was just something too weird at the time when he asked me.”

“Weird?”

“Yeah, see there’s this feather, and somehow he, well, never mind. Piiilooot! Come on. It’s time to turn around!” Pilot’s thumb-tail followed him perfectly through his u-turn atop a tree-lined knoll in the road that framed Mt. Bashful equally as perfect.

“Yeah, yeah, feathers, come on,” Jenny said rolling one coaxing hand before her chest.

Slowing the pace, Laura crinkled her face minus one brow and asked, “Jenny, have you ever been to a magic show?”

“If you mean with the slick guy showing how great his assistant’s tits are while he’s pulling a bird out of his ass, no. I couldn’t ever bring myself to fall for any of that crap. Why?”

“Well, let’s just say I know a certain magician that can at least pull feathers out of his ass, and apparently make himself disappear from my porch into thin air.”

Laughing, Jenny said, “Hey, maybe he’s the one that made the potholes down Patch disappear!”

Laura stopped in her tracks as Pilot weaved past.

"Podin' mi mon, din't see you stondin' dare! Popped up like a dom ghost ya deed. Are ya dokay mon? Yu lukin' at mi like I be da dom ghost. Ever ting gonna be oulright mon?"

"I'm sorry, you'll have to excuse me…I'm new here!" Cole replied, lowering his ocean-reflecting eyes to his bare feet again, this time actually seeing the warm white sand between his toes.

six

The southerly breeze zested around Cole's albino knees before brushing up against a woman with a large talking bird perched on her olive skin shoulder that cordially said its name was Gilligan as they passed. A young boy screamed wildly from the center of his mouth while being pulled to a tropical sky from the hands of his tan cheering parents. Cole shaded his eyes with a salute, admiring the bright yellow parasail and its sporty boat plowing the turquoise water.

Lazy trees with prickly skin leaned to the ocean, seeming to patiently storm the beach with huge leaves like those once gently waved by shapely gals dangling grapes over rich mouths before one of them rightfully burned her bra. Cole thought of the towering gate that King Kong destroyed to get at the tasty natives as his eyes ran down the rows of colorful shutters of the sandstone homes and trinket businesses, hurricanes, their rampaging gorilla. Sun kissed children drenched in sea salt cologne flirted with the dream of captaining one of the floating skyscrapers that crowded their romantic bay. Tall neon drinks with redundant blue umbrellas filled the hands of rich tourists looking for sunburns they could tote home to show coworkers in neighboring cubicles. Cole stretched his attention to the lush green mountains uncapped by snow, where instead he saw a smooth canopy of palm leaves swaying to cool its equatorial wildlife below.

Contently strolling under a sign made of painted stucco, *The Hickied Nipple*, Cole smelled blue booze and dried flowers as he swung the bamboo doors apart. The bar had become famous for never becoming famous after forty-six years with a name like *The Hickied Nipple.*

"What ya bee hovin?" the pleasant enough bartender asked, wearing his assigned flesh colored t-shirt embroidered with two bruised nipples.

"Anything local will do," Cole said, sliding his racing-striped shorts atop one of the eight staggered wicker barstools, his pale forearms draining to the bar from his only short-sleeved shirt. Looking overhead as the bartender reached for a dusty bottle hibernating deep in his four bleachers of booze, Cole found a guitar with five strings hanging as part of the cluttered decoration that littered the bamboo walls tied with yellowing sea grass. Like sitting inside a cool volcano, the roof chocked upward with a six-foot oval opening, letting the sunshine spotlight in as if God wanted a word with someone. Ceiling fans spanked a fly every-so-often sending palms over sweet drinks lined with local fruit.

"No pay if ya don'd like," the bartender said, presenting Cole with a polluted drink in a clean double shot glass. "Tizz called za Voodoo."

"Let's give it a shot," Cole responded, bravely bringing the concoction to his lips, smelling coconut and seeing the halved hairy shells still wobbling on stainless steel. A novice in his ways, he sipped, pursing his lips.

"Wholly jumpin' Christ...that's...Wow!" Cole gasped, his eyelids sucking back around their wet translucent balls. "Coconut...and...ah, yes...gasoline! I like it sir...and I'll be payin'!"

The wide bony smile of the bartender triggered another and another from the dread-locked locals that had anxiously awaited Cole's reaction to the hundred-and-ninety proof bomb. Trying not to swallow his tongue, Cole turned to the sound of a sliding cash drawer where aside it promptly sat a bald faced monkey, carefully watching the man's hands make change like a pit boss. "Hey, I don't mean to be a nit-picker...but I think this stuffs makin' me see monkeys!" Cole said, wincing at the idea of sticking his own finger down his throat.

"No mon, he be a real monkey, but try tellin him dat." The monkey shot Cole a beady look from under his evolutionary brow like a gun turret glances to the hostile sea.

"Hees name be Parasite. Watches za money when me bock is turned from dese dom thieves."

"Who ya be collin' a thief?" came from a gangly squint-eyed regular three stools down.

"Oh, now luk what I wend and done. I offend your pure ond tenda soul my good mon?" the bartender said with a turn, appearing to calmly reach for the man's emptied glass. FLAP! came the bartender's wet hand, pinning the man's left wrist atop the tile bar. "What ya coll dees!" the bartender pried, pointing to a string of teeth marks resembling a healed bracelet.

"I toul ya, I was makin' da change fo da car wash!"

"And I toul ya mon, ya dond own a car. Ya hove a moped, and ya stole dat from a tourist! That fat wouman dat owns da *Skyline Scooter's* across the island. She was here de next mourning with all her questions! Ya lucky I didn't throw ya to de dom hissin' goat. Damn fool Monty. There's note even car wash on de whole island!" the bartender said, freeing the guilty wrist with a round of laughter on the house.

An hour-and-a-half passed. Cole said, "I'll have another," twice and made three friends. The water spinning backwards down the bar's dirty toilet was kinda neat, Cole thought. He flushed it again. Contently ambling back to his barstool, he noticed Parasite had moved from his rectangular cat bed beside the register. Its jack-handle tail said he was digging for his wages in the long stainless freezer; three frosty pops a day, lemon, cherry made him gassy.

"How ya be gettin' around de island?" the bartender asked, presenting his friendly string of teeth.

Cole perked up, yet didn't let it show by only squaring his shoulders. "Oh…I'll be taking Monty's motor scooter," he said, with a calm James Bond glance aimed three stools down.

It took a minute for this to register over Monty's ongoing thoughts of the register. Through a curvy drunk he finally wiped his long pin-wheeled hair away with a genius reply, "What…my scooter, where?"

"O-sheet, I think he be serious!" the bartender howled as his arms fell open to his sides.

"I'll go out on a limb here, Monty," Cole said, pushing his emptied shot glass aside. "I'm guessin' you've been known to place a bet now and then. Am I right? Sure I am. So how about a little spin of the wheel now, amongst friends?" he asked, fishing in his swimming trunks for cash, pulling out twice what Parasite had been guarding all along.

"What…what ya bet to me mon?" Monty sneered, using the ball bearings of the old stool to swivel himself into full curious view.

Seeing the wad of U.S Presidents, the bartender slapped the dingy bar rag over his left shoulder. "Parasite! Come!"

"Would you be so kind as to share a shot glass of olives, my good man?" Cole asked, slipping a cool grifter's eye to the bartender, who was more than willing to assist in anything that promised egg on Monty's back-alley face. Parasite sauntered down the bar's runway with a quiet authority, lured by Cole's rainy day treasure. A pineapple shaped glass half full of olives came to a spinning rest center stage as Monty's liquor-shined bottom lip curled back after robbing his thick shot glass of its last hazy drop. Raising one brow, Cole made eye contact. "Here we have an olive!" Like a ring cradles its gem, Cole's tulip shaped fingers presented the olive before him in example. "And if you'll look above us, yes yes, way up there now," he said, gesturing to one of the six ceiling fans whirling overhead. Monty's long woven rug of hair tickled the top of his lazy ass as he strained his drunken head to see what appeared to be a half dozen remote controlled helicopters trying to rescue ashtrays from an incoming wave of afternoon tourists. Parasite, hunched and coiled, knew better than to take his trained eyes from the roll of green cash plopped down before him.

Real slow, Cole picked up and peeled hundred dollar bills off his tight drum of dough, counting to five, keeping the interest alive. "Your scooter sir, or whoever's it is, did you ride it here today?"

Actually proud of his steal of a deal, Monty whipped a string of his dangling dreadlocks over his shoulder and answered, "Tiz out bock! Pink, weeth za beautiful tie-dye seat." An upside down smile mixed with a nod from the bartender confirmed Monty's story.

"Well then, sir, I'll bet you these five hundred American boys here against the pink slip to your pink scooter, or I guess a key will have to do in your case. There is a key?"

Fixated by more money than he'd seen in six months, Monty gave up the small chrome key from his drooping shirt pocket, displaying it in the dent of his palm.

"My bet to you then," Cole said, aiming a finger as though he'd been asked where he hoped to go after he died, "is that I can give this olive a toss up to that fan, knocking it perfectly out of the park."

Monty's eyes followed Cole's finger and his low air-raid whistle to the ceiling's small open-air throat with a suckers-bet grin growing across his back alley face. As much an impossible feat as yahooing a wagon team to the rings of Saturn, the olive would have to travel a ridiculous trajectory. Reflecting first from the teak fan blades, then bouncing at least twice up the busily decorated walls in any desperate hope of throwing itself free the tee-pee styled opening.

A Frenchman, who liked gold jewelry, held the hand of his heavily perfumed wife tracing the unattainable through the air. Above such childish antics, the Frenchman's wife gave a snobbish gaze to no one in particular as she chose a spot on a distant wall with her eyes, while she hoped others groped over her with theirs.

"This some kind of bar treek, a game of words that will cost me my ride, mon?"

"I wouldn't cheat you, if that's what you're getting at. There will be no play on words, my sticky fingered friend. If this olive doesn't clear the room through that opening, I lose! The money is yours to keep. No catches or strings. However," Cole explained, leaning in a bit, "if the olive does go for the moon…your scooter is mine. Do you agree?"

"And you'll hove only one go at it ya say?" Monty asked, drunkenly jerking an eyebrow up during his question. The Frenchman freed his wife's rich hand to cross his arms about his round chest in allurement.

"One try," Cole smoothly said, with one finger held before him. "One."

Parasite gave a low howl as Monty cautiously released the moped's key, letting it slide from his palm, weighing down the American's cash between them on the bar's edge.

"Ya be watchin' him now my friend. He won't be takin' it well if you olive disappear in the sunlight like ya say," the bartender warned. "He would steal from his own mother on Mother's Day mon, and tell da police on Father's Day it t'was his father that went and done it, if there be a nickels reward to be hod." Monty gave a hiss from his yellow teeth in reply, never looking the man in the eye. Over his jutting jaw, Parasite spotted the pot as Cole stretched the skin over his adams apple looking from Monty to the pulsing ceiling fan, raising the green armored olive.

Like the Red Baron at his gun sights, Cole slow danced with the olive in mid air with his aiming eye. The Frenchman smiled from the corners of his thin mouth as his wife mentally spent his money like Monty was Cole's. Judging the speed of the fan against the angles and distance needed, Cole drew back the olive overhead. Everyone, less Parasite, was fixed, unknowingly holding his or her breath.

Cole flinched in a short flicking release. The olive cleared the whirling blades with a lingering u-turn bringing it back with a small wet fan slap, followed by another as it struck the Frenchman's wife in the left temple. The woman's hands flung to her affluent face, but not near as fast as Monty's to the cash. The bartender shared a wince with Cole seeing Monty's greedy hand instantly crawl off with its fresh kill to a nylon cave.

"You eedeote!" the woman fired at Cole, rubbing her temple, stepping back from the battered olive resting in front of her strapping open toed shoes.

"I'm afraid I'm forced to agree with her," the Frenchmen said, patting the small of his wife's back. "The sad thing is, we never agree! Your trick is impossible sir, why do you give your money away so?"

Cole held in a snicker, glancing away from the woman holding her frail arms away from herself as though she'd been splashed with a pail of pig's blood. Monty announced a round on himself, but only for himself, by shaking an empty glass at the disappointed bartender who answered with, "Daaaaa Monty, you'll be lurking around here drunker than the devil himself for a dom week." Reluctantly reaching for the aluminum ice scoop, the bartender got a 'hang in there' look from Cole.

"Well, my rich friend, it must be this punchy booze and tropical heat going to my crazy old head, but are you familiar with the term 'double or nothing'?" Cole inquired, lifting his chin, and the disbelief of others.

Monty turned once more to this silver haired man slowly counting out hundred dollar bills, this time to ten.

"Your scooter, and the five hundred, against my thousand here. What do you say we give it one more try?"

The Frenchman looked at Cole like he'd noticed bright red and blue lights flashing in his rearview mirror after leaving a bar that he vaguely remembered being at. Rolling her spoiled dark eyes, his wife disappeared through the swinging bamboo doors saying, "When you're done playing with the eediots, I'll be outside trying to enjoy the rest of my vacation." With a degrading chuckle, Monty reached deep in his pocket for his free cash and free key.

"The same es before, one try?" Monty asked, slowly waving his wager in front of the crazy northern tourist.

"The same as before. Agreed?"

Again Parasite was called to duty, hooting as Monty's thieving hand firmly placed his bet on Cole's stack. The bartender said to Cole, "I'm afraid only wishful thinkin' is gonna' be helpin' you!"

"Well, okay then…wishful thinking it is," Cole said, giving a confident glance to the unconfident bartender. "I guess all I can do now is *wish* for this olive to reflect from that fan, and bounce up those walls, to finally escape through that opening in the ceiling!"

The Frenchman followed Cole's words through this circus of an idea once more, trying to find the trick or scam. But he could see nothing other than a foolish man giving his money away as Cole placed a new olive on his thumb nail, never breaking his content stare into Monty's big lazy eyes.

"Are you ready?" Cole grinned.

"Yeah mon. I can use za money."

With a flick of Cole's thumb the olive sped for the spinning fan, and with a *tonk* it was paddled away. Monty's fat eyes caught up to it as it made contact with an antique cow bell shrink wrapped to the wall with blue fishnet where it awkwardly reflected with a *slang* across the five stringed guitar where it continued to end-over-end on its way, making a promising charge like a pole-vaulter at a retired bongo leaving behind an amplified *pop*. All widening eyes in the bar stayed glued as the olive miraculously ricocheted to freedom, disappearing in the sun belted sky.

"Be…domed!" Monty barked as his hand shot for the pile of dough. Instantly Parasite lunged, sinking his crooked razor teeth deep in the howling thief's forearm, again. The bartender howled as well, throwing his bar rag to the ceiling fan like a fan as the Frenchman's stunned face went limp watching the screaming monkey-fight whirl before him. Cole slapped his fist around the winnings, throwing a hundred dollar bill to the bar and tipping an invisible hat to the ecstatic bartender.

Running wild for the pink scooter, he squinted in the sunlight trying to watch for Monty, who at the same time would surely be in pursuit! He found the scooter carelessly lying on its side in the bar's tastefully graffitied alleyway like something an artist might try to capture on canvas.

Five barstools lay strewn in a circle of broken glass around a wounded Monty as Parasite was finally told to "Release!" Monty charged for the door holding his forearm, his squinting eyes, bunkers for the devil to cower in as God's sword of daylight ran them through. With his heart hammering in his chest, Cole lifted the scooter and ran like a child in trouble for leaving his bike in the driveway. "O-shit!" he yelped under his growing breath as he cleared the alley, jumping on the tie-dyed seat, flailing his bare feet. All six-foot-four inches of Monty seemed to come from everywhere, pounding at the pink scooter's rubber heel. Cole made the corner, bouncing to the main street, feeling Monty's dirty fingernails brush the air around the pores of his back with a swipe. Carried by momentum of his missed tackle, Monty's lank body blessedly went down in a knee and elbow scraping roll center of the sandstone street as Cole pushed on, tasting his own adrenaline.

Standing on his knees, flipping the barbwire hair from his satanic face, Monty yelled from behind, "Tiz za small island, mon! Tiz za small island!"

Straddling the anorexic motorcycle, Cole looked to the ignition switch center its chrome handlebars. After nearly fumbling the shiny key, he corrected it in his fist and stabbed the scooter between the horns. Its BB-gun tailpipe coughed up a pathetic gray wheeze, bringing an anxious smile to Cole's parting lips. As he scurried away on the moped with his knees spread wide, he broke into a full galloping laugh as he passed the French woman standing outside the bar with her oval mouth paralyzed open. Her string arms held away from herself once again as though splashed with another pail of pigs blood, the second olive resting in front of her white open toed shoes, right where she'd dropped it after digging it out of her mussed hair.

Cole's only pair of swimming trunks billowed around his white thighs like parachutes as he and the pink scooter headed for the other side of the island, wherever that was, mon.

✉

A half naked kid pushing another in a weathered wheel barrow, told Cole that *Skyline Scooters* was where that fat lady was always yelling about something or other. Pointing their fingers to the northwest, they swore Cole couldn't miss the place if he watched for a string of scooters that looked just like his. "Keep goin,' follow za ocean, she always dare."

Cole zinged the throttle, and the two laughed as he asked with a smile scattered deep in his stubbly cheeks if they wanted to race. But they didn't understand what he meant when he pointed to their wheel barrow asking "So…what cha got under the hood?" Fearing they were now certain he was a pedophile, Cole thought a wheelie might bring back the two's laughter as he left, and it did. He let the clutch fly like a cowboy riding off into the sunset, instead somehow running over his own foot, chasing the possessed scooter to a thorny ditch.

One palm tree at a time, the rural beach road buzzed by. Full on the throttle, the scooter limped to a crest overlooking what many only dream of one day seeing. All of the posters hanging in travel agencies around the world fell far short of making their point. The translucent waves charged the beach baring their sea foam teeth as Cole admired the flying white sails of a handsome boat and the people trimming them after tacking away to deeper water.

A small population spotted with offbeat tourist traps and fruit stands came into view surrounding Cole and the pink scooter with verbal advertisement. Like strolling through a carnival, the locals persuaded a few bucks from him. A half-dozen candy bars and a miniature wooden monkey later, Cole refired his hog, and headed for the edge of town where a thin dark man with tobacco-stained fingernails had directed him to, while making change. The monkey was for an obvious memory, the candy bars for the first kids that said please.

Sure enough, a string of scooters in a rainbow of scratch and dent colors came up on his right, lined up like assorted spices in a chef's rack. As the pink scooter's front tire pressed its knobby pattern into the white sand of the driveway, Cole turned the key and listened as the motor's patter faded between his legs. Raising one hand to shelter his eyes from the tropical sun, he discovered the business was more of a house really, told to say "Ah" from sunup to sundown, hiding its heavily lived-in backside facing a small uncrowded harbor. A modern sign, *Skyline Scooters*, had been o-so regrettably arched over the upstairs bedroom window of the withdrawn daughter who rebelled by taping four cardboard letters of her own on the sign after hours, then forgot about it, so Cole was actually pulling into, *Buy Fine Hooters*. Reading the sign, his instinct begged him to kick the hog back to life and save his own, seeing all three hundred plus pounds of Rosa Nomanino, the owner, break from the screen door beneath it in a boob-slinging gallop.

Slapping toward him, Cole could actually hear what sounded like several people having sex on a waterbed with no sheets, right down to the heavy breathing. He didn't know whether to run or yell, so he did both still straddling the scooter, scaring Rosa a little to the left in a veering motion.

"Numba seventeen! Numba seventeen!" Rosa screamed, starting a corralling circle as though Cole had been caught sitting on one of the beast's own cubs.

"Ma'am! Ma'am…I didn't…I'm just bringing…I'm not the…."

Like the needle of a record player, Rosa was closing in on him with each yelling revolution. "Numba seventeen! Numba seventeen!"

Cole reached for the sun, "STOOOOP! For the love of God or whoever the hell you pray to, just STOOOOP!"

The ring of dust beaten up by Rosa's stampeding blue and orange flip-flops was given a chance to escape, latching onto the light breeze.

"Now Ma'am…I didn't steal your scooter. Well, sort of, but I stole it from the one who stole it in the first place. I'm here to return it to you!" Cole pleaded, toying with the idea of cranking the key and taking his chances with the local police. "…I'm not the thief!"

Rosa's fists relaxed into hands. "You bring numba seventeen bock to me?"

"Here she is!" Cole said patting its skinny gas tank. "Now, I didn't run her through a car wash or anything because I understand there's not one on the entire isla…."

Rosa flared her fat-capped triceps at him again, heaving her hefty arms with a Santa Claus look in her begifted eyes. Cole saw her charge before fully realizing it, frozen to the tie-dye seat. Three stomps came from the flip-flops before the sun eclipsed. The last thing Cole saw was a canopy of repeating printed flowers across Rosa's sleeveless smock engulfing him with gratitude. Like pushing a refrigerator up a flight of stairs, his right foot cocked out to the side, digging in the earth to hold his ground as the scooter leaned with a creak.

Sixteen, seventeen, eighteen, the scooter took its place in the line once again. Curiously the daughter tiptoed down the roughed in stairs from her loft to have a look at Cole who said, "Hello!" Her eyes quizzed him, as Mom rarely brought anyone beyond the blue recliner boundary of the screened porch office.

"You will eat with us today!" Rosa ordered, snapping her thick fingers to the daughter with one hand, the other directing Cole to the head of a long hardwood table with eight miss-matched chairs surrounding it, he thought of his own. A light hoofed boy no more than six, came from nowhere popping up opposite Cole's appointed seat. The boy's lips made an upside down *U* inspecting this stranger's silvery hair with a thorn in it. The daughter, dressed in a hand-dyed t-shirt and blue jean shorts, stood resting her hip against the counter as she gutted a vanilla bean with her scooping fingernail. Flicking the bean's muddy entrails in a Ball jar of milk, she stirred it with the same finger and brushed her long dark hair over one shoulder with her free hand. She circled the table quietly and timidly offered it to Cole. With a soft tug and disguised giggle, the thorn was gently plucked.

"Oh…thank you. But you know, that's the big thing now up in the states?" Cole said, wanting to grasp his suspenders to build the story, but had none. "Sure, sure. Sometimes the rich and famous wear entire bushes on their heads! What…you don't believe me?"

The daughter laughed, fanning her cello brown eyes to the floor as a squeak came from the boy who was still staring at him the way kids do. "No, it's true, it's true. The more important you are the bigger the bush! Why you've heard of George Bush haven't you?" Cole asked, raising his arms high over his head as if balancing a giant vase. "When he became president, his name was honorably changed to George Tree! Oh, 'twas a lovely redwood," he said sifting a breeze between his teeth. "You should have seen him at Christmas, really a grand display of authority, except for the festive balls hanging in his eyes." Rosa, actually believing this for a moment, pictured the leader of the free world's knees buckling under the great weight as a wood tick crawled to his ear.

A wonderful plate of pepper chicken sausage and glazed pineapple dashed with cloves came at Cole eye level before resting on the worn table. More pepper than chicken, the burn on his tongue seesawed with the sweet of sugared fruit like a chef kissing his fingertips.

"Rosa, do you have a boat?" Cole asked, gesturing through a faded string of kitchen windows to the harbor where there floated a lonely fiberglass soul.

"Yes and no. Tiz mine, but do I be lookin' like a sailor?" Rosa asked, saluting with the wrong hand as she lightly marched in place. "My hosband died some time ago, and it's all his worthless carcass left behind. If he would hove cared half es mouch about he's fomily es dat dom boot, we'd be walkin' around with big beautiful bushes on our rich heads now wouldn't we!" Rosa said with a roaring laugh, bringing her hands to her first lady cheeks. The boy squeaked again as though keeping score.

Standing before the neglected sailboat, a whimper from the equally shunned dock told Cole's engineering mind to keep a piling or two between him and Rosa. Giving her hands to the saddle of her hips, she rolled her eyes and shook her head tisk-tisking at the derelict boat.

"Et hasn't been takin' out for some time. My daughter here only one to use it, she be sneakin' below to smoke that crap with her no good friends," Rosa snarled, spinning her disappointed head to the guilty. "You be getting' that ass of yours bock to the house, ond send numba seventeen my love by makin' her shine!" she howled in her infamous yell. Quick to replace it with a soft tropical rumble, she turned back to Cole. "You be a sailor mon, Meester Caffy?"

"No. In fact I don't care much for the water. Lost my nerve to it when I was a kid."

"Well you no kid now, and I can tell in your eye you want to go bock to it, yes? The boat need to go out, and so do you," Rosa said, landing her eyes directly on his.

"Oh, Rosa," Cole said, wrapping his hand around his chin. "I wouldn't want to hurt it. I don't know the first thing about sailing and this was your husband's."

"Yes, it was. And in dat case, you can sink the dom thing for all I be carin'," she scoffed, ignoring the moan in the dock as she stepped up close, lowering her voice. "Any one who bring numba seventeen bock, tiz sure to bring dis old ship wreck bock."

Cole wasn't given the time to think, let alone speak, before Rosa kicked her voice up a few octaves with, "Everyting work I think. My boy runs the mota now and then to chase the smoke out of itself and the sails are simple enough to learn. The wind teach you if you let it. If the boat go sideways to the wind, let the sails go loose to keep da boat from falling over."

Drawing in the palm of her hand, Rosa used her long lifeline to say, "Da wind come from here, so you want to stay like…dees," her index finger following the same line, less thirty degrees. "Today a good day, the ocean is offering a light breeze. You be welcome to drop the anchor for a night if you like. Just be sure to let out tree or four times more chain than ze water es deep, it keep you from driftin' away."

A nervous ill came to Cole's stomach as he swallowed hard and ran his hand along the teak cap rail. "Rosa, may I ask how your husband died?"

Regrettably hearing the electric echo of Metalica chugging from the daughter's loft, Rosa spoke through a sad smile. "He die in ze hospital, but he kill himself here on ze boot. He no drown in ze water, Meester Caffy, he drown in ze whiskey bottles below, and now I afraid my daughter will one day follow him," she said, gazing across the inlet, the sun reflecting just off center of her black pupils. "You should have seen her smile when she talk about ze ocean. She used to go on for days about how she wanted to study everyting that swam in it when she be old like her mama. Now, I cont get her near it unless it be sneakin' a drink on dis cursed boot, ond I know that's what she be doin.' I doon't have ze heart to sell it. I know she be gone ze same day, for good."

"My friend, Laura…my best friend, lost her husband six years ago in a plane accident. That's why I ask. I hope I wasn't too forward."

“Twas also six years ago zat my boy here missed meeting his father by only one month. I’ve hod my time to put it away, Meester Caffy, az I am sure your friend has, too,” Rosa said, putting a caring hand on her boy’s daydreaming head. “Taylob! Start da boot for Meester Caffy while his courage is with us!”

Soon after the boy crawled between the lifelines of the boat like a boxer enters the ring, the boat slugged to life, wiping a fresh gulp of sooty smoke from its sleepy eyes, putting a fear in Cole’s.

“You be fine now. Go on,” Rosa encouraged. “Taylob show you how to start and stop, forward and reverse.”

Cole hated to consider this a crash course, but couldn’t help seeing the irony in the words shouting through his mind. In less than five minutes, Taylob was untying lines from their precious cleats. Cole, standing spread-legged in the cockpit with an excited sick, watched the bowsprit creep to port, just clearing over the stern of a twenty-foot powerboat.

“Meester Caffy…who steel numba seventeen from me?” Rosa somberly asked, strolling along on the creaking dock as the Westsail eased from its slip.

Squeezing the mahogany tiller as he peered over the bowsprit like an eaglet from the brim of its nest, Cole answered without turning to her, “No one worth fussing over Rosa …no one worth fussing over.”

“I know who he eez. He be dat devil with big crooked eyes from town…ze bastard who help my husband drink himself to death.” Monty was right…it was a small island.

Rosa, running out of dock, stood watching Cole and the boat leave the harbor, knowing the two had about as much in common as the Dali Lama and drag racing.

Cole impressed himself with somehow weaving collision free from the small harbor, but was feeling a little lonely seeing it shrink behind him. On his tiptoes in the cockpit, the first wave of peace splashed across his racing mind. The boat was a Westsail 32, ten tons of a beamy girl named *Serenity* with a solid mast tall as an Alaskan spruce. The tiller seemed immense and awkward but reacted surprisingly quickly to the touch, driving the boat to God only knew where. Pushing right to go left, would take a while to get right though.

Eye contact and a nod from the helm of a passing vessel took some of the shake out of his hands. Cole answered with a forced smile under a nervous salute of sorts, jerking his hand from the tiller. His mouth opened when the passing boat's wake drank the bow first, then spit it up to taste the stern…and it was good.

Feeling the diesel popping under his feet, he looked across the biggest body of water he'd ever found himself in the middle of, and all without craning his neck from a bridge to see it. He tried not to think of Mary Pearson as he typically did whenever he was around more than a bucket's worth of water, but her excited little blue eyes were there in the usual place, leaving earth for the last time, shinnying up the oak tree's torso, reaching its long crooked arm, her henchman posing.

He followed the red-tailed wind indicator pop-riveted atop the mast with the lifeline of his palm aiming just so. He looked to the limp sails wrapped about the boom and bagged at the bow with his pulse matching the diesel's. The boy had done little more than point to the chest high winches on the mast miming a tug-o-war. Cole managed to starve the motor as he was briefly shown, bringing a still that quickly reminded him just how alone he really was.

Summoning his courage, Cole crawled from the cockpit on his hands and knees and scurried to the base of the mast. Slowly to his feet, he unwound a braided nylon rope from its cleat with his trembling hands and prayed under his breath without realizing it. Grasping the rope, he closed his eyes and tugged for all he was worth, hoisting the dirty mainsail that followed its track up the mast, filling high in the tropical sky with a snap to starboard. His adrenaline sent his arms around the mast of the heeling boat, his bare feet spreading apart, Mary Pearson, warning him.

The white tickle growing on the canal said the breeze had strengthened. The boat fought awkwardly, bucking the sail to port with a deep slap that shuddered across the cabin trunk where Cole was regrettably riding the bull, the safety of the cockpit seemed so far away. With his cheek pressed to the mast, he looked up with his eyes swelling as the words accidentally slipped from his dry mouth the way we all idly use the word going through divorce or watching the stock market.

"Shit, shit, SHIT! I just *wish* I knew something about boats or how to sail."

Before Cole could realize what he had said, his eyes calmly fell shut, and his grip loosened as a peaceful knowledge strolled around the teak decks, finding him embraced to the mast. With a warm kick in the courage, his eyes opened to what he somehow knew to be the main halyard dangling before him and that it needed to be winched tight and tied off properly.

From an aerial view, you could see the flapping mainsail fill and trim as it should, the boat coming into the wind with water beginning to break around its fat bow, thirty-degrees less Cole's long lifeline. You would also see a captain's arms reaching toward you with the same triumph of a writer noticing he'd made it halfway through his first book.

seven

Laura's yellow Wagoneer circled into the driveway of her favorite engineer. Pilot knew this stretch of a house and that the man who lived there liked to spin him in the air blowing saliva. Tracks in the morning snow said the Rover had been in quite a hurry leaving, but appeared to have returned contently enough, back to its garage. Laura knocked at the thick ash doors with her good hand, sliding the other away in a pocket lined with butterscotch candy twisted in yellow cellophane that felt like elevator buttons with pig tails.

Pilot winked as a snowflake died in his warm round eye when Laura gave the door's brass knob a clockwise turn. "Play out here sugar buger…mama's goin' in."

"COOOOLE!" echoed through the kitchen and across the bridge.

Closing the door behind her, she slowly coasted to the kitchen, passed the hanging antique phone that she always thought looked like her ninth grade typing teacher leaning in close to say something degrading. The home smelled of flowers, tulips actually, her nose supposed, leading her through the dining room.

"Cole, it's me, the boogie man, or I guess, boogie woman! I brought my attack dog who's circling your house as we speak, so come on out with your hands where I can see um!" Cautiously cresting the three steps to the living room lined with drying tulips, Laura muttered, "Jesus," under her butterscotch breath. Surrounded by the flowers, she stood wide-eyed over Spring Creek caressing one of the yellow petals between her thumb and forefinger. She could see that they had been frozen at one time, and the cowering arch of their bulbs said not long ago.

"What did he do, pull you poor things out of a dumpster?" she asked to the uprooted, spotting a small envelope with a colorful rainbow slung across it.

"Well, now…I'll bet you're the little love letter that came with this floral shop, huh?" she huffed, with a hint of hurt. Daintily setting herself on the lip of Cole's favorite chair, she dragged the envelope across the glass coffee table with her suspicious red nails, noticing what appeared to be a personal delivery finding no return address.

Being above invading other's privacy, Laura couldn't bring herself to read the letter stuffed inside, even though it was certainly from some slippery hussy! As she gave herself deeper to the chair watching Spring Creek lumber over the fall at the edge of Cole's property, thoughts of never being able to tell him how she cared, and cared in all ways, would certainly be postponed, if not destroyed all together if she were to leave now under the impression that there was another.

Realizing only she would be hurt by peeking …she peeked.

Cole chose a simple inlet just below the afternoon sun off to port. He counted three, then four other boats as he slowed the pulse of the diesel. The depth sounder told him when to run forward and let the plow anchor go, dragging its bulky chain from below with a rattling shout up the bowsprit, following its thirty five pound leader to the teal water. The boat's own momentum set the anchor as Cole began neatly lashing the mainsail to the boom with strands of nylon.

Going below, he quickly agreed with a frown that Rosa's daughter had somewhat claimed the boat after her father passed. Thumb tacked to the bulkhead was a poster of Annie Lenox, screaming into a microphone, back-grounded by a Scottish flag rippling across her stage. The hand-rolled cigarette butts in the halved Orange Crush can seemed odd somehow and blended with the old boat's smell. But what stood out most to Cole, was the framed photograph of a father and daughter holding up seashells on some never ending stretch of white beach. He assumed they were the same shells that had been carefully placed next to the picture in one of Rosa's Ball jars harbored to its shelf by a graying teak runner.

Hearing a youthful, "Hello onboard!" Cole made way up the companionway, finding an inflatable dinghy circling about the stern pushed by an excited little outboard motor. Its captain was a cheery kid that spoke through a high-pitched British accent who informed Cole his parents were having refrigeration problems and needed help eating everything in sight before it soured. Cole followed the boy's aiming index finger to the neighboring sailboat with brass ports and a navy blue hull moored at least three stone throws away, the mother signaling them with dark beer and something wrapped in tin foil. Cole surveyed the frightening distance with an alert glance back to the questionably tipsy inflatable.

Spread out across the dinghy like a cat held over water, Cole clutched the rubber oarlocks watching as the blue hull of his neighbor's boat grew to be a reasonable target of safety.

"Hello there! I trust your appetite has made the journey with you?" the English boy's father chuckled over the lifelines. "Now I cont say I've eva seen that technique before," he politely laughed, seeing Cole's limbs braced in more places than limbs.

"How do?" Cole said, scattering aboard in a way that brought an eye-widening smile to the wife as she delivered bratwurst to the grated killing floor of a gas grill. The boy, thinking Cole must have seen some sort of serpent, also leapt aboard quicker than usual, just to be on the safe side.

The dinner conversation overflowed with sailing and the wake of stories that always seem to ensue it. Filled to the gills with fish, Cole said, "no thank you," raising his hand in surrender to a slop bucket of what once was strawberry ice cream came round. The husband swallowed the last of many dark beers, telling Cole that his Westsail was indeed a well-proven boat.

"I'm afraid it's just an overnight loaner from someone on the island, but it's nice to hear just the same. Truth be known, I have a sizeable fear of water," Cole admitted, tracing the mouth of a beer bottle with the side of his thumb.

"I watched you bring her in this afternoon, and a handsome job you made of it."

"Yeah, well, that was just wishful thinking."

Taken with Cole's sudden gaze back to the Westsail, the father drained beer into his stomach by trading the bottle's ends. "We're from a very quiet place in southern England, Plymouth, if you've ever had the pleasure? Traveling here is indeed wonderful, meeting new people and seeing places we'll certainly never be forgetting. I suppose, I could do this for a living if there were such a thing."

The wife, dressed in a tan line-telling tank top and a pair of jeans amputated at the thighs, collected their plates in a clockwise motion about the knee-knocking cockpit, then headed below to the L-shaped galley. "Here, let me help you, my sweet," the husband offered, jamming his fingers and thumbs in the tops of ten empty beer bottles then wiggling them in the air as if he'd discovered something really quite amazing. The boy let out a snicker, knowing his dad never drank more than two beers a week.

"Thank you both so much for everything," Cole said below, craning his head in the companionway.

"Well now, you don't have to run off. You're more than welcome to stay. My husband's always after someone to lose a game of cribbage to."

"I'm afraid it's been a long day for me," Cole replied, gazing across the inlet. "I've covered more miles than you might think."

"Well thank you for coming over and for the wonderful company. Our limo driver will see you back whenever you're ready. He's always looking for an excuse to take the runabout out and about."

Sitting cross-legged on the bow of the sailboat, the boy's face lit up hearing this and he shot for the inflatable. Cole came to his feet in the cockpit, preparing for the crossing by telling himself it was only a short ride back to the Westsail, and that if he'd made it once, he'd somehow make it again. Approaching the gate in the lifelines, he said, "after you," as the boy's anxious feet tripped out from under him with a dull pound to the back of his head on the way to the water. His limp body never seeming to put up a fight, the boy was under.

Cole stomped on the deck yelling, "The boy fell over! The boy fell over!" The mother's face showed in a brass porthole with a confused shock. Cole knew by the time he repeated himself and the parents made it on deck to do something, anything, the boy would have sucked just that much more saltwater into his starving lungs.

Not so much as putting his fear aside as taking it with him, Cole inhaled, and jumped to the serpentine water.

His eyes stung from the salt, and his ears filled with that rubbery silence as the pressure squeezed at them. The father shot to the abandoned deck, finding only the dingy tugging at its line from the wake of bodies plunging overboard.

"Sam!" he cried…"SAAAAAM!"

Reaching the cockpit, the mother's hands went to her mouth saying, "NO!" between her fingers as the father peered over the side, clutching the lifelines. Cole used the man's pale face for a target, kicking wildly back to the surface.

The mother exhaled in a controlled burst, seeing the water explode, making a hole big enough in the ocean for two. "Oh God!" the father shouted, plunging his arm over the cap rail like he'd fumbled his car keys down a storm drain after yelling obscenities to a Los Angeles street gang.

"He's breathing!" Cole said, nearly forgetting to do the same. "Take his arm!" Being hoisted as though on the business end of a calf puller, the boy's ribcage swallowed his stomach in a silent wretch as he gave a cup's worth of the saltwater through what looked like an everyday face twisting yawn.

Seeing the father make way to the cockpit, cradling his only son, Cole followed hand over hand grasping the dull lip of the boat, his legs still paddling in the poison.

The boy's sun burnt skin shrink wrapped around his organs with a gasping exhale that quickly rebelled with a deep draw. "I…fell."

A relieved smile ricocheted around the cockpit, striking the mother in her pretty face after slapping the father across his thankful cheeks. "Just breathe, Sam, just breathe," the mother said patting the boy's wet slumping back. "What happened Sammy? Did you get ahead of yourself?"

"Yeah…GRRRROOOOOOPPP!" The boy's tongue danced like a retarded stripper center stage of his stretched oval mouth in a thunderous swimming pool burp, bringing a weight lifting laugh to the crew and putting the boy's door-ding dimples back in their happy corners.

"Thank you," the father offered, nodding overboard to Cole, still clutching the rail. "Thank you."

“Was my fault in the first place. If I wouldn’t have needed a ri....”

“We’ll have none of that,” the father interrupted, flashing his palm. “He’s always in such a rush, but it’s the unfortunate times like this that will have to teach him differently. I...we... are just very glad you were here.”

“...Thanks,” genuinely came from the boy, as he remembered Cole’s hand finding his in the deep.

“Not a problem, Sam! Next time I’ll take a cab, or just learn to swim properly and paddle myself home.”

“Speaking of that,” said the boy’s father, smiling over the rail, “how are you getting along down there, chap? I’m afraid your monster has you swallowed to the shoulders.”

“You know, I haven’t given it much of a thought, till now,” Cole mumbled, feeling nothing under his dangling feet, still bare.

“If you’ll find your way in the dinghy there, I’ll be right with you for that lift back,” the husband said with a brightened English curl in his spirited voice.

What happened next is only explainable by someone who has ever looked their own demon straight in the eyes and leapt at them with a charge of spontaneous courage. Through a due-south stare, Cole flattened his eyes and judged the distance of the Westsail’s plump white hull to be no less than eighty lingering yards to starboard.

“No need. Thank you again for the company,” Cole said, with all the romance of a prerecorded phone message. Sitting in the cockpit, the family heard Cole take in a gale of a breath as they watched his fingers free the rail one by one....then he was gone.

The sting of salt returned to his squinting eyes, eardrums beating as he kicked past ten, then fifteen feet, feeling the water cool with each fathom. He pulled back on the yoke to clear a sea floor of multi-colored coral like a crop duster avoiding power lines. Nightclub blue and pink with a harvest of prom purple and moon white passed under his torso as he pinched his nose and blew the squeeze out of his ears. A fish, or two, then three, sambaed by overhead, ironic, Cole thought, like flying over a bird.

His mind told his lungs to breathe as he pumped for the surface like riding an invisible pogo stick toward the sunlight that was leaking into the ocean through a kaleidoscope.

On his second dive, Cole could feel his fear of water still gaining on him as he neared the bottom. Like someone afraid of the dark smashing their flashlight, he swam on, determined to break his lifelong foe. Reaching the sea floor, his monster revealed itself in its liquid form, surrounding him with the same suffocating weapon that killed Mary Pearson over half of a century earlier. Again he saw her little blue eyes somehow saying his name as the rope crawled around her knees and fragile neck like lying on a pile of snakes, a pile of snakes that Cole had seen himself throwing to her, over and over and over again.

The thought of wishing it all away seeped into his frightened mind, but he forced himself to purge it, knowing this was something that had to be earned…something he had to face alone. Swallowed twenty feet deep in the belly of the water, the vindictive water, he floated… drifted…he saw Mary…saw himself…then screamed into the liquid beast like a fetus dodging a coat hanger tearing across its mother's ambient bag of life jelly that it called home.

Cole opened his eyes to the salty blur, his tears camouflaged. Mary and her snakes were gone…gone for good. She'd rode away bareback on Cole's defeated beast, jabbing its flanks with her Sunday school heels to rest in a place where the past is the past and the candy is free.

The following morning, Rosa dropped her hand fan and stood from the powder blue recliner, as she gazed with a proud smile to find the Westsail make its slow and steady approach to the bottleneck of the harbor. The spinnaker that she'd never seen flown was white with a red sash and bigger than the boat itself. The man at the helm too was white with a red sash, painted by the sun across his shy northern skin.

Taylob turned up under foot the way he always seemed to. "You go help land and tie da boot…if he be needin' any help, dat is," Rosa said, watching the spinnaker dowse to the deck as though Cole had performed this tricky feat a thousand times on many a long voyage.

Cole beat the boy to the cleat and tied it off neatly as Rosa built up speed descending from the cluttered back yard to sea level. The familiar cry of the dock sent Cole's eyes to once again judge his current position between pilings. He turned to her and stood tall with a peaceful smile stretching across his face, and without a word spoken, said thank you to Rosa, who understood the sparkle of a good thing when she saw it.

The daughter met them at the back porch, entwining her anxious fingers in a waist high knot, happy to find that her tree house had made it back in one floating piece.

"I'm a new man thanks to you, Rosa. And to you," Cole added, rolling his eyes to the daughter as the boy climbed up his left side like a palm tree. The daughter was taken back a step by Cole's genuine acknowledgement, rather expecting him to sail back to the dock with a payload of her strange cigarette secrets for a fiery tempered mother. She accepted his gratitude with a nervous smile to the floor, her hands slipping behind her petite waist like Laura's in a crowd.

"You will sit and eat with us again, yes?" Rosa asked, raising one hand, readying it for a snap to the daughter if the answer was a yes.

"You've all been so good to me. But, I need to get on home," Cole said, holding the boy out in front of him, inspecting each other with squint eyes and a grin. "Left so fast that I went and forgot to lock up. And ol' Rover's gonna need to go out for a walk."

Setting the boy down with his right arm as if weighing him, Cole took a lingering last look to the harbor and the wonderful boat tied there, sailing his eyes from bow to stern. From behind he heard the faint clack of the screen door shutting and the daughter appeared strolling to the boat across Cole's gaze. "Maybe I could trouble your daughter to show me around town though, if it wouldn't be putting anyone out. I'll need to know where I might catch a bus back to the far side of the island?"

Stretched letters spelling *Sky Line Scooters* anchored across an XXXL pink t-shirt was the last thing Cole saw before the sun eclipsed for the second time in two days, his bare foot cocked out to one side.

The daughter kept any thoughts she might have had to herself as she quietly escorted him the short distance back to tourist town where fishnet sacks of star fruit swayed in the humid breeze over stacks of floppy wicker hats and the occasional run of colorful sunglasses. Cole drew the wooden monkey from his pocket like a six shooter, aiming it at the man who sold it to him the day before with a no-thank-you-I've-already-got-one smile. Passing crates of drying coffee beans and cocoa, the daughter paid little attention as she weaved her way through a maze of back street short cuts to a small park and finally the abandoned bus stop.

"I think you miss that one," the daughter said, poking her pinky finger at the rear doors of a throaty bus getting smaller as it rounded out of sight in a cloud of dust. "The next will be in one hour."

Cole had no intention of riding any bus. His intention was standing in front of him with feet as bare as his. With the sun lazily idling directly overhead, Cole stood shadowless, tracing his thumb along his bottom lip looking for the right words to possibly make something right. "I'm sorry about your father dying," Cole said, catching the daughter off guard.

She slowly turned to him, dragging a shallow line in the sandy street with her big toe, her dark eyes watching this to avoid contact. "Yeah…me too."

"You sure are lucky to have your mom though, don't you think?"

Her long hair draped to the small of her back as she lifted her face to Cole's, "All we do is fight."

"Well, she's just worried. That's what mothers that love their daughters do…worry."

"She worry for nothing," the daughter rebelled. "I go now."

Cole watched her turn away, taking any hopes of a conversation along. "I met your father," he said with a brackish voice, seeing the girl's stride slow, but continue. "…Today."

The daughter stopped, and slowly turned to make contact with her eyes the color of soil that seeds would wish to purchase. "Why do you say this?" she asked, anchoring her hair behind the cup of an ear.

"Because he's worried about you as well. See that's what fathers do when they love their daughters…worry. He's afraid you might go and make the same mistakes he did," Cole said, glancing away to the jungle of trees bordering the park, finding not a single spruce. "Oh, you should have heard the wonderful way he said your name.

It was like someone summing up life in one word. You know you're about all that matters to him these days, and I don't think he's gonna' rest until he knows you're on the right path."

"Zess is crazy. Crazy ond mean!" the daughter snapped, figuring it to be an old timer lesson from some damn know it all tourist.

"...Is it?" Cole asked, tilting his head as if inquiring about the true condition of a used car.

The daughter let her eyes glide to the sanctuary of the park as a string of bleached sea shells the size of rosary beads tied about her bronze neck felt her fingertips, as they often did when times got tough.

"Your dad said he's afraid you might go looking for him in the bottom of a bottle or some drug that will take the hurt away, even for a little while," Cole said, watching her hand float from the necklace to her quivering chin. "He said to tell you he won't be there. Not now...now ever."

The daughter remained still, remembering how tiny her hand seemed as the doctor held it with his that early morning, clearing his throat before speaking the words that stole her father, driving the stock up on the sea shells still delicately lassoed around her neck. She saw Rosa staring through a cracked hospital window, cradling her unborn son with her entire body.

"Then where do I find him?" slipped between her lips and weaved around her fingertips.

Cole forced himself to stand his ground, not running to the girl. He knew she needed to try pedaling on her own, without life's training wheels forbidding progress. "I'll take you to him if you wish," he offered, overlapping his fingers as if ready to show all the people in the steeple. "Do you wish?"

The daughter lowered her arms to her side, widening her eyes, a small pop from her wet lips as they parted. "You con't do such tings."

"Okay, so you don't believe me. That I can certainly understand. But wouldn't you give anything and everything to learn I was telling the truth, even just some amazing small part of it? Look, you don't even have to go to some deserted neck of the island with me. I'll bring him to you."

The girl's face held still as a surveyor's stick, yet her eyes roamed from left to right in their wet sockets studying the park and the road that circled it like a moat. Unless her six-foot-two father with dreadlocks had been reincarnated as a potbellied boy going about flying a kite all wrong, he was nowhere in sight.

"All you have to do is close your eyes for me," Cole said, raising his hand in the same breeze that had earlier filled his sails. Like someone about to catch a frisbee in the forehead, the daughter closed her eyes in a prolonged wince to judge any last minute surprises.

"That's it. Now, I want you to put your hand on your heart, and follow it with your mind to a never-ending stretch of white beach. Do you see the seashells scattered around your feet? Have you noticed that there are two more feet standing in the circle of shells? Look up slowly, remember him? Remember his voice as he says, 'I love you,' his arms sliding around you in a way that says he'll always be right here for you, whenever you need him. That's because he's your father…and he always will be your father!" The daughter's eyelids pinched tighter, catching the cry, a second too late. "Now imagine breaking his heart the way he broke your mother's, and the boy's who never met him…and then yours."

The daughter allowed herself to feel like a daughter for the first time in six years. As she cradled herself with both arms, Cole approached. Her eyes remained shut, glued with melancholy and white beaches highlighting her father.

"There he is, and there he'll always be. Don't ever destroy that," Cole said, putting his hands on her olive-skinned shoulders. "I lost my father as well. But before he left he told me how to find him. He said that he would be a part of everything I would ever do, and that he was the reason I existed at all in the first damn place. So, he looked at me with those dishwater eyes of his and said, 'You just try and get rid of me! You can't! We're one and the same, son.' Well, this of course just tore my heart out. So I asked him if there was anything in the world I could do for him. He said, 'Yes, there is. Continue to make me proud…the way you always have.'"

The daughter's eyes opened full of tears to her sunburst feet and sandy street. Cole could feel the tremble in her shoulders trickling down her back like a parent calling the milk carton company to say thanks anyway, but you can remove the picture. "Why did he leave me?" she whispered, allowing herself to lean into Cole. "…I would never hove left him."

"Listen to me!" Cole ordered as he dropped to one knee, taking her firmly by the arms. "Your father's biggest mistake was not seeing you as he made the mistakes that killed him. And I can tell you, he would never make them again, no way, not in a million years, knowing what a wonderful daughter he'd had a hand in creating."

"He'z gone now, forever, ond I will neva see him again to show any such wonderful tings you speak of, so there es nothing for him to ever be proud of. Tiz all too late." The daughter exhaled, letting her mind slide back to the doctor allowing her to touch the cold hand of her father, realizing where the idea of sheets draped over ghosts came from. "I know you not see my father today, ond wont tomorrow, or the day after dat. Ond neither will I," the girl softly admitted, to this man that she knew cared, but could not prove otherwise.

Watching the daughter's fingers slowly chase her hair behind her ear again, Cole said, "Well, I best be getting along. Remember, I gotta' walk ol' Rover, left him in the garage you know."

"But da bus, it won't be here for some time," she said, wiping away the teary tributaries from her cheeks.

"You're forgetting, I'm magic! How else could I have had a sit down with your father to discuss your very important future, young lady?" Cole, saying goodbye in his own way, didn't. He simply turned away with a smile and strolled up the only knoll in the park, the daughter followed with only her eyes. Cole nonchalantly glanced back over his shoulder with, "Oh, I almost forgot. Your dad said something about hoping you wouldn't mind if he started making a necklace something like yours from a shell you'd found together. I didn't understand, but I agreed to tell you, so I did." Cole marched on, feeling a small seashell in his shirt pocket tapping his chest as he gradually summitted the twelve-foot knoll centered in the park. The daughter watched him take a slow turn to face her. "I understand you once loved the ocean," Cole said with a strong passive voice as to be clearly heard. "You know, I bet the life of an oceanographer would be a great one at that," he said, overlooking the ocean from the knoll. "Wow, can you even imagine how proud your dad would be? His little girl all grown up, studying those beaches the two of you walked on together?" he said exuberantly into the warm air, tracing the tropical skies with his iceberg-blue eyes. "Dreams can come true!"

Cole cast with this a look of promise, as he softly spoke wishful words for his ears only. The daughter's fingers spread wide at her side, again the small pop from her wet lips parting as the man with bad taste in swimming trunks and silvery hair vanished from the knoll, before her very eyes.

Left behind was a startled young woman, who that very afternoon dove from the long teak bowsprit of a Westsail 32, more interested in what was under it…than what was in it.

A draft of displaced air whispered around the iron flue in Cole's fireplace as he appeared on the glass floor overlooking Spring Creek. Pleasantly stunned by a new blanket of snow draped over the south thirty, he believed what his thermostat had to say and then some as he rolled his thumb across its belly to change its tune. Next, he crossed to the west end of the bridge, aiming his long finger at the stereo. He knelt, poking the POWER, CD then PLAY button. Ten, twelve, fourteen, he spun the volume. It answered by filling his home with Spanish music driven by a teasing tropical rhythm flowing over a great bass-popping riff in the background.

Reaching in his shirt pocket, he approached the toothpick bridge center the dining room table, its pointed trusses still resting on the airbrushed water. Pausing, he stared into the blue paper trickle with a sense of triumph in his mind and the taste of salt still on his lips. Introduced was a teak monkey the size of an empty toilet paper roll and a seashell spiraling from its waist to its smooth tapered ends like a barber's pole. They all went nicely together, Cole thought, as good memories always do.

He walked from the table on to the kitchen, leaving behind what looked like a miniature movie set. At its premier, people would have crowded on top of famous palm prints at Mann's Chinese Theater after seeing action packed previews of a giant heroic monkey crushing a bridge with an evil seashell.

Jogging his fingers along the copper countertop beside him like bum-rushing a pet fiddler crab, Cole stopped and turned to the answering machine that flashed with the heart rate of a two-hundred year old turtle.

Click, rewind…rewind…still rewinding…*click*, play…hang up. *Beep*, hang up, *beep*, hang up, *beep*, hang up, *beep*…then a final *beep-beep* said apparently a small army of shy mutes were trying to get their speechless point across. Cole's right hand and thicket brows flinched as the phone nap-jerked in its cradle.

"Hello there, Cole here."

The culprit behind the dozen or so beeps, spoke. Frail and sickly, Laura's voice crawled from the receiver like a wounded animal.

"Cole…Cole…I'm home…the…has fallen on…me. Oh please…I don't think I can…make it much…longer…hurry…oh, God,"…*cough…spatter…cough*, the thundering slam of metal on metal. "Hurry…Cole…everything is going black…." *gurgle-spat-spat-gurgle.* "I'm so…tired…." The phone fell darkly back to sleep in his hand.

Cole jumped in his own skin and his eyes flinched to the Rover's keys hanging within arms reach, his legs frozen, lungs expanding…Laura! He imagined her pretty green eyes fading behind a blink that could last forever as his squeezing fist freed its fingers in slow route to the ring of keys. The thought of her pinned to the linoleum by some possessed kitchen appliance or a foot long gash from a nasty fall, broke any dams of caution Cole might have been harboring…this was Laura!

His hand recoiled from the keys, his eyes shown to the copper countertop where he saw his own lips parting in its hammered blur reflection. "I *wish* I was at my friend Laura Day's home!"

Cole expected to find Laura's lifeless body being rag-dolled about the bloody kitchen locked in the gumming jaws of a run-amuck refrigerator trying to swallow her to its cool gullet, where ironically she would keep nicely for some time, or at the very least, lying at the foot of her turncoat staircase with one leg grossly draped around her neck. Instead, he wistfully appeared in the center of her living room, finding Laura crippled only by a gasping shriek and the sudden urge to run in place while sitting on the corduroy couch, her knees pumping, feet tamping, fry pan in good hand, green eyes far exceeding the elasticity limit of their sockets.

Cole realized in the moment that he'd been had, the jig was up, it was up, down, sideways, all over the place as Laura lit to her feet and bee-lined head on into a droopy hooded lamp that Daniel constantly said looked depressed.

"Now Laura!" Cole hollered without hollering, following her with his arms open. "Please, calm down! Just try to breath, and calm down!"

Like a drunken cheerleader, she ricocheted from the lamp into the breakfast bar with an acrobatic stumble, spraying the house with a high-pitched squeal! Cole tried to close in on her but retreated as she seemed to turn for him, flailing the non-stick pan over her red head as though desperately signaling from a life raft.

Pilot, bless his soul, made the corner into the living room to see what all the going on was about. He stood, not seeming to understand why Uncle Cole had come to call and not yet sought him out as to collect his frequent flyer miles for a two G spin in the air.

Cole bared his palms out before him, circling with Laura in an odd defensive powwow around the dinner table. "Laura, it's me!...Cole! We need to get ahold of ourselves here and talk about this! Everything is just fine, and you'd see so if I could just have a damn minute here to explain!"

She would have none of it! Pilot decided to take a later flight not wanting to get sucked into the jet wash of a nine-inch skillet tearing through the air. *Pu-tong!*

Cole's hand went to his opposite shoulder where his shiny new sailor's sunburn camouflaged the glow of the blow.

"OH...MY...GOD," Laura burst, walking her eyes down the red-fleshed alley of Cole's opened short sleeve. "You're literally the devil himself! Standing right here in my GOD DAMNED KITCHEN!" she shouted, then folded her lips over one another preparing for a blind charge at the antichrist.

"Laura, please, you're gonna kill me with that fuckin' fryer, and my body guard standing behind you is, trust me, going to take it personally!"

Laura spun on one foot with her pan reloaded, expecting to find another silver haired Satan offering a sports car for her soul. But as she stood spread legged with pan overhead, she saw only Pilot's bulging eyes staring back with the tiny reflection of Cole leaping over the table in a soft as possible body tackle. Pilot saw Mama go to the floor, cradled by Uncle Cole, then the empty stainless steel pan sliding across the linoleum, stopping at his knuckled feet as if to say the cupboards were bare.

In the fury of chasing one another's darting wrists, and Cole being extremely aware of Laura's knee, he recalled the mailman at the bridge, wishing he wouldn't go away mad, he remembered how his adrenaline pumping heart had slowed in his chest as the postman spoke the words. Winning the wrist battle, for the moment, Cole used the same strategy to win the war. With Laura elbowing her way on top for the second, and then third time, Cole let the words fly through the most composed tone he could muster in the moment.

"Laura, listen to me! I *wish* you would realize I'm still your best friend and for Christ sakes, calm down!"

Cole could feel his wish enter her runaway pulse through the wormy veins of her wrists like a serum of blue sky dripping into a test tube full of storm…his grip loosened.

eight

Forty-seven kilometers south of Perth Australia, the small town of Rockingham rests snuggly anchored to the edges of the west basin shoreline taunting its famous waves under a spring sky. Seven, then eight, all boys, running in single file out of sight. The last one rounding the corner into the alley ran with an empty shoebox lined with shot glass-sized holes tucked under one arm. Donny, the youngest of the lot, anxiously fell to his knees with the others as the shoebox was lowered to its milk crate podium. Rifling their pockets, the others pulled out bits of chocolate and tears of cotton candy. The bully of the bunch, peppered with freckles, proudly paraded an entire can of Cheese Whiz his mother would soon miss, while Donny had nothing but hope, and little of that.

Carefully lifting his stocking hat by its black button, the host of the game, a tall wiry kid that hated the fifth grade so much he decided to hate it twice, unveiled today's sporty mouse cowering behind his shock of blond cowlicks. After a chorus of "oos" and "ahs" admiring the clever permanent magic marker racing stripes running the length of the helpless rodent, the lid of the shoe box was removed.

"Okay, we all know the game, we all know the rules!" the host announced, displaying the mouse in a cage of dirty fingers. "The first one to lure him out of your given hole, gets the treasure chest!"

Five-cent, ten-cent, then twenty-cent pieces spilt into the teardrop mouth of a pop can piggybank. Donny reached deep in the front pocket of his worn jeans and offered his profits from a skipped lunch as he looked into the ball-bearing eyes of the captured mouse who had been primed by skipping many.

Above each cardboard cutout was a number scribbled in pencil from one to fourteen surrounding the box sponsored by Nike. Donny turned his empty palms upright as the others baited their fishhook fingers with a menu of poor man's appetizers. On a long shot, he ran his bare finger against the cuff of his only red sweater that he was famous for wearing day in, day out, no matter the season. With a quick pluck, Donny had his fat-free cotton candy, cherry one should think, hopefully the mouse would anyway. The cruel bunch laughed seeing the piece of sweater resting like a bad wig on the dome of his nervous finger as today's favorite hissed a slop of Cheese Whiz from nail to knuckle with a half troublemaker grin.

"You better not of shorted the can, Donny! There's not a one of us here that can't beat you silly and you know that now, don't you!" the host barked with a snarl growing over a string of knuckles, squeezing the mouse.

"I paid my share, just roll the mice," Donny scoffed, knowing all too well the threat was real.

After a gambler's shake at the host's ear, the mouse tumbled through the alley air, sliding his pink feet to no avail across the cardboard ice rink. *SLAP*, the lid stole the daylight except that of the portholes oddly smelling wonderful. The cheer that hopefully all of us were able to cheer as children, echoed down the brick alley, disappearing on a youthful note in the street.

Hole nine jumped out front with the lure of peanut butter, then the smell of chocolate leaked in holes two and thirteen drawing him deeper in the paper gallows. Then the Whiz kid made his move three holes down with an illegal smear around the cardboard window, keeping hole five alive. The confused mouse peered at each of the free meals poking at him just out of reach as he inched his way through the roulette buffet.

"Cotton candy damn you! There's nothing sweeter!"

"Don't listen to him mouse! Apple is where it's at!"

"They're fools! Go for the Whiz! The Whiz!"

"Macaroni! Get your macaroni here!"

Donny's narrow shoulders slumped as he sat on his knees staring into his dark number eleven hole, making sure the elbowing commotion didn't reveal his red-headed finger to be hiding under an inedible toupee. Pinched between the Whiz and some kid balancing a square of Hersheys, Donny saw the gray coat of the mouse brush past, ten, eleven, twelve, then yes, ambling back for a pause just beyond his shaky finger, the mouse's tiny face appeared! Dazzled with aroma, the mouse rose to attention, wiggling his nose at the choices, choices, choices. On his right, the Whiz pulled another cheesy smear as the fat Hershey kid on his left knocked on the mouse's door with a candy-gram that he'd have to sign for. Then suddenly overwhelmed, the mouse just let go and charged forward like a cannonball, mouth open, scattering into the daylight through a tunnel labeled…eleven!

Swoop! The pop can rattled with enough silver for a week's worth of lunches in Donny's little hand.

"You cheat!" the inhospitable host fired. "You're gonna' pay, dumb Donny, and so is that rat of a mouse! His guts will be splattered all over my old man's anvil by sundown!"

Weighing his doomed options, Donny held the treasure chest against his, looking for courage in the middle of poor loser's a foot taller than he. "Fair's fair, and the mouse came to me!" Donny piped, swallowing the fear in his voice while opening the shoebox to return the mouse in a quick sleight of hand move as not to let him squirm away from his certain miserable death within the hour.

"How could I have cheated?" Donny snarled back, puffing up his pounding chest. "I'd have to have a brain as small as yours to tell him anything that he could understand!"

The ring of towering eyes grew like those of a plastic clown at a water pistol shoot. Donny burst from the stunned mob with a fake dodge to the left, squeezing through a small hole created to the right behind the Whiz. As he shot for the street, he could hear their feet pounding out S.O.S for GET HIM!

Home was a fair lick away overlooking town from the cheap seats, but this was no time to consider pace. He ran as though every stride was priceless, or worth at least ten bucks in loose change. One could have tracked him by simply listening for car horns or looking for people turning their heads after a *woosh*. But instead, the gang relied on one another's clever communication system as Donny erased himself from the picture of buildings touching one another with traffic light cables humming over busy streets.

"Where'd he go?"

"I don't know."

"Shit!"

"My house! New game! I'll bet this mouse can't outrun my ol' man's hammer. Who's in?" Their fearless leader had spoken, cradling the Nike box that held his afternoon's revenge.

Donny finally slowed to a looking-over-his-shoulder walk as home came into sight. The fence was in as poor condition as the shoddy one-level home it nearly corralled. A shingle here and there on its roof as if gambling on where the rain was most likely to fall when the down under sky marbled over its ash-gray knuckles. It winked at its seldom visitors with an eyelid of cardboard, making the best of an embarrassing situation.

Dying on the graveled lawn, a pickup truck whose picking up days were long over, frowned with its under-bite grill as Donny triggered the chain link gate carefully with the side of one hand, still clenching the cuff of his red sweater. He felt a smile turning up at the corners of his peaked face as he spun the doorknob of this, the only home he'd ever known. Overhead, hand carved into the dilapidated house was:

Clara Tout & Donny Something
21 Dream Lane

The '& Donny Something,' had been added shortly after he'd been found stuffed in a sleeping bag by parents that weren't, and left curled up on the torn bench seat of the pickup, hence his last name. Clara had made it crystal clear time and again, "You're not nothing, Donny…you're something!" So it stuck.

Sitting at the barn-red picnic table that spilt over into the cluttered living room, Clara fumbled her paring knife into a bowl of octagon potatoes at the sudden racket exploding through the front door.

"Clara! Clara!"

"What? What?"

"I won!" he declared, waving the pop can victoriously overhead like mistletoe.

"Great fields of locust! You've spent your lunch money on soda? That's not winning Donny, that's just ludicrous. We'll make that one of your five works tonight," Clara said, aiming a grin with her weathered face the color of sandstone.

Donny waltzed to the table quite sure of himself, watching a single eyebrow sneak up Clara's suspicious forehead. With the lure of a magician, Donny sat the pop can on the table's edge, waving his hands over its top as though a cobra were about to rise swaying to the mesmerizing beat of a slow love song.

"I will now make an entire weeks lunches appear from this very can!"

"Ya know, that stuff will be flat by tomorrow, and when Friday comes round it'll be mud. I would have kept the money, Houdini!" Clara snickered, brushing a potato peel from her housedress.

"Pay no mind to this non-believer! She sees through crossed eyes and a head full of bats," Donny warned to the invisible audience of captivated onlookers.

"Abracadabra and hocus-pocus, look out for locust!" Donny commanded, building the climax with each magical word as he reached for the can now deep under his spell.

Expecting to see her tablecloth darken with sticky sweet cola, Clara saw instead a waterfall of copper-nickel jouncing to the table tallying like the slot machine eyes of a cash register. "Viola!"

"Donny! Where did you....?"

"It's just like I said, I swear! I won it fair and tape measure square!"

"There's a day's fortune here," Clara said, watching his excited expression slip a little south, stealing a pinch of sparkle from his hazel eyes. "Is there something more you want to tell me, Donny?" she asked, knowing him.

Fixing on the criss-crossed design the tablecloth offered, he inhaled and spoke slowly. "I don't remember the day you brought me into this house, I was two. But as long as I'm on this winning streak today, I'll bet I wouldn't have made it to three without you. This is asking a lot I know, but could we make room for one more that doesn't have a home?"

"Oh, Donny, I don't know. Have you met someone homeless in town?"

Lowering his arm to the table and unfolding his palm like a ramp, Donny loosened his grip on the sweater's worn cuff. "Yes...I did."

Clara's palms slapped the picnic table with a heave as she jumped to her feet. She'd never seen a mouse with racing stripes before.

"I'm impressed, Red…that was a pretty clever trick," Cole said, escorting Laura to the corduroy couch where she sat at its edge with the posture of someone waiting to hear back from a loan officer.

"This can't be Cole…it just can't be!"

Cole plopped himself in the modern rocker and scooted up, sitting face to face. "Laura, what on earth, ever, ever, made you suspect this?"

"Well…I started adding things together, like potholes and feathers, you know? So I took a drive down to your place looking for answers, any answers to put these crazy thoughts of mine out of their misery. "Well," she said, lowering her guilty green eyes to the white-carpeted floor, "you weren't there. So I…."

Cole's grip tightened around his chin, figuring a little rainbow had spilt its colorful guts all over his coffee table. "So you went in…and?"

Laura still trying to swallow the whole thing, shook her head at the floor and pushed on saying, "I called, yelled really, but everything stayed so quiet and Cole, those tulips…they were everywhere! So I just sorta' followed them to this pretty little envelope staring back at me."

Cole exhaled through his fingers, lowering his eyes to Pilot nosing a beach ball to his bare feet. "And let me guess?"

"Yeah…I peeked," she admitted, sitting up straight and tucking her handful of damaged digits behind the moon of her thigh. "Please don't hate me, Cole, please! I can't imagine what things would be like not having you around."

Cole leaned in even closer, bringing an angry frown along for convincing, flushing her poor hand out of hiding with his. "Do I have your complete attention right now Laura May Day? GOOD!" he demanded, squeezing her hand tighter. "You could walk in my house unannounced and burn it to the ground, now I might be pissed, sure, but you still wouldn't get rid of me that easily, my friend!"

Laura leaned back in the couch as though the loan officer had returned to his desk saying 'yes' through a highly trained smile. "I just don't believe this, Cole. Tell me it's a trick, some crazy trick you've concocted from having too much time on your retired hands."

"Oh…I've kept busy these last days," he said letting a tropical grin unfurl across his sun burnt face.

Laura's green eyes rolled to Cole's winter blues, if blended they would be the color of a wave being x-rayed by the sun. "Your face. Have you been droppin' tokens in one of those electric skin fryers?"

"Nope," he truthfully answered, letting the smile crawl deeper in his red cheeks.

Speechless with wonder, Laura's face tried to catch up with a sudden flush of its own.

"Oh, you think it's a lot for you to grasp? Dear God!" Cole nearly shouted, shaking his head at the floor. "Can you imagine what my wrinkles looked like seeing a haystack of yellow tulips creep out of nowhere under my ass?"

"Okay, okay, now you just lost me when I was already lost. We need to slow down here. You're telling me you had a haystack of tulips creep out of your ass?" she asked, revealing the small stash of dental gold buried in her mouth mine.

Cole laughed, picturing himself fluffing his vibrant ass plume after so carefully getting out of his Rover down at Johnson's Grocery.

"Oh sure, you just keep giggling while I sit here trying not to convince myself that one of us is a few shingles short of a roof!"

Cole simmered his laugh and looked at Laura as never before. "You still don't believe this?"

Even Pilot seemed to hear the question, and quickly responded by doing absolutely nothing. Cole raised his grinning eyes up the wall behind Laura, letting them idle on the Ruddy Turnstone's feather proudly arching its spine, standing at attention in the row of other Alaskan quills. Laura felt herself sink, knowing what he was slyly grinning at.

"The feather…where did it come from?" she asked, not knowing what to do with her arms, then nervously crossing them. "You're probably going to say you just wished it there?"

"No, Laura," Cole said beaming into her eyes. "I'm going to say I *wish* there were two."

She slapped her blue jean knee with an uncertain snort in a fearful stall of looking up her own wall. "Now that's rich, and this isn't funny anymore, Cole, enough is enough!"

He answered with nothing other than a casual glance back to the teak plaque.

Sliding forward she said, "You old fool, I knew you wouldn't survive retirement without cracking up one way or another. So here, I'll look at your dumb feather, then we'll have a little chat about what nut houses are and why their walls are made of user-friendly rubber."

Cole saw for the first time her crippled hand make a jumbled fist as her eyes ascended to the teak plaque, finding now a second Ruddy Turnstone feather crowding the first as if an Indian had been promoted.

"Sweet Jesus!" she shouted leaping to her feet, the backs of her knees caught the coffee table, allowing a handful of yellow candies to ride a sweet wave to freedom, only to be quickly recaptured by a bug-eyed warden with stick-legs and a barrel chest advancing their scattered positions.

"Laura, you're forgetting, I just appeared in your house, out of nowhere…there's no tricks or rubber walls here," he said standing from the rocker, offering his hands to her trembling shoulders.

"Cole," she whispered, cupping her mouth and turning back to his sun burnt face, "What else have you done…where else have you been popping up besides my living room?"

"Wheal now' moy dear," he answered, curling his words with a perfect Sean Connery accent. "You moight say I've been here and there, traveling abroad about the countryside, making a friend or two."

Laura threw herself wearily onto the couch with the grace of a thrown sand bag. Her finger trembled as she aimed it at his sloping mouth. "That accent…I used to cringe when I felt it coming on…tell me you've just been watching more of your *007* movies," she stammered, retracting her good hand to a confused temple bordered with autumn hair. Cole found the closest thing to a Scottish grin he knew, and let it seep out between his lips, spreading to the corners of his cheeks.

"…You didn't?" Laura gasped, with her eyes bulging like Christopher Columbus being handed a world atlas.

"...I did!"

"The…the movie star?"

"Yep."

"Noooo."

"Yeeesss."

"Noooo."

"Yeeesss."

Pilot watched the conversation more than listened, trying to follow the ball ricocheting between Laura's stunned face and the proud bend of Cole's lips.

"Met him on a train."

"Noooo."

"In Europe!"

"Noooooooo," she exhaled, taking a step back as she slapped her good hand around her forehead.

"Laura, yes. And stop before Pilot spits up a load of that expensive crunch you stuff him with morning, noon and night."

The small no hole in Laura's pretty mouth closed like a valve governing bewilderment, but reopened with the flood of another thought. "Pot holes?"

Cole pushed back in the rocker like another job well done. "That one was for ol' Rover."

"Dear God!"

"Oh yeah, and that's another one you won't believe."

"God?" Laura muttered, unable to move her lips.

"No…the deer!" he answered, making his eyebrows do a little jig. "The damn deer. They like me!"

"You're scaring me again," she said, picturing a buck saying "Sorry I'm late, Cole, I'll have whatever you're havin'."

The far ends of the rocker's floor rails pointed to the cathedral ceiling as Cole leaned in to whisper something like a kid preparing to spill his guts about a slingshot and a cracked windshield. "If you want to hear something scary, last night before I went to bed, I stood on the floor…the ocean floor!"

"Ocean?" Laura gasped. "You hate the water! You'd rather bomb your own bridge than swim a lap in your own bathtub."

"Yes, well, I guess there was just something in the tropical air that coaxed me," he answered with salt in his hair, feet still bare, putting an end to her next sun burning question. "Laura, let's just say, life is reminding me that it's an adventure, this wonderful amazing adventure that I've been putting aside without realizing it."

Laura collected herself to nearly the point of calm once again, her collage of misunderstood thoughts beginning to see the amazing light like grasping a Picasso for the first time. She looked to the tan of his skin, the gleam on his eyes under a neat mop of sun-streaked hair. She sadly glanced away and pattered toward the kitchen. "Well then, guess I won't be seeing you around very often. Pilot's gonna' miss you more than he'll let on to, but that's just life now isn't it, Sugar Bugar," she said to Pilot, who understood no words, yet knew when Mama was upset.

Cole hadn't thought of this, but began to as he stood from the rocker and turned to the oval breakfast bar he and Daniel had drafted on an airport napkin. "Laura? That sounded a bit…dark."

Not wanting Cole to discover the hurt in her eyes, Laura opened the pantry door just to open it and stood staring into a rolling Italian vineyard offered by the label on a bottle of white wine. "It's going to take some time for all of this to sink in, but so far it's clear that whatever this is it's bound to be better than hanging around me….my wishes don't come true, Cole. I've tried."

The home was silent for the next few moments. Cole came to the opposite side of the breakfast bar as she stared at her own circus reflection in its stainless steel countertop. "I remember the stormy night Daniel and I sketched this out. He claimed he wasn't hungry but hoped they wouldn't mind him using a napkin just the same. I thought he was busy making lines and curves in his head like me, but that wasn't why he said no to the red eye special. You see, we were there waiting for the white stripe of your Cessna to poke out of those black clouds and touch down. Well, as soon as you did, Daniel threw a twenty on the table and rushed us to the Rover like we were being hunted, yelling, 'she'll have both our asses if she catches us out here spyin' on her!'

"He just stared into the ditch all the way home without a word. Christ, it was like he'd went and shit on his head again, but no hood. Finally, we stopped in your driveway. He climbed out and looked at me over the engine hood saying, 'Cole, a man can only fly with fake wings for so long, and something isn't as right as it used to be. Been having these dreams, the ground's rushing at me like a zoom lens. Cole, if my wings give out, you have to promise me something more important than life itself…. Will you always be there for Laura?' Well, I started in with the usual this-will-never-happen speech, but he interrupted with, 'Promise me, Cole!' So, without hesitation of course, I gave him a direct answer, as it was plain to see he wasn't about to accept anything less. Then he smiled with that big row of teeth of his and said, 'Thank you my friend,' and looked up to the storm rolling in from the south."

Laura pushed back from the counter and turned to one side to wipe her eyes. "So, I'd hate to think the only reason you're here is due to some old promise, because I can take care of myself just fine, Caffy."

"Oh, I know that, and so did Daniel. I knew that long ago. I just like being here, Laura. You're my best friend…I would never leave you behind!"

Cole rested his hip on the breakfast bar, knowing how to settle this thing once and for all as he looked into his own reflection shining back at him from a countertop, just as he did before he appeared in Laura's living room. Letting a grin push into his red cheeks, he flashed his eyes to her under his prickly brows. Laura stood her ground as his hand slowly slid across the stainless steel to hers. Then with a gentle squeeze, he took her crippled hand. As he leaned over the counter, Laura couldn't help but stare into his wintry eyes as he softly whispered… "Hang on."

Before she could jump, he spoke the words, words that Laura couldn't believe she was hearing. Pilot held his breath without realizing it as he shuffled to the outlet looking for answers after Mama and Uncle Cole vanished in front of his jiggly eyes.

Laura's hand jerked away from Cole's, her fingers fanned out wide in a balancing gesture, green eyes exploding in a frozen stun. Refrigerated air pushed in and out of all three holes of her pretty pink face as she first saw the top of a great mountain, then another craning even higher just beyond that cradled an earth-scarring glacier between its shoulder blades.

"That's it, just keep breathing!" Cole said, wafting his right hand in circles.

"Light…Light House Lake? Oh, God!" Laura shouted, slapping her hands to her face, peeking between the gaps in their fingers.

"Yes, yes! She freezes up early livin' this high life. But isn't it beautiful?" Cole casually said, in the tone of a realtor.

Laura's shocked expression held on, unwilling to sip from the reality glass just yet. Her eyes lowered and crossed a little as she blew a tornado of warm breath into the cold, watching it flicker from between her lips like a ghost snagged in an electrified fence. Standing on a lake of ice smothered by a foot of new snow, she managed, "I could hear…color?"

"Isn't that something? Scared the b-Jesus out of me the first time," Cole said, putting his hand on her shoulder. "Once I heard purple, it sounded like pirates rowing to shore. Beats the shit out of elevator music, huh, Red? Which by the way, sounds like people cheering."

"This just can't be happening, Cole!" she shouted, in the middle of a frozen lake, a hundred-and-eighty miles from her counter top. "This doesn't happen!"

Slowly, Cole took a few steps back as she turned in place for a panoramic view, her hands warning off invisible dogs. At full circle her eyes landed on him. "Wishing, Cole?"

"Wishing," he agreed through a beaming smile.

"Everybody knows wishes don't come true!" she said, noticing Cole's short sleeve shirt billowing open in the biting breeze, his sunburned thighs matching the color of tropical sunsets. "Aren't you freezing?"

"*Wish* I wasn't," Cole cheerily said, raising his arms to the sprawling Alaskan sky.

"Stop that!" she cried, watching as he let his arms fall to his side as if to say, 'it's not so much the heat as the….'

"Cole!" she scowled, covering her temples with her palms. "We're standing on a frozen lake miles from home, a home I was in two minutes ago!"

"It *is* amazing," he grinned, massaging the east with his eyes.

Laura's pointer finger sprung from her fist, switchblade style. Wagging it aside her tilted red head, she said, "Wait a minute. This is why you came sniffin' around wanting to know what my three wishes would be, isn't it?"

"I....Yes," Cole admitted, looking to his foot lightly tamping the snow.

"How long has this been going on?"

"Few days, that seem...more like a lifetime," he answered, unable to wrangle his wonder.

In silence, the two friends stood under clouds that smeared into one white mass hovering a thousand feet overhead as it tried to hold onto a gulp of crystallized water it had inhaled over the Alaskan Gulf. Failing, it began to cry its jagged tears as though casting Chinese throwing stars to the wind that herded them across the sky. Cole thought one nimbus breaking free the flock looked like a fat woman with one leg throwing up down a crooked chimney. Another ambling deep into the north resembled a paper hat held high in the sky by a baton, then somersaulting, it only added to Cole's growing smile as it pleasantly took on the lines of a sailboat.

Laura took a second breathtaking lap with her disbelieving eyes following the granite-accented skyline of Light House Lake that had been named for its mile long tapering shape the mountains allowed by stepping back from one another. An avalanche spill of boulders trespassing its slim end reflected sunshine to satellites and spy planes. In 1946, a snicker came to a smoke filled room of Russians when they received labeled maps of the northern territory, discovering their nickname for the lake was coincidentally correct, but then scattered to have another look at a lake in Minnesota they had been affectionately calling the Big Gun!

Jumping up and down like a jackhammer, Cole reassured their foot thick gap between pleasure and panic to be true. Convinced, he turned to Laura, rubbing his bald tummy, then thought to pat his head at the same time.

"Ya, that's great, Cole. Next you'll break out a fuckin' hula-hoop. This isn't funny!"

"No? How bout' this!" he said, adding the ever amazing hop on one foot move to his one-man talent show. Laura looked to the ground fearing her sudden giggle would only encourage him to break into some plate-spinning encore.

"Laura, I know when you're laughing, your forehead turns as red as fruit punch and your toes curl up, and don't look now but there's the cutest little lumps in the ends of your shoes," Cole said lowering his eyes, his shirt still open to the unpenetrating freeze, naked legs full of wished brave, feet slowly melting what ground they stood.

Laura approached with crossed arms, the lumps gone from her favorite house shoes. “I’ve wished for wishes since I was a little girl watching my dog die from thinking she could befriend coyotes. I was too young to dig up the earth that buried her, so my dad handed me the shovel afterward to pat the ground smooth. Then he held the cross real careful, knowing my swing could go either way. As he led the way back home, he told me ‘part of life, pumpkin, is understanding death.’ Since then, I’ve given up on Tooth Fairies and Santa Claus.”

Cole began to corral her by plowing a moat with his bare feet like a child discovering seasons. When the sphere was complete, he stopped at his own shuffled footprints and spoke his question softly. “Laura…what was your third wish?”

Realizing he’d remembered the first two, she buried her scarred hand under the other, and certainly didn’t sing. Cole caught a surge of harbored poetry in her widowed eyes before they looked to the miniature pyramid her right foot was nervously constructing out of cloud tears.

“I believe the words you used were, ‘It was something only a wish could ever make come true?’” Cole asked, knowing full well he was skating on thin ice.

Laura continued to gently tap the crown of the pyramid flat, leaving a three-sided igloo with no loft for the natives to snuggle in.

“Laura…I also know when you’re crying. Your dimples do their job, although reluctantly, and your weak hand goes to your strong heart,” he said, narrating it as it happened. “This isn’t you, Red. What have you been keeping from me? I’d think something this upsetting, ought to be shared.”

Cole’s skin went cold again as a chilling thought crept its way into his mind like four kittens tied in a burlap sack wondering why the fifth was made of stone. He looked to her poor hand doubling over at her chest, painful knuckles knuckling. The thought spread, had her poor hand sold its crippling idea to the rest of her once healthy body out of some jealous lashing? Would her walks with Jenny slow each day under the weight of oxygen bottles in tow before inevitably turning into wheelchair rides with drugged eyes?

The heels of Cole's hands slipped from the resting notches of his hips, snowflakes matching the color of his eyes. "…Laura?"

Shifting the weight of her small frame from left to right, she found the courage to speak from the center of Cole's circumnavigated moat, ignoring the warning label in the eye of a hurricane. "Do you remember the two days I asked you to watch over Pilot when I tagged along with Jenny to drop off those kids of hers in Homer, Cole? You'd been on me for months about the rusty grind my Jeep screeched when it stuttered to a stop. Well, you said, 'brakes are the way of the future.' I said distant future. So the day after I'm home, I make a run down the hill to Johnson's. Like usual, I started flirtin' with the brake pedal long before the bend at Temple's mailbox. I thought I could smell a trace of your cologne sneaking around just as Old Yeller reigned back without so much as a whisper, tossin' Pilot head for tails." The bulb dimmed in her light voice, the welled poetry in her drowning eyes finding a leak. "I just sat there, hogging both lanes of Patch, trying to convince myself not to…fall in love with you."

Her words collided in Cole's stunned mind. His sticker-bush brows lifted in the chill, seized by ponder. His first response stayed to himself. 'Thank God…no wheelchairs!' The second was slightly aloud…"Love?"

Hearing that word leave Cole's mouth made Laura want to run to his still hovering steam of breath that it took to frame the word and capture it in a Ball jar for safekeeping. Instead, she stood completely exposed to the lingering of the moment, waiting for what the next puff of steam might have to say. Letting her hands be swallowed by the warm mouths of her sweater sleeves, she rolled her emerald eyes shut and asked, "Could you do anything right now, except just stand there with your eyes doing that…thing?"

At times, Cole's expression had its own way of coming to a lifeless pause like seals between winch-handle blows from fur pirates. Bewildered, he stood at the rim of his snow moat with his tongue playing the bony keys of his teeth in wonder, wet sanding ivory.

"You don't have to say anything, Cole. Eventually something along the lines of 'still friends' would be nice. But I probably just single handedly destroyed the one…"

“Still friends!” he interrupted with a commanding tone, allowing himself to blink.

Where the mountains curtsied to the lake, Cole could see the centipede shape of the summer dock he and Daniel had tied the balloon-footed Cessna to, uncountable times. He remembered the wisp of a brown feather Daniel pulled backwards through two belt loops for safekeeping. Most were brown, but not to him.

Looking with a flattered smile back to Laura, Cole said, “I’ve often wondered in my lengthy collection of single years what I was doing wrong. Now after all this time it comes to me, I should have been showing up on those doorsteps of beautiful women holding boxes of brake shoes, not candy.”

“Beautiful, huh?” Laura snorted, forcing the corners of her kissless lips to bend towards the sky.

“Laura, I fixed your brakes…two years ago.”

“And lemon bars don’t grow on trees, ya know,” Laura said, caring less if they’d cost their weight in gold.

As Cole turned away to survey the land, and what he’d just heard, he gently bit the flesh of his bottom lip, searching desperately for a response. His thoughts trotted free, nor came to any conclusion until he saw a familiar site in the distance naturally anchored to the lake’s edge. He only inhaled and did not look to Laura as he softly spoke, fondly remembering the past. “Daniel hated seeing the end of my fishing pole wiggle from these very shores. I think he tried too hard. Saw him hook the plane once with this crazy backhanded toss. I ducked into the tree line as his eyes scoured high and low for me, knowing I’d never let it go. He always worked your name in one way or another, no matter the topic. I brought up cow tipping once just to see if….”

Laura stopped him short. “I’ll always love Daniel, he was my first everything, maybe my last. And with that respect, I’d like to settle this without bringing his name into it. He’s asleep, let’s not disturb him.”

Cole went to work on the word ‘settle,’ it didn’t. “You have nothing to settle, Laura. I could never see you for anything less than the red-headed angel you are.”

“I didn’t expect ‘I love you back,’ Cole.” Her frozen breath escaped her mouth, riding on the backs of her irretrievable words.

“You’re cold, Laura.”

"And you're scared."

"...I'm sorry."

Cole ignored the moat and its toothless alligators with big hearts, offering his bare arms dangling from short sleeves. He hugged Laura harder than the morning he'd flown here six years ago to throw her husband's ashes to a magical land we each silently hope exists. Her eyes pinched shut with tears as Cole's lips wished beside her ear. Next she heard the sound of kite tails quarreling with wind. Pink.

Staring from his kitchen window after showering the salt out of his salt and pepper hair, Cole thought it amazing how snowdrifts swaying back and forth with each other perfectly were perhaps the finest example of structural engineering he knew. The worse the storm, the more articulation their engineer was demanded.

He liked when Daniel's face visited his memory at times like this. Seeing it hidden deep in a fur lined hood brought a warm grin, then his laughing eyes the day he agreed to teach him to fly. Cole found himself thrown into looking at life from a sharply different angle, wondering what Daniel's eyes might look like from now on. Instead of pleasantly stopping by time to time reminding him he would have a friend forever, dead or alive, would he now tear down that hood in his memories with a bewildered huff to stare at a fair-weather friend he would have never believed capable of what he was thinking.

When alive, we have our own personal gag orders protecting some thoughts better left just that, gagged. But dead is dead, there's nowhere to hide if someone were listening from beyond. Cole knew he couldn't walk down the street hand in hand with Laura, whispering sweet nothings then hollering 'thanks for the lug wrench' to a sky full of invisible ears.

Breaking his concentration was the bouncy little van full of wishes sliding to a stop at his mailbox. From across the south thirty, he was pleased to see the mailman's red mitten stall high in the chill with a friendly wave. Cole pressed a hand to the window in return as the brake lights dimmed after feeding his box then disappeared from the center of Patch as though late for the next, wherever that might be.

After a three-day bare foot chase, boots finally captured Cole's feet and kept perfect time with his long stride as he strolled up his snow-packed driveway. Midway, he discovered the does had left their split-toed tracks dotting away towards the creek perhaps en route to more tulips. Cole looked to the shaded spruce hemline where he suspected the spike buck had chosen to spy on the does as they pawed and pondered their way across the south thirty, his yearling nubs skewering the undergrowth.

The aluminum mouth of Cole's mailbox complained open with a whine from its lower jaw, exposing a manila envelope it had just been fed by a Fed. Labeled only 'Cole,' he brushed his hand over his own name in raised lettering and sauntered back down to his heated bridge.

Happily leaving his snow boots to melt cloud tears on the garage floor, Cole passed by the kitchen, figuring mail of this stature to be something best read sitting in a favorite chair. As he put his feet up on the glass coffee table, he blew in the gaping end of the envelope he'd torn open. Finding first a handwritten letter, he read:

Wonderful Cole, you're doing wonderful! So much so that I'm inclined to ask an important favor of you. I've gotten behind here and thought you might enjoy helping me deliver something. Remember, Cole, good only produces good.

Mail Man

PS, Your new tropical friends made a sign together this morning that I thought you'd like to read.

WESTSAIL FOR SALE

With a warm smile, Cole gave the manila envelope another shake at the coffee table. However, his expression changed as a familiar looking little envelope slid out...all covered in rainbow.

Clara Tout
21 Dream Lane
Rockingham Australia

nine

Clara Tout's mother looked to her home delivery nurse with screaming eyes full of labor sixty-two years ago in this quiet town of Rockingham, Australia. Afterwards Clara got taller, not much. At five feet flat, she'd pattered through life watching first her mother, then eventually father, fall prey to the facts of it, cancer, massive stroke at the wheel. Left behind was a surveyor's dream of stretching land the Tout family once caressed wheat from. With the growing city of Perth just a roo's hop up the coast their bushels bustled. "From way over there, to clear back here," Clara would say if someone asked about her sprawling acreage, her finger a magic wand blessing each distant knoll as she spoke.

Greed sent a slim man carrying a fancy cane he didn't need, glancing through her open door before knocking a decade ago. "Community," he said, speaking through the center of his mouth. "Elbowroom for the city to grow and you'll be rich."

Clara inquired what would be constructed on the earth her father struggled. The answers came out as the lies she'd expected and clearly knew he had no intention of mentioning casinos or pawnshops, nude dancing or double A meetings that always followed like pilot fish on the backs of sharks. Her answer was the same as the many that would follow, "NO!"

She became a saint at church, Satan at town meetings. It was when death threats came calling that she made her move by toting the Tout deed with her one Sunday morning. "Don't get your collar in a knot," she told Pastor Hammond. "Half of any money the church makes from my donated land will go to the homeless, the rest do as you will. I never believed in Heaven and halos much, but the walk once a week does me good…now let's see if you can." Pastor Hammond rarely raised a brow, he did.

Word traveled. Especially to those with no home using newspapers for blankets that one early morning showed a picture of Clara's garlic-textured face while she asked not to be interviewed.

Rockingham Woman Gives it Away

The church later sold the land, less fifteen of the eighteen-hundred acres where an inviting shelter of brick was built by the homeless who now reside there tending its ever-extending gardens. On a nearby bump of earth stood a new church with a spire of spires one could see from downtown to the next town. The land had been sold to the Australian Parks and Management for the future possibility of a zoo, still pending.

Over time, Clara's caring reputation preceded her down the West Australian Basin where a failing sixteen year old single mother cried her way through another down under day. The following late Saturday night, she hoped the squeak of Clara's old pick-up door wouldn't wake up her way out. Duct taped to the sleeping bag he quietly slept in, was the name 'Donny.'

"A hug is what the world needs!" Clara would always say, wiggling a finger to the heavens she questioned. Donny had learned not to put the picnic table between them on his way out the door. She would only squeeze him that much harder…that much longer.

Clara Tout never had any children of her own, but she did fall in love once...once.

Ten dollars and fifty, fifty-five, sixty cents, was counted for a third time, the sound of five-cent pieces sliding on vinyl last. The mouse's name, "How about Coin?" Donny declared, more than asked, "Coin Something!"

Sniffing a stack of what he was named after, Coin then went on to the silage pile of potato skins cast beside the towering bowl of their carved yellowing innards with smoke colored spots, the eyes severed optical nerves. "Donny!" Clara snipped. "New rule, I don't care if you bring home a koala bear holding a sweepstakes check, no one walks across the table, especially on all fours."

Three jars, each taller than the next, held first sugar, Donny's money, and then decaffeinated coffee. The day's fortune was denied a fourth count with an, "enough is enough," nip from Clara. The top of the third jar was left ajar after the sound of loose change rang out across the paint thirsty kitchen.

"Be careful with that, Donny. Even though that shampoo says no tears, well, go ahead. Probably his lot they tested it on first," Clara winced at the idea, just as they certainly did.

Donny spun from the sink, pulling his elbows in close to his tiny rib cage hearing Clara say, "There's somebody sniffin their way up the walk. Probably another auto collector wantin' to bother with the Ford."

As Donny stood petrified, all he could picture was one deviant cleverly stacked atop another on stilts, disguised as a wobbling zombie with lying eyes for used-up Fords, just waiting to be invited in like a swarm of juvenile vampires after his ten dollar hide. A cautious tap-tap came at the front and only door with sprouts of silvery hair lining the bottom corner of its rectangular window.

"Truck's not for sale!" Clara howled through her funneled hands. Another knock in reply, even softer. "Great Peter Paul and Mary," Clara muttered, turning the doorknob like a hawk landing on the three o'clock blade of a windmill, exposing half her portly face. "Yes?"

Donny looked to the stranger's size ten feet. They seemed real enough, no wooden ankles.

"Yes...Hello," Cole said, still amazed by the sound of playing cards slapping bicycle spokes; turquoise. "I didn't see your mailbox."

"Used to have one, damn thing just kept filling up with bad news and bills. Which you got?" Clara asked, wiping her hands on her flowered apron to ensure a good swing of the door if this strangers next words where 'might I interest you in...'

Cole cleared his throat and anxiously brushed his silver hair back with the tips of his fingers. "No ma'am. No bills...just good news."

"You read my no trespassing sign?"

“I’m sorry…no,” Cole answered, swiveling his head to the left, then right.

“Yeah, I aint got one of those either.”

The boiling potatoes overflowed from the blue speckled kettle with its lather reaching the flame, following the spiral shape of the wrought iron burner below. Clara’s half face tottered away with a yelp to Donny for her matching potholders, gardening gloves patterned with smiling cactuses. The commotion overwhelmed Coin still in Donny’s soapy clutches. A reflex nip to an index finger set him free with a sud fueled pop to the counter where the erupting kettle met him a hundred times his rodent size. To the pine floor with a scatter, his wire tail followed as a wheelie bar, pulse his tachometer. Knotty potholes left and right on the road to daylight glowed along the rubber rims of Cole’s soles. Coin zinged between his size tens like a tri-colored pipe cleaner on a missiles tether. Next was Donny in pursuit, same path. Cole raised a leg with a fancy spin bringing the repentant Ford into view.

The chase ensued about the yard’s crevasses and stony terrain leading back to the jumble of a pick-up. Scurrying on his hands and knees using a light come hither voice, Donny coaxed to no avail. Clara arrived on the scene remounting her happy cactus mitts. Cole shot to the left, Clara the right. Dust stomped from the earth beneath their racing feet, Coin here, then suddenly there.

Flat on his stomach, Cole’s arms reached ahead, superman flying under the truck’s rusty privates. Clara, now a perimeter of worn blouse, joined in from the opposite end beneath the truck’s pitted chrome jaws. Coin launched, and Donny’s eyes went limp seeing his homeless friend skip the length of the truck’s underbody past Cole in a bouncing shot.

“Let him go, Donny,” Clara said, knowing it had to be said.

Cole jumped to his feet wooing and hawing, beating senselessly his wriggling leg in a tornado of red dust. Looking at this stranger going crazy, possessed full of some phobia, Clara removed her gloves by tugging at each finger separately as though counting the seconds before calling the police.

Donny went silent, staring beyond the yard’s chain-link where Coin would have to fend for himself from now on. Cole approached catching his breath, offering a hand to the boy’s slumped shoulder. “Sometimes you win, and sometimes…you win.” Donny’s mouth fell open, his hands reached out before him, taking a mouse named Coin from the stranger's cupping palm.

"Handsome mouse. He's as fast as he looks!" Cole said, admiring his racing stripes. "Thought I felt a little tug like a junkyard thief was mistaking my kneecap for a hubcap."

Through a contagious smile, Donny said, "Thanks! Who are you?"

"Well…I'm Cole. Who are you?" he asked, matching the boy's matter of fact tone.

"Something, Donny Something."

Cole thought of Bond, James Bond, but kept it to himself. "Not Tout?"

"I'm Clara Tout," she said, hands to her squat heavy hips. "Are ya sellin' something?"

"No Ma'am. And if I were, I'd be out of luck. Sounds like you already have a Something!"

Donny's smile shifted into giggle, and Clara's lips curled up, too. "You after the Ford?" Clara asked, cocking her head to one side.

"No, no, forgive me…I have a very special delivery for you, Mrs. Tout," he said, reaching inside the pocket of his flannel coat as if another homeless mouse were about to appear. Instead a small rainbow was revealed.

"Pretty little thing," Clara said, feeling her own name and address all fancy in raised letters like scripted Braille. "I need to sign something?"

"No, there's no need to draw on the boy," Cole said hearing Donny's giggle grow.

"You scrub those stripes off that rat yet?"

"I tried," Donny said, combing what was now permanent with his thumbs. Clara's dimpled chin went flat against her chest, her curious eyes narrowing at the rainbow, the wisp sound of an envelope's hinge in human hands.

Congratulations

Her dissuaded eyes switch-backed left to right through the imaginative words, then back to Cole's anxious stare. "Lot a work for a chain letter, mister. Wishin' never got anybody nowhere."

"Got me here," Cole said, though the world had changed without her knowing it.

Clara lowered the letter to her side, rolling his answer over a few times. "You don't seem like no, postman."

"You should meet mine."

Clara's judge of character did its job up and down this stranger and gave him points for not pounding Coin flat against his run-away leg. "This letter…you brought it from where you say?"

"Alaska."

Her reply was silence. They looked at one another as if sharing in it. "What time do you have, Mister….?"

"Call me Cole. 3:15," he mundanely answered, pulling his sleeve back…four hours early.

If he was a con he was at least thorough, Clara thought, looking at Cole's bulky flannel jacket in the ninety-six degree heat. Lowering her brow once again to the prismatic question in her hand, she offered, "Got a pot of spuds, meat loaf from yesterday. Donny calls it spotted slab. You just as well gather around if you like. It'll give you time to change your watch."

Donny crowned his mound of mashed potatoes with a button of mustard completing the spiral that wound from the heaped paper plate. The color of ketchup was next to reflect across Coin's starving pewter eyes, Donny's nightly hand at culinary art.

"Your plate, it looks like Christmas," Cole said, admiring the engineering.

"Not mine…Coin's."

"Donny!" That was all Clara had to say in her special way, Coin ate from a different plate. As the four ate, the envelope stayed locked between the plastic handicap rails of a napkin holder, waiting. There was to be no silly talk of wishing for this or that at the dinner table.

"So, has there ever been a Mr. Tout, Mrs. Tout?" Cole politely asked, curious about the branches in her and Donny's family tree.

"Clara," she said. "Was once. We met and said goodbye all in the same year."

"I hope it wasn't ended by death," Cole said, thinking of Laura, remembering how the bent Cessna looked like the shoe of a basketball player just before releasing the shot.

Clara looked to her spotted slab. "A part of somebody always dies when things end."

"I think I was out of line on that question, forgive me. I'm just curious about you, it's not everybody that gets one of these little rainbows," Cole said, aiming his fork at the napkin holder.

Clara denied the lure. "His name was Morgan, a nervous sort, always biting his nails over what he figured others might be thinking. He was a good man, just born with the pulse of a virgin peeking through keyholes."

"Virgin?" Donny asked, thinking of a state in the Americas.

"We'll make it one of your words…next year," Clara retreated, then continued. "I watched Morgan's conscience turn into a curse, kept him from being what he could have been. Seems the whole world goes against the grain sometimes, doesn't it, Mr. Cole?"

"You loved him then?"

"Still do…wherever he is," she said after a pause. "And no, he didn't run off and die, not all of him, just the part that reminded him that I loved him. You, Mr. Cole?"

"No, I never married."

"Well, most people aren't married when they fall in love, didn't ask if you were married."

"That's a tough one to answer, Clara," he admitted, carving a stream for gravy with the side of his fork leading under a bridge of meatloaf.

"What's tough about love?" Clara asked, resting her fork on its plate then crossing her arms. "It's simple to fall into, what can be tough is the landing. Some stand up brushing lust dust off themselves wondering where the hell they are. Ever land in the right one, Cole?"

"Right or wrong, how do you know?"

"You just do. That's why it's easy. You must have had other loves in your life to be learning this lesson just now," she said, watching Cole pat his bridge, one of many. Sitting up tall as if stretching, Clara drug back her hair that used to flow, now receded real slow, the color of raspberry cream divided between her garden tanned fingers. "You sound like a man who wouldn't know he was in love if the perfect woman knelt right down and bit him on the ass."

"Ass! A - S - S," Donny piped, "Somethin' you better be haulin' if you're late for spotted slab!"

Clara's eyes bounced off the last S to the ceiling. "One of last year's treasured words," Clara scoffed.

Cole brought one leg over the other and a hand to his chin as he pictured Laura biting him square on his spotted slab. He stalled before his question, "What would you do if it were, your best friend?"

"Best friend? Well now, I would think half the battle to be won already," she answered with a subtle authority like a paddle in the sea, resting her arms on the table to look Cole closely in the eye. "Wonderful, wonderful. Her eyes tell you a story of passion, do they? One that cuts loose the baggage of seeing yourself alone?"

Her words crawled up close to him and struck deep. He looked away as if just completing an indecent thought, grimacing at the concept of Daniel's bewildered eyes like he'd been caught firing up a stogie in the space shuttle. "Six years ago, her husband was killed in a plane accident. He, Daniel, was the first to be my best friend."

Clara lowered the tone of her next question, "And now you're afraid to be choked by hands beyond the grave. Is that it, Mr. Cole?"

"Wouldn't you?"

"Were you 'his' best friend?"

"I'd like to believe so, yes. But…."

"Six years you say? That's a lot of water under the meatloaf bridge, Mr. Cole," she said, noticing his spotted slab now had mashed potato people crossing it, fat white folks with wavy gravy hair. "Only so much time flows before it trickles away all together. Do you love her?" she asked, leaning in yet closer with her suspicions. "Or have you always loved her somewhere in those valleys of your mountainous respect?"

Coming full circle with his gravy trench, Cole highlighted the center of it with a tap, right where Laura had stood in his snow moat at Light House Lake. How she must have felt, he wondered with his face falling slack as though he'd called 911 and got an answering machine, the message loud and clear.

"I'll bet you *wish* I didn't ask your soul that one, huh?"

"Easy…that word!" Cole said dropping his fork, horribly disfiguring three groovy gravy guys.

"Oh, yes, Mr. Cole. I'll be real careful with that magical word from now on," she said rolling her eyes to Donny, fanning the flames of his chuckle.

After the paralyzed potato people were pitch-forked and drug through the Great Gravy River only to be sacrificed in the hovering black hole, Cole found himself in the living room by simply throwing one leg over the red bench seat he'd dined on. Clara collected the rainbow and gained on an opposing couch the color of Thanksgiving with a pondering stroll. "I've given you enough time to flip your lid, if you were a lid flipper. Seems you're still convinced this letter of yours is more than just a letter. Tell me, have I won some grand prize, or is this a way to raise money for something along the lines of Make a Wish Foundation? Because, I'll admit I've become a bit of a celebrity to the homeless. So, how about you just come out with what you're after? I'll listen, but I have to tell you, Donny and I, are, well, we have little left to give."

Cole liked her just that much more from that moment on, he admired the direct honesty backed up by give-a-damn eyes. He stood, and clearly said, "Mrs. Tout, will you please read once more?"

With a hint of play along, she agreed, and her lips whispered down the page with each magical word.

Jenny lowered a motherly finger aimed to the lesser of her two evils for the last time. "Get THAT gum out of THAT dog!"

The free football phone barely rang as though mumbling its own last rites.

"Hell-hole."

"Hey…it's me. It's letting up out there. I was thinkin' about a stroll up Patch."

"I'm afraid it might be more of a plow than a walk, Laura."

"I talked to Cole."

"Wow, and I have a dog I can chew, blow up, and pop."

"No, Jenny…I 'talked' to Cole."

The line was silent.

Clara finished. "I'm sorry, Mr. Cole, I don't understand. Wish for what?"

Cole leaned forward as if catching her words. "Easy, Mrs. Tout! You want to be a little careful throwing that word around from now on."

"Wish fish," she mocked.

Cole flinched, bringing his fists to his temples as if snugging a rain hat under a downpour of Rainbow Tout trout. Clara was teetering back toward lid flipper again, seeing him look side to side, perhaps thinking the walls were at her command. She let a soft chuckle slip imagining this to be a wonderful game between the realistic and wishful thinkers.

"Wishy Washy Wish Wish Crockadile Dishy!" she laughed, Cole's eyes shot to the kitchen's linoleum, no gator maid in an apron, then to the front and only door. Her laugh flamed as she turned to Donny who was quick to jump in, his eyes the texture of glazed cherries. "I wish I could leap over a thousand...."

"NOOOOO!" Cole cried, throwing himself center of the wishing lions. "Now Mrs. Tout! You have to listen to me! DON'T use the word 'you know what' jokingly! Please!" Cupping his hand to his mouth he whispered the 'you know what' as if there were an unmarked van with tinted windows and tall antennas curiously parked across the street.

"Now, Mr. Cole, I enjoy a laugh as well as the next, but really, why all this bother for little ol' me? You don't seem like the homeless type, and a good-looking rascal like yourself must have better things to do than knocking on doors sellin' nothing for nothing."

"Oh, you'll soon see this is better than playing cribbage or peeling spuds," he said, still hanging on her every carefree word. "I'm not sure what to do here, Mrs. Tout. I was just told to deliver this. It knocked me over too, but I now know it's true."

"Oh!" Clara smirked. "So you've been graced with this amazing gift yourself?"

"...Yes," Cole admitted, fearing the worst of his ribbing now certainly lie ahead.

"Well Dancin' Dingos! Why didn't you just say so? And here I was starting to doubt you."

Cole felt the back of his teeth with his tongue, his silver mane resting on his ideas. Coin hunched in the pocket of Donny's fingers, saw a wedge of Cole's eyes traverse on him.

"Mrs. Tout, why don't you start with something small like ridding that mouse of those racing stripes, or tulips did the trick for me."

Clara squinted back at him as if he'd just pinched her butt when her head was turned. "Okay, Mr. Cole, okay," she agreed. Looking to the living room window, Clara stood with a levitating gesture entertaining Donny's grin. Slowly waving her arms about the air as if telling a neighbor hello before telephones were invented, she shot a wink to Donny and Coin, flattened her lips to Cole.

"I *wish* the old Ford would just start up like it was ready for a race!"

The tattered Tout home was still. The only sound was Coin's delicate feet retreating deep in Donny's palms. Cole…waited. Filling her lungs, Clara's waving arms frozen in time, her inflated eyes bubbled under her forehead, grin slipped to her chin. RooOOOOOoom!

The windows trembled, so did Clara.

Wandering down the powder dry hill into Rockingham, a hill once owned by the Tout's, Cole allowed himself to be lured by the Australian streets. Sugar white beaches disappeared behind touristy buildings and the sounds of city grew as he descended. He'd left Clara and Donny with a new wonder, left them to lead their lives as never before, that much he was certain of. There were no goodbyes, no last words of wisdom, only a long hug Clara was famous for and Cole pointing to the little rainbow as he saw the questions welling up in her eyes. It had done its own job well enough guiding him and he thought it to be right, thought everything to be right.

He walked the same streets Donny had run with a mouse up his sleeve as he lightly chuckled again at the idea of Coin's racing stripes and shook his head at his feet over the kids nowadays. It brought back the memory of catching two boys grinning ear to ear, gawking skyward through the glass floor of his living room from the creek bank below. It had been a dinner party, thrown for Philip, the men in ties, women in…dresses. Cole remembered chasing the boys back in the house, he also remembered noticing the way powder blue lace curved with Laura's inner thigh, the vividness of the memory stopped him, forced him not to think about it like he'd done standing under the bridge.

"Podon me, matey."

"Certainly," Cole said stepping aside. A coffee house pinched between two brick bullies exhaled the smell of cinnamon and crushed beans from its open door mouth, its eyes half blinded with blinds. Inside were neat rows of colored bottles its customers would point to, vanilla and strawberry, orange and peach, banana. The sound of cups and saucers for those who drank from a string of little round tables and padded seats with wrought iron back rests bent in the shape of hearts. Styrofoam, for those inflicted with the modern disease of going too fast.

"Something fancy, maybe with a hint of mint?" Cole cheerfully answered, looking at a green bottle plugged with a shiny hollow tooth like a single barreled viper. A man ironically topped with an outback hat made of rattler hide reached for sugar. He'd been recently fired for scheduling a tampon commercial during a drag race, eyes snuggled up close like a Cyclops, belt buckle saying something about nineteen-eighty-one. The woman next in line, eyes bulged a little as though life had over blessed her with curiosity, nervously recounted the silver in her rhinestone coin purse.

"Here ya be!" said a lively young thing, draped in a stark white apron spotted with coffee that looked like Eskimos wandering about for a little blubber to fill their igloos in a wash of spring light. "Thank you. Keep the change," Cole said taking the cup from her hands.

As he sat, he saw a frustrated man drawing blue ovals around want ads, another across from him read the paper's remains. Kitty-corner was a woman that showed a mustache of wrinkles above her lip when she used the word 'no' to her anxious child, letting its finger be the judge of hot milk. Pictures of places and things showed captured moments of places and things nailed to the wooden walls. *The Coffee Drop* in letters the size of typewriters worked as a fine backdrop for the stainless steel machines humming behind the counter.

With a sudden stoke of wind, the shop's mouth closed, capturing its patrons. They began to notice one another more as if looking for answers in the belly of a whale, a garbage can overturned out front, spilling its guts in the freak whirl, styrofoam cups with a single coffee drop logo advertised across the street and under cars pelted with the blow. Then it was no more. The cups' dance ceased, their mother coffee pot had waddled center the street with a stern finger.

Cole knew he could smell magic behind this gust as he smiled, his eyes looked to one of the iron hearts of the backrests and he wondered what color Clara might be listening to. He thought of cheering red and suddenly missed Laura at the same wonderful time.

Raising his eyes, he discovered the man in rattler hide opening his arms, strolling toward his tiny table. Cole stood, not really knowing why, and his arms fell open in suit, wide like describing the state of Alaska. They embraced, with the man's hat riding against Cole's ear. A hug. Over this stranger's shoulder, Cole saw what the entire world would only see once. He saw it spreading in the shop and in the streets where the gust of wind had passed through to blow elsewhere, leaving behind people embracing one another with transfixed eyes closing in the grips of precisely what they needed.

A towering crane lifting skyscraper bones to the commercial heavens in Vancouver B.C. came to a rest swinging its load of steel over the city. A stick figure lowered rung by rung to the soaring deck of unfinished support beams and thick-ended wires. The engineer watching, hardhat, big thoughts rolled and tucked under his arm, seemed to know why the crane's operator was hugging him and allowed a laugh as he did the same in return. Over his shoulder, through neighboring building windows, the engineer could see they were not the only ones. Square plate glass windows worked like free peepshows for the perverted who got off on care and compassion.

In Russia they hugged, in Spain they hugged, in Cairo the owner of a factory argued with an environmentalist in front of giant gauges monitoring how much a smoke stack smoked. The owner lowered his angry finger and tone in sync. Two things shocked the environmentalist, first, this man hugging him, second, hugging him back. Grass later grew at the base of the factory's mighty stacks as though children had gone mad with green crayons on dirt canvas.

Mr. and Mrs. VanLeer, soon to be Mr. and Miss VanLeer, sat across from their divorce lawyer. One crying. The other tapping his finger on a pile of pay stubs, both thinking of their two daughters. The secretary burst in, circled the desk, arms around her boss. The husband and wife? …Still husband and wife.

Cash registers and gas pumps stopped their tallies, stock graphs flat lined. A rock band in their recording studio caught the moments of silence on tape as they laid down their instruments to embrace. It was later played at a World Peace Concert.

Paris, France, traffic jam to the horizon and back, a woman in Gucci stripes weighed down with gold and diamonds stepped from her muscular Porsche, wrapping her perfumed torso around a mother of three hungry kids, staring at them from the back window of a car held together by junkyard donors with the same blood type.

North of Anchorage, Alaska, a dog named Pilot, home alone, approached his feared outlet. He licked, dragging his wet tongue over its snake bite eyes…it did not shock him.

Pilot's mama, walking center of a road with no potholes, too, was engulfed by the urge to hug. Crying, she fell in her friend's arms, certain of committing the crime of attempted passion, guilty by not hearing, 'I love you,' back.

An assassin in South Africa did not pull the trigger. A drunken father in Seattle did not strike. Those alone did not feel they were for that warming moment, crossing their arms, gripping their biceps, rejuvenating their own sense of security.

Clara Tout first struck life in the heart of her old Ford, then…all. "A hug is what the world needs," she always said.

Nice job Clara…nice job.

A rouge wave of wind drug its icy comb through the giant spruce as if dolling up for the silver-haired rascal it was leaving behind in one of its winding car scars. As Bashful Peak came into view jetting from the Chugach Mountain Range, Laura took her eyes from the center of Patch, raising them slowly, seeing a new life come into view. Her breath ceased. "…Cole?"

Her eyes filled with him, all else was not. His hands came from his pockets, extending those arms that she could spend a lifetime in.

She went to him, each stride greater than the next. Jenny could feel her vicarious life, coming to life.

Cole took the shy hand he always preferred, his eyes the color of sky ten minutes before it rains.

"I love you."

ten

While Cole and Laura were born from my imagination, I must treat them as if I've been invited to their amazing Spring Creek homes for a hot game of yard darts, or their characters in the end will lose something, that creative something, for me, then unfortunately trickling down to you. So I believe, Cole would be far above speaking of his and Laura's first remarkable night together to just any passersby. Therefore, neither will I. However, I will tell you this much, they both heard the same color, violet, the sound of people making breathtaking love…in Italy.

The sun rose over Cole's bridge and the south thirty, shoving clouds aside as if it were being escorted from its orange flame painted limo past those waiting in line to the greatest play of all time, every human on earth playing a role, starring as themselves.

One green eye opened, looking over Cole's tan forearm as if it were saying 'go' to traffic in a desert made of skin. Laura whispered, "Cole?"

"Mmmmm."

"I had this dream. A legless man was demanding I race his fancy car. It must have been a block long. The steering wheel turned by itself through the corners. The dash kept getting smaller, the rushing pavement closer, there were potholes. You went by in a blur waving a sign beside the road. I tried to read, but the tiny dash lit up with all the colors of a rainbow. The car swerved. I could see faces, faces in the bleachers, curious faces getting closer and closer changing into the faces of…deer."

"Did this fancy car of yours have racing stripes?" Cole rattled into his pillow.

"Here's where I have a problem with it, Cole…either I'm still asleep at the wheel, or the deer faces are real."

"Mmmm, remember to always pump your brakes, never just sla…."

"Cole…Cole!"

Opening his eyes to the bedroom wall, Cole expected to find the shadow of a one-eared donkey smoking a cigar, a morning reflection from a pencil holder sitting atop a roll-top desk centered under a string of one, two, three French windows. However, the reflection seemed to have found its lost ear, and multiplied across the wall looking more like two-dozen fuzzy arms pushing vacuum cleaners. Rolling his groggy eyes to the new day's light, he sprung to life with, "Well, good mornin' ladies!"

"My God, I'm not driving! Ladies?"

"They look hungry don't they?" Cole grinned through a half maze of wrinkles mirroring his pillows.

"That one, right there," Laura scoffed, poking in the air. "He's looking right at me like he knows I'm naked under here. Yeah, sure, I've had the dream of classmates staring at me naked, but this?"

"She."

"She?"

"Yes, she. They're all she, except for Spike. He's probably off feelin' sorry for himself. He never warmed up to me like the girls here did."

"Warmed?" Laura snorted, picturing one of the does saying, "Hey thanks, it's only until mine's out of the shop," then throwing Cole's Range Rover in gear.

"Good morning, Red."

"Yes…it is," Laura said, loosening her grip on the quilt wrapped about her chest.

"What's this monkey for?" Laura asked, drawing circles with her thumb on its teak chest plate as she sat at Cole's dining table.

"That's to remind me of Parasite," he said strolling from the kitchen.

Laura quickly placed the wooden monkey back beside the toothpick bridge, her finger and thumb grinding like grasshoppers attracting the opposite sex. "Your bridge, it's fallen in its paper river."

"There's a little Irish lass in this one, lass," Cole said handing her a *Here to There Engineering* coffee cup, with a picture of two men scratching their hard hats from opposite shores.

After a sincere pause, holding the seashell that would always remind Cole of Mary Pearson, Laura showed him what green eyes were supposed to look like with, "Thank you."

"Well, I'm not used to making coffee for anyone else, so I'm glad you…"

"Not for the coffee, Cole. It tastes like you poured it from the ass of something hung over. Thank you for…you."

The shell was slowly placed back at the monkey's feet, her left hand out of sight hanging from its strangled blue wrist under the table. "Cole, I can't help myself from asking you something. Have you tried…big things?"

"Things?"

Tracing her bottom lip with a long nail, looking to the toothpick bridge, she muttered the words, "Cancer?….The starving? ….Peace?"

Cole's eyes went to the collapsed bridge as well, Laura's flashing to his, waiting for the answer to one of the biggest questions she or anyone would ever ask.

"I'm sorry. Waves in the ocean."

"Waves?"

"Yes…I'm afraid it doesn't work that way."

Laura saw for an instant, herself lured from a shore, swimming against an impossible tide charging with wished waves of passion and pity. "Cole…am I a wave?"

"No! And don't you ever think it! You are you, and I am I. Together we are we, and I think it's a we that is meant to be. Besides, if I were to have wished this, I'd be havin' coffee with one of James Bond's undercover gals about right now."

"You old shit, you wouldn't have a clue what to do with one of those racey little spies!…Well, but then maybe you would," she admitted, finding her good morning smile, red nail circling her top button.

A knock at the heavy maple doors brought a confused look to both their faces. "Oh God, what if it's Pilot? I've forgotten. I need to run home."

Leaving the table after a smile and kiss, not necessarily in that order, Cole said that he would wish her there in a moment. "You can surprise the little guy! Oh," he said, looking at his torn boxers and shirtless body, "could you get that for me?"

Watching Cole dance his way across the glass floor, mocking the way they had just hours ago in an Italian vineyard warmed by flaming barrels, Laura found herself still, and always to be, amazed by the power of a wish.

In a wonder of a mood, she pulled both doors open in a *wooosh* to a mailman in black rubber boots holding a manilla envelope under the arm of his blue-grays.

"Hello there!" the postman jolted through a half laugh, catching Laura off guard with a fast question. "Do you know that Cole can wish?"

She thought of Cole's late night story under the stars of how things had occurred and knew this lively little man had been a key player.

"…Yes."

"*Wish* you didn't!"

"Didn't what?"

"Exactly! Hello there, is this the Caffy residence?"

"…Yes."

"Would you be so kind as to see that Mr. Caffy gets this please, there's no need for a signature."

"…Yes." Laura's face remained blank as the cold air climbed her bare legs to cuddle under the hem of Cole's long white shirt.

Recrossing the bridge, buttoning another one of his shirts, Cole said with a chuckle, "Maybe I should have you appear in the broom closet, you could jump out like a witch, that'd thrill his baggy little hide."

"What in God's earth are you rattling on about? Are you already calling me a witch?"

"No…Pilot. You could really get his dander up, huh?"

The doors closed, her face still happy, yet fighting some distant wonder. "There was a delivery for you," she said, presenting the envelope.

Cole's heart didn't know to sing or choke. "Little guy? Earflaps?"

"Yeah, a mailman, but not mine."

Cole knew there was something missing as if the postman had left with more than he'd delivered. He took the envelope with a follow up kiss. Laura went to stand on the glass floor to watch the surprisingly friendly deer chew the darkened tulips Cole had harvested about his living room and flung from the French barn window, the grooves of their teeth matching the tulips color. Laura turned, hearing the tearing sound of mail reaching its destination.

Deer Cole, (get it?)

Remember our talk on the bridge. We can't have water running where others know there is not. It would only be a matter of time before they're chasing upstream looking for some great fountain of youth. Your love for Laura is real, as hers is for you. We just can't have her wandering upstream. Do you see the questions I've planted growing in her eyes? Look into them and repeat these words, as I felt they should come from you.

"I wish for you to accept the events of the time we've shared. There is no need for questions, only to know, I love you."

This is far from a scolding, Cole. Again, you're doing just wonderfully. This is all part of learning to walk on those wishing legs. If you and Laura were to one day marry, to become one, the water would be allowed to flow between you again. It is far too great a secret to keep from the one you've chosen to walk through life with.

My next stop is to come up with an explanation for the entire world stopping for a hug, 'A wave in the ocean.' It will be worth it.

Mailman

Cole lowered the letter to his side, bending it in two. Laura stood letting the sun warm her legs with its reflective glow like the deer below, her eyes filling with the questions the mailman warned. "I saw you standing there once," Cole said with a sad smile.

"You've seen me stand here a thousand times, you old billy goat."

"One time stands out."

Laura's expression was as monotone as the words she spoke. "Cole…how did we get to Italy last night?"

"It was several years ago," Cole said pressing on. "That party for Philip and his wife. You left early, but not before I stood down…there," his finger aiming through the glass floor, beside a door. Laura followed his gesture to the frozen ground below, reflecting back up to all of her from the same view the deer now had, that certain one seeming to smile again as if saying, "ah ha, I knew you were naked under there."

"Cole," she blushed, with a rush of schoolgirl. "You dirty old man."

"I saw powder blue lacing its way around your thighs, tracing those amazing curves of yours. I would have never thought you would be standing here like you are now."

"Well," she said undoing her top button, then the second, "I am." Her words slipping out from the soul she was about to bare.

"That's why I need you to listen to what I have to say." With his words forced, letter at his side, he crossed the room and took her by the hand, regrettably looking her straight in the green eyes. "I *wish* for you to accept the events of the time we've shared. There is no need for questions, only to know, I love you."

Her buttons unbuttoned, questions in her eyes, answered.

It was odd to see someone else behind the wheel of his Rover. The garage door closed, Laura pressing the clicker over her shoulder then blew a long kiss to him over its black rectangular end, her shock of red bed head piloting towards Pilot.

Leaning in the frame of the garage's side door, Cole thought of many things as he watched the Rover slip away up Patch, his friend and not foe Sean Connery, also Rosa and her daughter loaded with potential, Laura and the fact that she may never hear color again. Would he have to say he was going into town for groceries and hope not to come home with a tan? But he knew he could not lie, not to Laura. Were his wished travels at a close? Then finally, huggable Clara Tout's face came to mind, her question repeating clearly in his mind, 'or have you always loved her'...."Yes," Cole admitted to the south thirty and the eavesdropping spruce. "Yes, I have."

Crossing over the bridge and through the French doors of his den, gently dragging his finger across a certain poster, Cole rounded his desk and plopped himself in the leather chair. Two letters were written there, only one with proper postage torn from a booklet of sticky back-sided geese and pheasants.

The first;

Miss Rosa,

I have enclosed a check for $40,000. If this is acceptable, I would like to purchase your Westsail. The extra $1,000 is if you could look after it until I discover its future. Incidentally, this would cover the fee of a fine oceanography school. If your daughter was to graduate, please escort her down your dock with her diploma, to the Westsail, and tell her it is hers again...forever.

Your friend,
Cole Caffy

The second;

I made the Tout delivery. I now know it was partially a set up. Clara made me look for Laura in places I would have never searched... I found her.

Thank you, Mailman.
Best wishes, Cole

The letters were tapped into formation on the kitchen counter and loaded in the pocket of his black and red flannel jacket. He thought of the postman's ear-flapped hat as he picked his own from the garage's wall, mittens snapped free from their plastic tear-dropped handcuffs, tattered red scarf for old times' sake. He argued his feet into their boots, and felt his breath grow with the upward slope to Patch realizing if he just kept wishing his way here and there, the love handle signs of a lazy man would start choking his slim waist. He inhaled deep and thought it all too amazing how his coat still smelled of smoke from the Italian vineyard. The mailbox said *ahh* and so did he.

"You," was written in neat letters under a hand-sketched rainbow, the first treat for the box. The second, nearly followed until the color of melted sun on the frame of Cole's hand brought a cheer to his cold face. The envelope and its tropical address escaped the box's fish jaw as he laughed a shot of breath into the Alaskan fall. Only the black spruce could hear his next words as he clinched Rosa's letter and heard the color of copper come at him from east and west, north and south…mainly south.

The string of scooters in a range of colors with steel spokes bent like rusted lightning strikes, chrome gas caps that made it appear you were hanging on the rear fin of a fighter jet when actually impatient car horns were their uphill motivation. Copper, the pounding of wild horses running where they please.

The sun felt its way over Cole's coat offensively like someone asking a five star chef for ketchup. His arms swimming high in the wave of heat, his waffle stomp footprints yet to be seen in the sandstone street. As he turned, a shocked child stood, mouth open as if all fairy tales had come true at once, breath leaking from his tan tummy in a rough hiss, tongue purpled with his chosen sweet.

"Ahh, hello there son. I'll bet your wondering how I…." Cole looked for an excuse, but found only, "BOO!" The boy dropped what was left of his snow cone and ran wild left and right out of sight, the fading sound of a fart with each Olympic leap. Cole had to laugh, and laughed as never before. Through his tearing eyes, he saw that *Skyline Scooters* apparently no longer sold fine hooters, and the white masthead of the Westsail towered in the skyline, ironically just beyond the word *Skyline*.

Approaching, he threw Numba seventeen a salute standing in its racked ranks and saw a rosy figure eject from the blue recliner in a charge for the screen door.

"Roooosa!" he shouted, cocking his right foot out of instinct before the equatorial sun eclipsed again behind a sheet of shirt.

Pilot, the poor little crap factory, pattered in circles at the front door waiting for its hemline to darken with the shadow of Mama, the scrape of worn brakes no longer his cue. The door opened, opened to a new woman, a woman about to say goodbye to her husband for one last time, a wonderful husband that would well understand that life must, and will, go on. A husband that knows she will always love him…wherever he might be.

"My daughter, she work all da day after you left," Rosa said, stepping from random fists of grass to the wood slats of the dock. "She clean everyting, even shine da port lights until she see herself."

The Westsail floated in her slip, prouder of its bowsprit than ever before, sun glowing from its scrubbed cabin trunk, the smell of Simple Green floating from below. "I don't know what you say to her Meester Caffy, but she took the shells her father collected and toss them from da bow after she say something to da ocean. Then she come bock talking about a school in da United States. She now on da far side of da island putting up signs to sell dis boat. I don't have da money for school," Rosa said gazing across the harbor. "I've neva wanted for money more than now. I am her mother. I want everyting for her."

Subtly, Cole turned to look at Serenity's stern thinking the teakwood sign, hand painted with a wash of white letters, was clever indeed.

'Selling what floats to study what does not'

'Westsail for sale'

"What does a handsome boat like this cost nowadays, Rosa?"

"She waiting for someone to call from dis fancy school, in Florida I tink. She will have to pay for place to eat and sleep, then there are da books."

"Oh yes," Cole agreed, unable to count the pages he'd turned discovering what it takes to suspend steel. Rosa turned to him, unknowingly stinging him with her question. "Your mama, she proud of you, yes?"

Cole didn't answer right away. He stood before Rosa slowly unbuttoning his coat and searching for words before he spoke. "I don't know, Rosa. I don't think she knew what I went on to do."

"I sorry, Meester Caffy. Did she die when you were little boy?"

"....Something like that. I would like to believe she thought well of me, when good days gave her the chance to anyway." Cole let out a false smile, his eyes drowning in the wake of her questions.

Rosa saw their void, realizing she'd stumbled into something that hurt, something that was starving for resolve. She stepped forward and turned into Cole's direct view insuring her next words would hit home. "I don't know where your mama go, Meester Caffy, but, I do know she would be proud of you. If she is in da sky now, she knows you are good mon, ond believe me when I say no one knows their child, more than da mother."

Cole's stare left Miss Rosa's round brown face and climbed the Westsail's mast to the tropical sky where she believed Misses Caffy to be keeping an eye. "...Not mine, thank you Rosa, but not mine," he answered, staring down at his snow boots.

"I wish you see my daughter sparkle after you speak to her. You would hove seen da reflection of a very proud mon," Rosa said, leaning in close as if wanting to use her own eyes for proud mirrors.

Cole's stare wound up the mast like the stripes of a barber's pole, "Trust me Rosa, your daughter will make you proud...I wrote you a letter this morning, here," Cole said, rustling his flannel pocket. "This is to keep that sparkle of hers sparkling."

After passing a finger over her own smartly written name, she glanced back to Cole's winter coat and heavy boots topped off with an ear-smothering hat she'd certainly never seen before. "Meester Caffy, aren't you hot in that getup?"

Meester Caffy only smiled, as Rosa's motherly eyes grew with each line they descended. It was obvious when the word 'forever' registered. The sun once again eclipsed behind a blur of bewildered t-shirt, then a final time as he attempted to make his way past Numba seventeen's pink soul, Rosa had herself a grip. Tucked under Cole's left arm was the sign he'd asked for in return, 'Selling what floats to study what does not.' His mind's eye saw it framed with teak, hanging near a monkey of the same tropical grain. His mind's eye also saw the tears pooling in the saddle of his own mother's vacant eyes. Saw it all too well.

After Cole reminded Rosa that he knew his way to the bus stop, he watched her portly frame samba across the white sand of her rutted yard. Out of the blue, the Westsail shifted in her slip from a spook gust that sent Rosa's hands to her chest as to keep a dear friend's letter from blowing away, like most dreams do.

Bloom House
346 Plunge Street
San Diego, California

A home for those who no longer knew where home was. Cole remembered its address from the series of checks he'd written for the past seventeen years. Before that they were sent to a characterless building in Colorado where hanging family photos were seen as just another nail hole in the wall by its affluent owners.

With his earflaps patting his ears, Cole walked up the paved driveway's gentle grade, seeing that waves collapsing under their own weight bordered the sunny side of this historical four-story home sprawled out about its knoll, comfortable in its own shingled skin. Remodeled as a high care facility, the subtle exterior appeared as though it was once the rich kid on the block before being drafted as a medic. In trenches the size of gravel pits, the home would reach deep in its back porch to reveal pictures of itself saying, 'Yep, that's where I live,' to a wounded doublewide, mini malls and fast food restaurants calling the shots between explosions of termite mortar. IV bags dripping golden varnish, hammer and nail first aid kits, one hour photo shacks capturing the horrifying moments of battle.

Wheelchair ramps like someone shook out the cement steps, doors two nurses could pass through at the same time discussing car payments, the florescent ceiling leading to where Cole stood clearing his clear throat half surrounded by an L of plastic chairs, somewhere the sound of plates clicking with silverware and the smell of buttered potatoes.

Perma-freckled was the young thing rounding the corner with her professional smile just off a ten-minute frown break, finding ear flaps and mittens accented with a ratty red scarf worn like a pilot. "I'm sorry, sir, have you been waiting long?"

"No, I…."

"Is your escort with you today, sir?" she asked, with a rapid glance impolitely masking the room. Cole's thorny brows spelling V over his confused eyes took a lap themselves, hoping not to find two men stronger than he with a coat that lured magicians. Two and two were put together and added up to him being taken for a new patient. He looked back to the shrapnel of freckles judging him. “Oh, I’m sorry, does it appear I’m soiling myself as we speak?”

“…Sir?”

“One moment please, miss,” Cole said making fists at his side, looking to the florescent heavens. “Okay, okay, in the home stretch now and…there! Could I trouble you for a sturdy handkerchief or a nice big roll of paper towels?”

The star chart of freckles in the center of the receptionist’s face parted ways, making room for her gaping mouth as though a blackhole were swallowing unfortunate planets in its timeless inhale. She rounded out of sight as though showing others the proper way to exit a burning plane, feet shuffling, hand over blackhole.

“Do I have an escort?” Cole grumbled to himself, chuckling a bit as he shook his head at the tiled floor.

Contestant Number Two entered the room with his own brows in a V seeming to have caught the highlights from unlucky contestant Number One. The fit of his sport coat told Cole this one must be a fair bump up the totem pole, round glasses reflecting the memory of his own worn as a child.

“Look, before you say anything, no, I didn’t bring a date and I’m well in control of my ass.”

“…Okay then, I’m Doctor Woodland. Most of our new guests arrive with an escort, and I doubt you’re in need of one. How may I help you?”

“Doc, my name is Caffy, Cole Caffy, and I’m here to see…”

“Caffy?” the doctor interrupted, head straightening on his white collared shoulders, “As in…Madelyn Caffy?”

Cole had not heard his mother’s name spoken in seventeen years. It rolled off the doctor’s tongue as smoothly as Ben Caffy’s after finishing the minister’s lead in; ‘I take the….’

Doctor Woodland spoke with a relaxed fist wrapped in a palm held before him as if taking a short break from raking. “I’m afraid she still will not recognize you, now, or after you’ve gone. She has to study me for a spell before the clouds clear away, and that’s usually for a very brief time. She is, however, in very good physical condition for a woman of eighty-four. We tried to take that ring of hers away as we feared it could do more damage than not, but let's just say she's still wearing it and I have three staff members that will tell you it's going to stay right where it is."

"Let her keep the ring, Doc. To my knowledge it hasn't left her finger in over seventy years. Says she found it before she got lost. I guess she keeps thinking it'll one day repay the favor," Cole said, reflecting back to how his own reflection had grown from learning to walk to running from base to base across its black onyx face. He remembered how she would stare for hours into that blank stone trying to hang on to those memories her demons took pride in taking.

"It's good of you to come, Mr. Caffy. But, as you are aware, it can have its downsides, leaving an even more confused person behind in a world that is already against them."

"The last time I saw her, I was told to say I was just a visitor. Who am I today, just some goon with nothing better to do?"

"Aside from being a goon, I think that may have been good advice. In her apartment, there are mementos of her past that have tagged along from home to home, but to her they're just something that came with the room, like leaving the model's face in a store-bought frame. I have to be perfectly honest with you, Mr. Caffy, somewhere inside of your mother is a good hearted, and amazingly strong person, but her long list of mental problems are simply too much for anyone to bear for a lifetime, and she is just naturally getting tired. Schizophrenia is a beast that only those placed directly in its path can barely describe."

"Doctor Woodland…has she ever tried to hurt herself, again?"

"…Not in the physical way," the doctor answered, knowing Cole could not have stopped things that had in fact taken place. "I'm sorry, Mr. Caffy, mentally, she just never had a fair shot."

Doctor Woodland led the way to the third floor as Cole glanced over the handrail of the pigtail staircase. He wondered, how had his mother's mind described this view to her; a mineshaft leading to a hell worse than she was in?

The hallway smelled of colorful pills on stainless steel and paper shot glasses. He walked by an aluminum walker parked in the carpet driveway of someone that missed how they used to.

"How would you like me to introduce you, Mr. Caffy?"

"No pun in that one, huh, doc?"

"I think it would be fair to say you were a friend who wished to say hi."

"Yeah, no pun in that one either, huh, doc?"

For a fleeting moment, Doctor Woodland glanced at Cole's earflaps and toyed with the idea of a genetic problem. Cole inhaled and reached for that last minute courage as they reached the door quietly standing guard against things the good doctor and engineer could only dream of.

"I think you'll find your mother's words just as colorful as you, no doubt, remember them to be."

Cole's hands crossed at his waist, again he cleared his clear throat, then tried to add seventeen years of time to his last mental photograph of his troubled mother. The doctor's knock was soft, yet screamed in Cole's stomach.

A frighteningly still moment passed. Then a mocking knock in reply meant she was nearby. Doctor Woodland caught Cole off guard by raising his hand high about the door, then slowly knocking downwards clear to the floor as if estimating the amount of water in a steam engine. The mocking knocking came again in perfect sequence and Cole became uncomfortably aware of the peephole.

"Who's that ridin' shotgun with ya, brain boy?" Cole felt himself being x-rayed by an eye that lived in a lie.

"This is a friend from long ago who's come to say hello, Miss Caffy," Doctor Woodland said, squaring his shoulders.

Cole smiled at the door and its tattletale hole as though looking into the lens of a driver's license camera.

The door pulled back, a wrinkled woman came forth, eyes used up like parachutes after the fact. Her hair the color of the paper these words are written on, slumping left in one neat piece on her bald head. Tip of the nose, resembling Cole's. "Well, let's settle things and get out of the rain," Madelyn said, glancing to a blown hallway light the staff had yet to change, one of her many suns.

"Miss Caffy, I thought you might like some company, but if not, that's okay, too," Doctor Woodland said with a professionally trained smile.

"Who are you?" Madelyn snipped, wondering if his wire-framed glasses where just part of a clever disguise.

"I'm your doctor, Miss Caffy."

"And you brought me another pill to swallow? This feller here?…I'll choke."

"Not a pill, Madelyn, just someone to talk to."

"Hi there…Miss Caffy. May I call you Madelyn?" Cole asked, as though he'd happened by one of his old high school teachers at the movies.

Doctor Woodland studied the two studying each other, his prognosis was to leave. He did not smile as this could smear the words he'd chosen. "This is a good man, Miss Caffy. I've checked him out, turned over every stone. Why don't you invite him in and I'll be just down the hall if you need anything." He then allowed a departing smile, leaving the ball in Madelyn's court. She stepped back a little deeper in the door's frame, straightened her wig like Cole would a tie, a jack rabbit stare at the floor, looking for all the right words, any words.

"Are you comfortable with my calling you Madelyn?" Cole asked, feeling his palms start to sweat. "It's just such a nice name that I thought maybe…."

"Madelyn's…okay," she interrupted, not wanting her fleeting moment of courage to pass.

"Thank you, Madelyn. You know if you'd like me to leave there won't be any hard feelings. I just don't want us to stand out here in the rain all day."

As Cole had hoped, the word 'rain' stood out to Miss Caffy like the word 'boobs' does in this sentence. Her blaming finger started to poke at a grayed light bulb, then paused, pulling together every drop of lonely sanity, "Would you like to come in? Only long enough for them to take your picture though, okay? I'm always alone in all their photos. They think nobody wants to sit with me because I know things most don't."

"We both know things others don't, Madelyn," Cole said, remembering things.

She liked the way this man said her name, reminded her of something, perhaps an old song she'd forgotten the words to.

The apartment had its own smell, its own face. Cole's father made eye contact with him in the entryway as he made his way past other pictures Madelyn knew not. Feeling like he was walking onto the set of a sitcom, Cole followed Madelyn into the living room lit by a dozen suns sucking on electric umbilical cords. He was becoming more familiar with the smell of the sea lingering in from the deck where at the sliding glass doors his mother stood eyeing the ocean, her tattered frame three inches shy of when her name was Mom. Cole's lips parted, his breath trapped deep in his chest, as his eyes found a piece of the past resting where a cat might sleep. A bridge made with Popsicle sticks ten times the size of the ten little fingers that engineered them carefully into place, fifty-five years ago. He'd nearly forgotten this childhood piece of work and his father saying, "This will help your mom remember you while she's away, this time." Above it, Cole looked into a black and white mirror of himself. A picture of those little bridge builder fingers crossed just so under his carefree smile, he remembered having to work at that smile, it wasn't natural.

"Madelyn…who is this?" Cole asked, removing his winter hat, subtly turning his head in her direction like a lineup.

She turned from the ocean, seeing this stranger standing before a picture of a boy from long ago she didn't know. Forced into a five-cornered routine of fear, she let the three-pound jockey snickering under her wig crack the reins of her runaway wagon team. Her answer was slow and broken, clipping the ends of her words. "He's the neighbor boy. He rolls sideways in front of me to cover the cracks in the sidewalk when they make me carry the building's laundry up to the city of Lost Angels. He's very polite and calls me his best friend every time his face is upright, it's like putting a speaker on a tire."

Cole's eyes closed in her answer, the boy before him fading as though he were never there. Madelyn brought her hands to her temples as blinders to hide the obvious tears her fucking mind was again celebrating with, a mind that Cole would jam a pitchfork through if it would die and leave his mother alone.

His approach was cautious as he lifted his hand to the plateau of her shoulder that shied away, a son failing to touch his mother. "That boy is your friend."

With her slouched back to him, Miss Caffy spied on the ocean she believed spied on her. Cole saw a woman nearing the end of her battle with creatures bearing long swords stained with the blood of her sanity. A mother that wanted to be, wanted certainly to be many things. A widow widowed from herself, left running alone from bunker to bunker across fields of nightmares.

“Madelyn, you said you wanted to have our picture taken together?”

Her makeshift blinders slid down, taking tears with them on purpose, a pinch of skin on the bridge of her nose, from behind a web of fingers, she spoke. “Yes,” she carefully said, gesturing to the small balcony suspended over a sidewalk that wound along as an apron for the beach, the sky the color of gifts if it’s a boy.

Cole followed Madelyn to the sound of children, roller blades, and finally the crash of waves spotted with surfers that she nervously pointed to. She wore the fake smile of a slave being asked if all was well on the job by his master. The sliding door left open for a quick retreat as usual, her left foot remaining just inside as she sat, a pretty square of black onyx on her right hand, looping veins the color of pirates rowing to shore.

“Them,” she said through her porcelain teeth like a ventriloquist. “Them.”

“The surfers, Madelyn?” Cole asked, joining her on the bench seat.

“Not surfers. They’re high paid spies with envied assignments. Them too,” she whispered, nodding to a young girl in the middle of breaking a young boy’s heart near the water’s edge, hands pulling away from his, flicking her blond mane over a sun kissed shoulder.

“They watch me. Did you know they have cameras nowadays the size of jewelry?” She asked this twisting her ring over to face her palm, half waiting to hear a faint click in her fist.

“Madelyn,” he asked swallowing. “…Do the trees still whisper things about you?”

His mother’s fake smile collapsed in slow motion, something behind her eyes made them look away. “How did you know that? Are you a surfer?”

“No, Madelyn, I’m not. I wouldn’t even get into the water until recently. I’m just an old friend that came by to say hi…Hi,” Cole said cheerily as possible, with a thin line of water growing over his helpless eyes, the same way it had fifty-five years ago.

Madelyn was unfamiliar with the idea of someone else crying. She’d always assumed she was the only one…the only one ever. Those who did come around carried glasses of water half full, not half empty, delivering happy pills with on-the-clock smiles.

Cole brought a hand to shelter the quiver of his jaw, stared at a wave creeping up under a couple of spies. Paddle, crouch, stand, lean, carve the water. His mother touched him for the first time as her finger crept to his cheek to see if his tears were as real as hers. They were. She whispered to Cole like the trees did to her, "You know, one day, I'm going to stand up as tall as you and march right out to those so called surfing boys and tell them the jig is up. Right off this little scrunch of a deck I'll go, that'll help catch 'em off guard. Which reminds me, I'll have to sneak past that lifeguard, he's their ringleader. One day he just jumped up and ran after one of 'em, drug him right out of the water and sat on him, started beating him square on the chest he did, right in front of everybody circling around, and didn't stop until the hospital police came in their paddy wagon to arrest the beaten one. I don't know what he did wrong, but I think they wanted to keep things under wraps because they didn't even play the sirens. I've never seen that agent here again. They must have fired him," Madelyn sighed, letting her eyes drift to Cole's. "Why are you…crying?"

"…Because," Cole said, watching another wave in the ocean, not a ripple, bringing his palm to tremble before him, "when I was just about so high, I wished I could make you better. There wasn't anyone listening…then."

Miss Caffy allowed her pose to soften, uncaring at the moment if spies were focusing their birth stone zoom lenses packed with microfilm. She spoke even further behind her own breath, her butterscotch eyes on guard, darting side to side. "Who's listening now? I have a list, we can compare."

Cole took her hand. She almost pulled it away to her side and then did not. He spoke slowly, clearly, now was not the time for a Freudian slip. "Madelyn…Mom, I *wish* I could make you better."

The corners of beach towels lying on their own reflection flapped against the tanned legs that kept them from flying away all together. Several of the undercover spies covered their eyes, sand getting up and leaving in a grove of wrinkled lines. The freckled receptionist paused before lighting her Camel, a wind from nowhere, going somewhere.

Miss Caffy's hump of wig hung on by one finger at her ear after flopping over like the sheet metal roof of a Gas 'n' Go in a hurricane. Cole hugged his mother, tears windswept across his cheeks in tributaries of shine. The blow passed.

Miss Caffy pulled free the flipped wig that she'd flipped years ago. Her bald head under construction, she felt the crew at work. Electricians uncrossing a nest of wires, plumbers clearing drains clogged with the inability of reason, sheet rockers fitting their clean white squares over soiled walls finger painted by the insane. The foreman, standing center, new plans rolled out before him, hand wrapped around a pleased and nodding chin, "She's looking good boys, looking good!"

Madelyn sat up straight as a pin, ignoring the mundane slump of her spine for the first time as though Geppeto were leaning over the balcony above, his stringed fingers spread wide, palms gently rising in front of a proud smile saying, "Tiz okay Pinocchio, go on now…dey love you."

Cole could see his mother's eyes wiping away the lies, her speechless mouth open, the crew collecting their tools and gathering to admire their finished work. Madelyn looked to the beach, she saw people, people enjoying the day because the enemies had gone away. The lifeguard guarding lives because they were worth guarding, innocent jewelry bouncing on the sun drenched necks of the playful. Rings, beautiful rings, like her own, just rings.

Miss Caffy brought a hand to her small mouth curling up at the ends all on its own, un-powered by smiling pills that had a way of frowning away anyway. Cole gripped his mother's arm as she looked to the deck, wondering why her left foot was slid just inside the sliding door's frame. Her eyes led deeper in the apartment following an enigma of extension cords leading to a dozen light bulbs burning for no apparent reason. Then to where a cat might sleep, the bridge of popsicles popping up in her renovated mind. Cole closed his eyes as she spoke between her trembling fingers. "That bridge…my…son…my son, made me that bridge. I…I have a son."

Her tired eyes only knew tears of sorrow and endless confusion, these were foreign, different, special tears trickling over a smile that wasn't posing for hi tech jewelry. Lucidly her stare rose, falling deep in the young framed eyes of a black and white photo of whom exactly she was speaking.

Both hands now at her mouth as she slowly turned to face this kind man sitting quietly at her side. Her pause was long into his eyes…his cresting eyes.

"…Cole?"

Wig (□wig) - An artificial covering for head which imitates natural hair.

Schizophrenia - (skit-sə-ˈfrē-nē-ə) - Psychiatric disorder of many and varied manifestations in which person loses contact or misinterprets reality.

Wave - (ˈwāv) Advancing ridge or swell on surface of liquid.

Sanity - (ˈsa-nə-tē) State of being sane (ˈsān) - of sound mind; not deranged; reasonable; lucid.

Bridge - (ˈbrij) To bring together two things once separated.

eleven

Toothpicks and Popsicle sticks, two bridges side by side, one a broken boy in the bubble, the other quiet and humble. An eye the color of sky that sea captains fear closely inspected its round-ended timbers then stopped, hovering just above its single A-frame load tower like the Cyclops pyramid on a dollar bill. The eye rolled to the sky hearing the garage door motor bitch to life, hand over handing greasy chain into its tin mouth, to Cole, the sound of an old love arriving home with a new one.

The kitchen door eked open with a series of soft and cautious taps. Pilot with less uncertainty, greatly so, went in to this whirling thing he did when all the stars were aligned perfectly, or when the universe was becoming one, or maybe just when Uncle Cole was near. Whichever, he wiggled out a barrage of snorts as his pudgy shell lifted from the hardwood runway in a hot round of 'Pilot to co-pilot.' The map of the land chosen for today's flight was on a direct course set for Mama, who got closer with each of Uncle Cole's mid-air loops and propeller-pausing inhales. Banking high and to the right, Pilot was ordered to open the Bombay doors, the mighty sound of wet pink propeller fell silent as the bomb exploded below, Cole's free falling kiss hitting its mark, long and slow.

"Landing gear down!" stick legs fanned out all about, stump tail rudder thrown hard to starboard.

"Nose up! Pthtaththtp-p-pthtthzzzzppththtzzz."

"Cole."

"Pthththp-pzzzzpptatatp-p-pththzzz."

"Cole!"

"Zzzt"

The sound of delighted dog nails clicking on varnished oak floors. "Oh, I'm sorry, Red. Didn't mean to leave ya out all these years, come here!" He came at her, arms out, tongue warmin' up for another run, "Ground control to Red Baron, control to Red Baron. Need help over hostile enemy kitchen floor!"

"Cole, now don't…."

"Pthtatatzzzz-pop-pop-zzzzting!"

Clutched at the waist by Cole's talons, amidst a spinning twirl, Laura pulled the wind out from under her favorite pilot in a screaming laugh. "Cole, I've been trying to tell you, those deer you been rubbing elbows with are cheatin' on ya. Somebody's right out front pettin' at 'em just like you do! Which, by the by, is kinda freaky if ya ask me."

"Well, fair's fair," Cole said, wobbling at her, waving his noisemaker tongue around like the cane of a blind man in a doorway.

Laura's laugh carried across the bridge, to the den, and down the spiral staircase to where she'd slept, filling Cole's home with what he'd wanted most of all…another's voice.

"Come with me, Laura," Cole said, wrapping his arms around her. "I want you to meet someone."

"Okay…who?"

"Someone I've known all my life…but just met."

A string of unplugged suns, a chopped broom handle pinned behind the sliding glass door's aluminum heel. An old class project missing from the corner, an armful of now treasured pictures gone, leaving a truer shade of six and eight inch squares where time had carefully painted around them. Neatly left behind in Madelyn's own rare handwriting was:

Dear Doctor Woodland,

I'll be moving along now. You see I've met my son Cole today. He says he lives in the heart of big beautiful trees on a bridge much like the one I now remember he made for me all those years ago. Thank you for your equally imaginative stories it took to get me to choke down all my pills. I'll never forget the one about the frail yak on the mountain that didn't. You were a fine doctor, and friend, Jeffery, and you'll just have to trust that this is the most wonderful pill of all.

Wishes can come true,

Madelyn Caffy

Amongst a baker's dozen Sitka blacktails, Miss Caffy, Mom, stood as her renovated mind twirled with splendor. She stared beyond the deer her son had *wished* to greet her to the bristling wooden towers of Alaskan spruce. They were silent, gentle beasts, simply going on about their own natural business. Her bald head was warmed by the ear-flapped hand-me-up, mitten handcuffs dangling separately high overhead about the great outdoors she was inhaling, her cheeks stained with cloud nine tears. From behind, her name sang from her son. Thirteen tails rose in sequence like readied hairbrushes waiting for the whistle at the International Makeover Finals.

As Cole approached down the slope of Spring Creek with Laura on his arm and Pilot plowing snow with his barrel chest at his side, Miss Caffy freed the muzzle of a beige-coated doe and lit up to say, "Well, hello all!"

"Mom, I want you to meet someone, someone who I care the world for. This is Laura Day."

"...Mom?" Laura said, crinkling her face. "From what little I knew, I thought your mom was...."

"Bonkers?" Miss Caffy said, finishing the job. "Hi, I'm Madelyn, Cole's mom," she proudly announced.

"I'm sorry, I was just under the assumption that...."

"That's perfectly fine, love, and not a drop of offense taken," Madelyn said, politely interrupting. "In fact, when I woke up this morning, you would have been right on the money and then some, but now...Oh!" she cheered, twirling in place, arms up as if she were trying to plant a tinfoil star atop the tallest spruce.

Seeing this, Pilot thought certain he'd just missed his connecting flight and stood transfixed, brandishing the hackles of his spine as he realized the deer weren't scattering for the tree line like the marmot in Jenny's woodpile.

Tickled at how her very own laugh didn't so much as pause to look both ways before spring boarding from her bottom lip, Madelyn stopped, looking to Laura and Cole with their own smiles, one holding the other's hand, "Do I see love?"

"Yes, Mom…you do."

Trying first to come to terms with having this crazy conversation amongst thirteen wild deer, Laura grabbed Cole's arm and squeezed, saying, "Miss Caffy, forgive me, but I have to ask, did you just wake up as if something wonderful visited you in the night?"

"Not something, someone wonderful visited me and just two hours ago. It was this lovely boy who's arm you're holding that turned the light bulb on in my mind, or I should say, turned off."

Laura began to assume she was the crazy one as she stood trying to piece this mystery together. "Weren't you in a home somewhere in Colorado or California? How could you possibly get from Calif…."

"Blue."

"I'm sorry, blue?"

"Oh yes, this indescribable ocean of blue. I thought I'd slipped back into, well, things. But then Cole heard it too and just kept holding my hand! It sounded like a river with children playing in it. Then all of a sudden, there I was, standing right over this one on a big glass floor with my son, right up there," she said, pointing upriver to Cole's house. "Now, if I have gone crazy again, then so be it! I like it, actually love it might be the better way to say things," she admitted, with her fawn-colored eyes sanely falling on her son's.

Laura no longer knew Cole's talent of a wish, no longer knew color could be listened to. She stood with her snow boots pressed together, loading another round of questions in the back of her mouth as the blacktails impatiently pawed in place, hooked on what a couple of Madelyn's fingers were capable of achieving behind their hairy tube ears. Miss Caffy couldn't shake the smile from her face as she walked with her arms stretched out center of the herd, dragging her fingers across each of their coarse hides as if carpet shopping.

"Okay, Cole," Laura said shaking her head. "Obviously, there's still a little crazy here, and I'm not so sure it hasn't spilt over to you.

And what the hell is with these deer? That one just double, no make that triple checked to make sure your mom isn't secretly your dad!"

Watching his mother smile to the world, Cole said, "Everything is near perfect."

"Near? Near what? Your mother, who's bald by the way, is playing with a herd of wild deer and is convinced she paddled two thousand miles holding your hand while listening to a Sounds of Nature CD! What does she mean she heard a blue river then just popped up in your living room? Cole, I damn well know she wasn't here this morning, and I've had your Range Rover all day. My tracks leaving and coming back are the only…."

"Laura, I said 'near' perfect."

"Okay then, okay, I'll play along, Cole. What would make this fiasco of yours 'perfect'?

"This morning, you would have understood everything clearly. And then it was taken away from you as if it was never there."

"Okay, Caffy, you're getting yourself in deeper here. Is this some scam you brew together after waking up with just some girl you had your yahoos with, trying to get rid of them? Because I'm not just some damn yahoo, Caffy!"

Cole squared himself to her and braced his hands on her shoulders. "The last thing you are is just some girl to me, Laura. And I'm about to prove it to you by once again making everything clear here on Walton's Mountain, and this time it's going to stick, damn it!"

The deer's heads began to rise slowly like clockwork, looking to the tree line for that something beginning to linger as Mom closed her eyes.

"Laura, I *wish* you knew everything as you did when we woke together this…."

Suddenly, the deer discovered their lingering beast. It shot at them swerving from Patch Road to the south thirty in a howling metallic bounce. A sound like Clara's race ready Ford screamed in Cole's ears as his eyes shot up to see a mail van careening wildly across his property, kicking up frozen earth from its four black heels between short leaping jolts in the air.

"MOOOM!" Cole shouted. For an instant he saw her crippled mind slapping itself against a rock again, the trees' mouths stretching open to let out their terrible words, words Cole knew she couldn't take again. He left Laura's side in a bull charge up the slope screaming, "NOOOOO!"

Miss Caffy stood with her back turned, her eyes pinching tighter. Her mind a pro at seeing things go to hell, knew what was about to happen, yet she put up a last minute battle by whispering to the bright Alaskan sky, "Please, please, I beg of you, don't take this from me. If you do…let it be my end."

"NOOOO YOU SON-OF-A-BITCH!" Cole bellowed, charging the chrome eyelids of the mail van thrashing at them across the south thirty. Laura was left stranded with her confusion as she watched the deer's tails wave high and good bye. "Miss Caffy, what's…."

The mailman's fists tightened around the wheel of his boxy white monster as he commanded it skidding side to side across the snow-packed field, his earflaps flapping, black rubber boot to the floor. Cole dodged in its direct path, bearing his row of knuckles overhead. The mighty mailman and his van peeled to the right in an obvious swerve, but still gaining on Miss Caffy to make his mind-stealing delivery. "YOU LEAVE HER ALONE!" Cole cried, as the bull washed past with its sliding door open exposing its determined captain throwing a letter to Cole's running feet. Cole ran flailing on beside the door, his fingers just managing to strangle the mirror's gooseneck.

The mailman hung on, spinning the wheel. He hollered to Cole who was straining aboard, bearing his teeth. "Let it go, Cole! You knew when you wished this, it was no little ripple in the pond! Let it go!"

Miss Caffy turned to see the mail van's square face bearing down with her son shouting behind its bulging window, "I *WISH* THIS VAN WOULD COME TO A STOP! NOW!"

The mailman's seatbelt guitar stringed, capturing his half moon belly in an eye-popping halt. Laura's hands shot to her face as Cole launched from the doorway, snowballing to a stop at his mother's feet. His snow packed eyes opened, the sound of black rubber boots approached, crunching snow at his ear. Three faces haloed overhead. Laura Day, his love, the sole survivor of a twisted aluminum wreck that wrecked everything. Miss Caffy, his mother, pulled from the crazy jaws of crazy, and finally the mailman, the *WISH* giver, the *WISH* taker.

"Please leave her alone," Cole pleaded before opening his eyes.

The mailman leaned over him with a genuine compassion driven by the physics he obeyed, eye level with Miss Caffy and her new sane brain, earflaps to earflaps, "You know I can't do that."

"Yes weal, thot's joust the way things goe I guess, ae?" Cole coolly said, borrowing James Bond's smooth accent. "Go on ahead and zap her then."

As Miss Caffy and Laura snorted in sequence to this cold-hearted reply, the mailman politely began his song and dance of soft words eking over his lip's edge like a barrel at Niagara. "I am sorry, Miss Caffy, but we can't have you running up stream looking for…."

"BAAAAAAAAA!" Cole's hands rifled skyward, throttling the mailman's thick squatty neck. "OVER MY DEAD BODY!" Cole yelled as never before.

The mailman retreated from the huddle, dragging Cole and his iron grip along like an unfortunate warthog that had regrettably peeked in the wrong den. From there things got ugly. The mailman answered back with a stumpy-legged rib jab and a gasp as the talons freed from his neck. With Cole quick to his feet, the two fell into a spread-winged circle dance staring deep in one another's fierce eyes.

"What has to be has to be, Cole, you know how this works!"

"That shell of a woman never hurt anyone in her entire tragic life, and she's going to live, and live well!"

"For Pete's sake, Cole, I'm not here to kill her!" the mailman growled, blowing snow from the corners of his mouth.

"That's just it, you may not realize it…but you are! She can't take anymore!"

Cole swung in the Alaskan air, the mailman winced as a fist whistled just past his earflap. A five-foot wall of federal gray lurched forth with the grace of a charging walrus, "GAAAAAAA!" Again Cole went to the ground, bringing the postman along for a thrashing side-to-side roll in the snow.

Laura ran to the fight loading their guns without realizing it. "Knock it off you two!" Laura demanded, raising her own row of crippled knuckles. "This is the weirdest fucking day of my life! I wish you would both just stop this!"

Cole and the mailman did stop, frozen by that triggering key word…*wish*! Their eyes grew as their fists tightened. Cole took the first big swing, grinding his words through his teeth. "I *wish* your little boots would catch fire!" *Pop, wooOOSH!* The smell of burning rubber, the yell of postman as he stomped wildly in melting circles like a drunken clod dancer on hot coals, Cole's hot coals! Bond, James Bond. To Spring Creek the earflaps flapped, in a way the Wright brothers might have looked at twice. The mailman's boots hissed at each other as he dove them through the thin layer of ice skirting the creek's edge.

Cole stood upon the bank of Spring Creek, his creek, this stretch of stream that his home straddled as though time had frozen its glass-bellied leap. "Ya had enough there, hot foot?" he yelled across the scathing water.

Glaring at Cole, the mailman hopped atop a rock center stream to let his boots smolder. "You don't want to mess with me, green horn! Boots are rookie stuff!"

Cole felt the blood slow in his veins as the mailman's spellbound eyes slowly paddled up river to a handsome two-legged bridge he affectionately called home. "No," slipped out from under his silver mop. "Not my house."

"You do remember our chat on a bridge don't you, Cole?" the mailman said, huffing and puffing his words. "I guess I'll have to walk ya through it one more time, say, to show you the difference between a ripple and a wave!"

As the postman's stubby finger popped free his fist and pointed upstream, Cole fell to his knees shouting to the sky, "I *WISH* THIS BRIDGE WOULD NOT FAIL!"

The finger only halted long enough to wiggle side-to-side. "Your words, Cole, we can't determine the future or what it holds. You're speaking out of turn."

Again the shrewd finger rose as Cole took his shot at a fifty-yard dash to no avail. He only brought himself that much closer to the sound of pleading steel, the creaking of wood beams, floor squares of thick glass rattling in their wrought iron frames. "DAMN YOU AND YOUR WISHES!" Cole yelled, turning away from the sky thundering with French window debris.

Laura's face turned a lighter shade of pale, her gaping mouth still unable to swallow even the spontaneous combustion of black rubber boots, falling to her knees, struck with awe in the bridge's shifting screams of torture. The mailman roared a laugh and slapped the belly it came from, watching a white leather wing chair slide front and center inviting its matching couch along as though it were far too nice a day to just sit around inside.

The middle of Spring Creek started hopping and popping with pieces of broken home, carving a hole in the thin ice big enough for a bridge that would soon follow. Cole held his face fleeing from the collapsing monster, the machine gun sound of failing rivets unzipping just behind. Then with a horrific steel shriek echoing down the valley, the weight of the single span gave in. Tearing with it sections of den and dining room from either side, clearing bookshelves and tables that began to follow by peeling varnish from the hardwood floors like candle wax stripped with a thumbnail, a poster of the world's greatest crime fighter, losing the fight, its maple frame becoming its roll bar.

Turning to the crash, Cole sucked in his breath and held it there as the entire spine of his home fell before him in a gut wrenching M. Blocks of shattered glass mixed with punctured furniture, bent steel hot to the touch, a teak monkey bobbing. Cole released the wind from his lungs in a trembling gust as Spring Creek began trickling around his memories. A few unable to hang on just went with the flow.

The still chuckling mailman standing center stream atop his stone island, bent down and picked up a single popsicle stick. "Hey look, a tongue depressor. Now isn't that depressing?"

Cole felt anger as never before. Not anger like discovering your identical twin had a facelift and boob job ten days before your twentieth class reunion, but pissed! It flowed from his fingertips to his stunned head the way heat travels up a fry pan's handle. A last rattle from the fallen bridge rode down the pinball machine of wreckage to rest upright in plain sight. All eyes stared at it, then shot to Cole's, waiting for the explosion. A now broken glass case, housing a now mocking toothpick bridge, settled itself center the carnage, a wounded soldier slumping out of a bombed building, Cole's bombed building. Again his blood sickened to an ill pumping gray even the mailman could feel as the bridge's engineer turned, letting go the frayed ends of his old world manners. Cole spoke his next words like a guitarist strumming all six nylon strings then pausing before gently striking the final note for an unmistakable emphasis. "I *wish* you would just go…away."

Shoulders slumped, head dangling somewhere between, just as the bridge before him, Cole heard what he'd expected, the sound of treaded black rubber splashing then pattering up close.

"Ya like my boots?"

Turning humbly in his defeat, Cole found unburnt feet. Boots with healed heels, saved souls, shiny rubber as though meticulously waxed and buffed for the funeral of his fallen home.

"You *wish* I would just go away, where? A wish doesn't know what to do on its own, Cole."

"Your boots, huh? I lose my home and the mother I just met, and I can see my worthless reflection in your dumb assed boots."

"Yes, Cole…my boots…your answer." His knobby eyes happy and brimming with hint, blue postal eagle riding casually back and off to one side as though it swooped in for a tasty ear and found a fly papered head instead. Cautiously, Miss Caffy and Laura took baby steps toward the ruins of red steel and glass. The blacktails did not, twenty-six eyes, somewhere deep in the spruce.

"Take it all. Take everything if you have to. Just leave my mother, my girl, and myself alone. I'll wish here and now to never wish again. Whatever it takes. Just leave us alone," Cole muttered, watching his favorite James Bond videotape float past. "I've tried to be a good man. Always stepped out of the way for those after the almighty buck. I got up in the mornings, these wonderful Alaskan mornings, and I went to work trying my best. I've felt the pain in the many ways life can bite you before you even realized she's charging, hooked on your scent wiped across her face by a sweaty rag you don't even remember dropping. I've never tried to hide in self-justifying my mistakes that I knew to be just that, I got off my ass and fixed them!" Cole raised his voice, turning face to face. "Then somebody comes along with a little rainbow, saying life owes me because of all this. Well, whoever you are, Mailman, have a good look around and just keep laughing it up, because if this is all my life is worth, thanks for nothing…I'm off to rob a God damn mini-mart!"

Cole couldn't bring himself to make eye contact with his mother, and only lightly touched Laura as he slowly went to summit his home's gut pile long enough to carefully collect the tooth pick bridge cowering in his father's cracked case. He stood beneath one collapsed bridge, holding another. Pilot, sniffing at the backside of an outlet, figured the torn free jumper cables must have been the evil one's optical nerves.

"You never answered my question, Cole. How do ya like my boots?"

"Yeah…real nice, shiny to boot," Cole mumbled, staring into his trash heap as the word shiny led to the word fixed, as in repaired. "I wished my bridge wouldn't fail. Well, it failed all right…and then some."

"Lessons, Cole, lessons."

Silence, except for the grind of heels in broken glass as Cole descended, cradling the toothpick bridge. "Tell me this. You said yourself you were off to find an explanation for why the whole world stopped for a hug. You said it would be well worth it! A wave in the ocean."

"Yes, Cole?"

"Well, how in the hell is it the entire damn world can flip out for no apparent reason and squeeze each other, and yet this poor little ol' lady who knows no one, and has endured far more than me, can be denied exactly what she's fought for all her devastated life?"

"Lessons Cole, lesso…."

"Yata, Yata, Yata. I'm tired of your words. You better stop talking out of your ass and start spilling some answers mail boy, or you just might find I still have a little hocus-pocus left up my sleeve!" Cole said on the verge of shout.

"Okay then, Cole…fix your bridge," the mailman matter-of-factly said. "Go on."

"What's to keep this circus from going on? Am I to fix something only to see you break it again?"

"Think of how you want things to be and wish it so, Cole. *Wish* it so."

Standing before what once was his home, Cole closed his eyes. "I *wish* this bridge was fixed!" Anxiously, they opened to the same heap of ruins, spotting the torn drafting of his home in the wreckage just for a cherry on top. His hand shook as he shifted the glass case to the notch of his hip, the other to his long and hopeless face. "This makes you happy, doesn't it?"

"As I told you before, reword your words, Cole. And if you'll notice…your bridge is fixed!" he said, nudging a waist high aim with his plump chin. Cole brought the toothpick bridge eye level, his bushy brows weighing down with his discovery. Though still through a long crack, he saw toothpicks, toothpicks butted up against one another in a neat row from here to there that a gravy boat could float under. A smile came to one side of his unshaven face, then flattened again like his home. "This bridge means a lot to me, but am I supposed to live here?"

Laura sighed from behind. She'd seen the fallen toothpicks this very morning, but what the hell, she just watched Cole's house fall to the river while standing beside a once crazy woman who this so-called mailman with new boots was here to make crazy again. Her sigh was of relief. The small miracle of toothpicks holding hands again was almost explainable in the scheme of things.

The mailman brought a hand to Cole's shoulder, which some might have seen as a suicidal move. "Just like before now, just like before. Try again," the mailman said, bringing his hands together to create a small clap.

Remembering the words used on the old forest service bridge, Cole spoke. "I *wish* this bridge, my home, was as it was before asshole here trampled over it with his voodoo!"

Laura jumped, pulling Miss Caffy with her in retreat as the giant red support beams moaned to life, lifting their heads from the carnage, spilling glass and tumbling furniture with its own mind as the once wreckage clawed along for an uphill lift. Ironically, thick engineering books were sucked from the water, defying any laws they supported, torn leather healing before their eyes, a brass floor lamp rocketing from the creek bank in the metallic whirl. Floor girders inhaling glass blocks back into their wrought iron jaws. French windows showering back together in their country white frames, ceiling beams beaming, the evil one's optical nerves plugging into its central brain system. James Bond's sly sloping grin a cool and confidant smirk again. Laura, hands on red head as if being frisked in front of Cole's home as it finished its own perfect touches, stereo on low, dining room table aglow, heat coming in a warm flow from a thermostatic click that told it to do so.

Cole had well known all along his home could be spared by a wish, that lesson had been learned a few exciting days ago. He'd been stalling, waiting for the right words to slip from the mailman that he desperately needed, and slip they did. Cole pivoted, meeting the mailman face to face who'd been dancing in place as the bridge crawled back together.

"What are you so happy about?" Cole scowled, noticing his mother out of the corner of his eye, her arms again waving in the Alaskan sky, but as if to say goodbye.

"Well, Cole, I never intended to destroy your home."

"No…just my mother."

The mailman's joy fell back to earth. "I am sorry, Cole…I am."

Miss Caffy and Laura glanced to Cole and his postman without blinking. Madelyn felt more than heard their following words. "This morning, your letter concerning Laura, you said you thought the words should come from me."

"Yes, Cole, I did."

"You still feel that way?" Cole asked, looking to the ground, his bottom lip failing, words spaced and broken.

"Cole, yes, I do. But please understand, I'm only following the rules, rules that we all have to learn getting our wishing legs."

"Then so be it," Cole grievingly said, his white face full of stare like the owner of a sick dog reaching for the family shotgun. Miss Caffy, Mom, watched her son approach with this unruly fact in his eyes. As he stood before her, she inhaled and let out a string of old fashioned tears looking to the silent Alaskan spruce, awaiting their twisting words to jump from their barking bark mouths. Cole's hands reached out to hers as Pilot looked into the sudden gust of wind that once brought savior to Madelyn, a wind now hungrily circling for a fine. As her candy store eyes closed, the mailman turned away, awaiting for the shot to be fired.

"Mom, I need you to listen to my every word. You'll never know how sorry I am, but we, it, can't have you chasing up stream looking for water running in a dry creek bed. So…I *wish* your sanity would…Never! Ever! Leave your side for the rest of your long, full, and happy life!"

The mailman spun on one foot, stopping in a squatted hat holding stance. "COLE!"

Miss Caffy, Mom from now on, felt the pardoning wind wisp gracefully away as she inhaled, drinking from its invisible glory. Her good son turned with a certain confidence to the dazed postman. "I did exactly what you told me to do, Mailman…I *wished* it so…just so!"

Cole expected the worst, but didn't care. He felt his sane mother was safe now and always would be. That's what truly mattered. He quietly awaited the rain of furious words, or to be wished away to stand in front of some jury with enraged miracle eyes, much like the postman's. "Do what you wish to me, but I think you'll have a hard time robbing my mother of what's hers forever. And Laura, remember, innocent Laura, who knows nothing other than thirty-minutes of crazy, is harmless. You saw to that this morning. And no doubt you'll steal that too before you run along."

The mailman squinted, licking his lips in a circle then corrected his postal eagle forward with both hands as if it were cleared for take off, one boot firmly aside the other. "You think you're a pretty smart feller don't ya, Mr. Caffy?" he quizzed, emphasizing Cole's last name as an angry principal might. "You must be under the impression you're ready to just jump up and kick a field goal with those new wishing legs of yours, huh?"

Cole let a confident smile unravel across his still sun burnt face. "I don't believe in ego, it's for the shallow folks we spoke of in one of your lessons. This has nothing to do with win or lose, maybe it does, but not in that light. I love my mother. I love the woman standing next to her, too. You're looking at everything that means anything to me. They're safe. The rest, I don't care, bring it on."

The mailman pulled mittens the color of stop from his deep pockets and tugged them on while shaking his head at the cloudless sky. "Well, Cole, you're right about Laura here. I'll have to fix this little problem, then I'm going to have to set you straight."

Cole felt a thousand scolds huddling to go over their play as the mailman walked past, flashing eyes to back up this theory. Laura crossed her arms then took two small steps back as all five-feet of mailman fatly swaggered up close to her.

"Miss Laura May Day, I need you to listen to me very closely. I *wish*…you knew everything you did this morning when you woke up beside this clever man of yours here. In my line of work we have to look inside peoples' hearts. His is a good one. That's why things are the way they are. It's plain to see you'll be by each other's side for some time. You might say he's already chosen to walk through life with you, he just hasn't gotten around to telling you this yet, but something tells me he will, soon," the mailman said, glancing to Cole with a slight grin. "Also, would you be so kind as to let Cole here know he's graduated. Tell him I won't be looking over his shoulder any longer. His wishing legs are strong and ready to walk on their own. And, oh yes, you might mention to his simply lovely mother, that I would have never done such a thing as sweep her mind back under the rug," he said, turning to warmly touch Miss Caffy's arm. "I'm sorry for it seeming so, Miss."

The mailman's eyes were soft and full of pride as he set these words free. Cole was nearly as stunned as Laura, who slowly began to remember the sound of violet and how she'd gotten to the Italian vineyard, snow moats and potholes, feathers and the tan hide of Cole's hand.

Miss Caffy stepped forward and kissed the mailman's pudgy cheek, whispering, "Thank you," as she hugged him. Pilot wished he could understand words.

"I *wish* you well…Mailman," Cole genuinely said, knowing the blue postal eagle was about to fly away to bless another life. Listening to the snow crunch under the mailman's black boots for the last time, Cole tilted his head to ask, "Hey, do you have a name?"

The mailman stopped, and half-turned just enough to let the others know he was smiling. "They used to call me…Ben. But Mailman just has a ring of its own, doesn't it?" he said, letting his legs do a little jig as he continued on, shouting into the breeze. "The trees are all done whispering now, Madelyn! Cat's got their tongue for keeps! If you need anything…just drop a line."

"Ben?" Cole whispered, turning to his speechless mother, a part of each of them wanting to believe what was stirring in their minds as they took each other's hands.

The mailman reached the white van and paused as if having a high school portrait taken with his favorite car, one red mitten raised in the freeze with a big wave. Resting axle-deep in the snow-packed trench it had plowed coming to its gouging halt, the postal van fired with a tin-throated roar echoing across the south thirty. It only shuddered back and forth once…then vanished.

After weaving from the apron of their spruce sanctuary, the does vigilantly paraded down the east slope with their fur-lined frames playfully bucking and thrusting, the spike-buck not in sight, but full of shy nearby. They ignored Pilot, busily finding the courage to advance for a sniff at their split-toed hooves, and corralled Madelyn, who was quick to grasp their ears and plow her fingers into their winter coats.

Laura stood her ground on a small rise of earth the south thirty offered as Cole quietly shuffled another moat around her. When the sphere was complete, he took one step back and spun in place to form a diamond. Her good hand came to her mouth to catch a gasp, she knew, she just wonderfully knew the way you do. She felt her crippled hand warm with his as he knelt before her. Tears, much like Mom's new ones, lined the bottom of her glazing green eyes as the Crazy Man Who Lives On a Bridge, spoke. "Miss Laura May Day, I've fixed your brakes, and you've stuffed me full of lemon bars. In my rear view mirror, I've seen you watch me from your window each time Rover and I left bouncing up your driveway. All this time, I thought you were just afraid you'd poured too much Irish in my coffee. Well, I want you to ride off with me this time, Laura, to anywhere you wish…forever. I love you…will you marry me?"

Before Laura could answer standing in the center her diamond engagement moat, Madelyn stepped forward politely clearing her throat. "Forgive me, but this has seen me through more than a million sane people could ever imagine." Cole watched the square of black onyx twist free from his mother's finger for the first time ever in his life. It was passed to him with a warm squeeze from motherly hands and a trembling smile, his reflection in it, the best one yet…yet.

Cole held the ring before Laura. Her purple hand wanting so badly to gobble it up forever, instead pulled away to her side, embarrassed of its gnarled knuckles. Cole saw it hiding there ritually over the moon of her thigh. He took it, bringing the crippled hand forth with his and cradled it there between them. He stared into the web of scars, wishing just under his breath. As he began inching the black onyx ring over the twisted bone of her finger, Cole watched as her entire hand amazingly erased itself of any tattered tissue, for good. Feeling only a tiny tickle deep in her palm, Laura batted her emerald eyes open in disbelief to smooth pink skin the color of health. Speechless, she wiggled her new fingers one by one as if counting the ways she loved him.

Struggling to keep more tears from coming, Laura Day failed, and fell in those arms she could and would spend a lifetime in.

"Yes, Cole…and forever."

twelve

Cowboys have the endless western range while astronomers have the solar system and beyond. Mechanics have the '69 z28 and photographers have what the eye beholds. Prisoners have cell floor sundials made of striped sunlight as the Ruddy Turnstone has unbarred flight. Coyotes have dirt holes they call home, but rarely alone. Cole and Laura now have one another. Life goes on unfolding under our idle feet, so hop to it!

Wedding Invitation

Who would have ever thought that a guy like me would have found a gal like this?

Laura May Day

Has accepted my proposal of marriage. As I should do this quickly before she changes her mind, you are invited to the Crazy Man Who Lives On a Bridge's bridge. This Saturday, November twenty second, at one o'clock in the afternoon. I wish all those who receive this will be able to attend.

Thank You,
Cole L Caffy

Before Anna could finish, her happy finger depressed a clear button marked P. "Philip! Are you in?"

"No, but as long as I have you on the horn, could you please call the police. I hear there's an extremely handsome cuss rattling around behind my desk. Just give them my description and they'll catch the bastard right quick!"

"It's Cole…HE'S GETTING MARRIED!" This was nearly muted by heel clicking jolts of joy, her chair's spider legs skating to one side then the other of its protective plastic rink, her small fists striking in an offbeat drum roll.

"Married? Holy shit! If my secretary calls, tell her I'm out. Something big's come up!" Philip left the phone glued to his hairy ear and poked a plastic button still marked C.

"Yes, this is Bridge," she answered, staring at a three-sided ruler as if it were lying to her, rows of black hair trickling over her soft face to the tilted drafting table, one long leg resting just so around the other.

"You in?"

"No, I'm sorry you just missed me, but you better call the cops, I hear there's this amazingly beautiful woman working hard at my desk."

"Yeah, no shit," Philip mumbled, raising a brow above the rim of his round glasses like the fender of a bicycle's tire that could see.

"What was that?"

"Uh…nothing, never mind. You won't believe this one! Cole's getting married!"

"Married? I was about to dash out and give Anna CPR, sounds like she's spotted the only roach in Alaska pitchin' camp in her pantyhose!"

Philip thought about beating his desk until Bridget rounded the corner, mouth open throwing one of those golden legs over his savage chest while screaming his name, the other brow raised, dual fenders.

"Married…to who?" she asked, waiting for Philip to start banging on his desk until she rounded the corner, mouth open, throwing a leg over for improper CPR.

"Be damned, I'll have to call ya back!" The letter A glowed under his finger. The stamping of pointy navy blue work shoes magnified as A picked up. "To who, Anna?"

Atop her excited lungs, she let the name "Laura May Day" fly through her happy lips from clear over Here to There.

✉

Cole Caffy's close friend the Alaskan morning was the first to attend that Saturday, bringing the best gift of all, itself. The sun crept over the south thirty with the ease and grace of a good story filling its reader with warmth and possibilities. Pilot didn't think much of his black bow tie until Uncle Cole pointed out with his noisemaker tongue that it resembled a propeller, twisting it side-to-side, "ptpt-zzz-pop-zzz-t."

From the passing Ruddy Turnstone's aerial view, one would see the red and silver twinkle of an airport van winding its way to a house that comfortably stretched over a river. The driver coming round to offer a hand with luggage and then a pine crate from the swinging rear doors where in the round-eyed mirror a pretty dark skinned girl who loved the ocean said, "Tiz cold." The small boy ponied-up a squeak as his eyes climbed trees taller than the mightiest of cruise ships, his mother offering her tropic hands to the Alaskan sky as if reaching for the ledge of a winter's window to see if this guy Santa Claus really did live nearby.

Spying through the sheer haze of living room drapes, the name "Rosa" softly poured from the groom's lips while admiring the vibrant colors of her traveling wardrobe, her shy daughter anxious to see the man that vanished from the knoll of a park near her island home. The driver thought it funny how the three stared at one another's breath pumping out in short amazed laughs, the boy bending down to touch the snow as if he'd dropped a secret.

Laura's new hand came to Cole's back. "Are you alright?"

"Yes, yes I am…and today is going to be a wonderful day, Miss Day."

Pilot and his bow tie shot across the glass floor in a huff. As Laura turned to the sudden commotion, her mouth fell open seeing not just a mouse, but a mouse with racing stripes making a scurrying charge for the kitchen. Cole caught this out of the corners of his sky blue eyes and calmly closed them over a smile as a familiar voice poured softly from behind. "Mister Cole, we heard yellow. It was the sound of the seasons changing….I'd like to think it had something to do with an old friend turning into a new love."

"Yes…I should think it did, Miss Clara Tout," Cole said, wiping his eyes before hugging the woman that knew what a hug was worth, leaning over to pump Donny's small hand as if waiting for water to pour from his mouth.

The next to pop up from Patch was Anna's red Blazer, proudly driven by her son Brett. Anna darted from the four-wheel drive with presents in hand toward the Minister and others told to gather atop a flat spot the south thirty offered. Brett, bright headed, tall and quiet, paused and turned to the kitchen window where Cole had been secretly watching him walk past, fumbling with his only black dress tie. As Brett made grinning eye contact, Cole realized that he was looking at the closest thing to a son he would ever know. Literally his best man.

Jenny Massey hopped from her Volkswagen bus waving an exhausted finger, threatening to leave her brats tied to a tree draped with raw lox of bear pleasing salmon, then letting nature run its course if 'things' didn't cease at once! The fattest one suddenly wanted fish.

Philip held the Suburban's door open as Caroline gracefully slid from the leather bucket seat. He liked how her tight thigh escaped its skirt for an instant.

Laura's dress flowed from the curve of her shoulders to just below the knee like Spring Creek over its smooth stones, her cinnamon hair thick and alive highlighting her charming face just so, lumps in the ends of her white shoes.

Madelyn did her job well, of directing traffic away from the bride and groom, easing guests outdoors where they found themselves perfectly surrounded by the sound of running water disappearing over a stony edged fall, blackberry bushes kneeling before the massive feet of the giant spruce, offering their fruit in return for protection from wind storms and summer hail. And a bridge, a bridge designed by a fortunate man that knew it.

Cole let his hand slide from Laura's. She thought snow boots to be out of place and said her last words to him as a single woman. "Runnin' off on me already?"

"Only long enough to have a word with the ring bearer," Cole answered. "I love you Laura…and I'll do whatever it takes to let you know that each and every day."

As her eyes glassed over, Cole pulled the door closed and tromped away in the snow.

A new white Subaru with dealer tags came to a stop beside Philip's gas hog. Bridget stepped out all covered in a dress suit that told no lies. Her date closed the passenger door and reached for Bridget's hand before joining the others. "Bridge, are you still comfortable with this? I don't know Cole that well. I think he likes me but he might jump up with a fit just the same."

"Cole? No. I have a feeling everything will work out just fine, Holly, just fine."

As all gathered on the south thirty, Cole removed his earflap hat while shaking off the snow boots and slipped into a couple of nice black leather dress flats. He looked down to his amazing group of friends gathering for his and Miss Day's wonderful day, thankful for each. Laura and Madelyn, standing just behind the downstairs door that exited ground level to center stage, embraced. Trotting to the kitchen, Cole exhaled as he roamed his gaze up to Patch, one invitation unanswered. He sadly smiled and understood this as his handsome reflection faded from the window.

Brett and Cole, side by side, no words needed, both equally proud to be standing in front of such good people. The big French barn windows swung open and music washed over the river and through the woods right on cue as the entire wedding party gasped seeing thirteen Sitka black tailed deer prance from the tree line as if apologizing for being a touch late. "Good Christ, it's even hunting season!" Philip whisper yelled. Rosa had never seen a deer and thought that Alaskan Airlines must have really doctored up their pamphlet on grizzly bears, a lot!

Laura stole the attention away from the fearless does as she was escorted by a woman who just days ago silently wished for her life to end. Madelyn was the first to grow tears, and then Anna, as Cole reached for his fiancée's hand. The smiling minister, spotted tie draped over a half moon belly, short dress pants neatly tucked in shiny black boots. Laura had said she would take care of the formalities, so she did. Cole so pleasantly taken back, saw the man that had seen to the prompt delivery of wedding invitations, saw the man responsible for his standing here in more ways than he knew. "You're a man of the cloth?"

"Physics, Cole, what goes up must come down," the mailman whispered through a grin, then pointed a stubby finger toward Patch. "Your last guest, I assume?"

Cole's eyes shined, as he spotted the gleam of a black Range Rover ambling down his drive. "Yes, my last guest."

The others turned, thinking Cole must have lent his Rover out before one small detail caught their eye as its driver stepped free the British 4x4, *Last Frontier Rentals* reading in thick letters across the front bumper. As the man and his life-long wife approached, Holly was the first to suck in cold breath and hold it there nearly too long.

"Please, forgive our tardiness. Driving on the wrong side of the road is a bit unsettling, somewhat like finding a dozen deer masquerading as bridesmaids you moight say," he said in that wonderful Scottish tongue, looking to the line of fawn-colored girls. "You said the last frontier was wild, Coole, but I had no idea."

"Thank you for coming, Mr. Connery," Cole said, proudly nodding to his lovely wife and softly shaking her hand.

"Let's just say I was intrigued," Connery said, tossing one brow up with a sly grin.

All were still as the happy-go-lucky minister sprinkled his uniting words over Cole Caffy and Laura Day, but reeled as he gestured to the silver haired groom for the exchange of rings. Amidst the gasping and now standing crowd, two gold wedding bands poked forth from the spruce high about the spike rack of the shy white-bellied buck, one slid perfectly over each pointy antler. "Good God, I'm standing ten feet from one of the biggest movie stars in the world and now there's a wild deer delivering wedding rings!" Philip leaked under his breath, receiving a sharp nudge in the ribs from Caroline who was trying to remember the name of a certain submarine movie.

The spike buck cautiously lowered his head and Cole carefully plucked the rings like fruit from a gem-bearing bush, Laura covering her mouth as the spike buck's tongue gently drug across her healed hand. As Laura said, "I do" her chin trembled a little, as well as

Rosa's and Anna's, Philip managed to look away before Caroline could see.

The minister leaned in close, lightly resting his hand atop theirs. Proudly he pronounced them husband and wife, then *wished* them a wonderful future together…his gift.

Two cakes connected by a frosting bridge were cut with a double-fisted knife center Cole and Laura Caffy's glass living room floor. As the newlyweds held their pose long enough to be machine-gunned by Anna's Canon, Cole saw Bridget near the back of the crowd saying everything with a smile that he thought was made just for him…it was.

Sean Connery made his hand shaking rounds after leaving the den where he'd been grinning at his own grin, then stopped before the bride and groom. With a curly little smile of her own, Laura said, "I understand you two met on a train?"

Leaning in close to gently raise her healed hand to a kiss, Connery smoothly said, "I had no idea how fortunate a man I was meeting that day. You're simply beautiful, Mrs. Caffy."

His Scottish accent rolled off his complimenting tongue as he shook Cole's hand, pressing a leather Range Rover key ring in his palm. Stitched on the backside was: *Friend, not Foe.*

There went the sun again behind Rosa's tropical gown with Cole wrapped inside. He then lowered his eyes to the daughter as she quietly offered her present. It was a piece of paper carefully tied with blue ribbon. He opened it, found it to be an acceptance letter from Florida State University. Cole whispered, "Your father would be so proud," as he hugged her and smelled the ocean in her hair.

Anna threw her arms around Cole and squeezed, then loosened to draw in a breath before squeezing again. Brett gave him an engraved Forest Service badge that said, *Thank You* across its silver banner, Anna still squeezing.

Clara Tout came from the group holding an envelope with Donny's hand colored rainbow dancing from edge-to-edge. Cole grinned as he opened it and pulled out a picture of a bright cherry red Ford pickup gleaming as though it had just left the showroom floor. "Clara says I can get my license in just six and a half more years. License, L-I-C-E-N-S-E. What I need to drive that!" Donny's piped, his finger anxiously bending the picture's corner.

Philip pounded at Cole's shoulder after embracing him as Caroline kissed his cheek then spun in place to wrap her arms around Laura. Bless their souls, but they'd arrived with the one gift the Caffy's didn't need, luggage.

Yellow haired Holly inched forward and climbed up between Cole's forearms to leave a small kiss, then left behind a gift certificate that showed people eating in a fancy restaurant as others played golf just beyond. "From what I know, you have a great lady here, Cole."

"So do you," he said, loud enough for Bridget to overhear.

The ever elusive little mailman came front and center the very bridge that once lay fallen in the river below. "Well, Cole, you've done it, just like I always knew you would. And Laura Caffy, as I've told you before, this man has a good heart, just as you do. Sometimes life has its way of bringing things together as they should be," he proudly said, before catching Cole off guard with a hug, another for Laura. He then quietly dismissed himself for the last time after kissing Madelyn softly on the lips. He vanished with a wide smile moments later from the kitchen when Cole had everyone's attention.

Taking Laura's hand, Cole stepped to the center of their home. "Could I have everyone's attention please?" his strong northern voice carrying well across the bridge.

"I retired just three weeks ago. I won't lie to you, I was scared. I was scared of wondering what happens to an old lonely guy that didn't know much more that how to build a bridge. Now as I look across the one I, we, call home, I see there's nothing to fear. I want each and every one of you not just to know, but to remember from here on out, you are my friends, and that is what matters in this life we all share. Now," Cole said, smiling to his bride. "I'm going to take my wife's hand and lead her to those distant places we've both only dreamt about. Thank you all so much, for just being you."

Anna, drowning behind a smear of happy tears, cleared her throat and fired a sharp, "HEAR, HEAR!" that everyone loudly echoed, creating another snapshot for Cole's cherished mental photo-album of memories, Laura's healed hand coming to his chest felt like Christmas morning.

"Meester Caffy, Meester Caffy! You did not open our wedding present we bring for you!"

“The best for last Rosa, the best for last,” he said through a smile, following all of Rosa out to the circular driveway, where again he saw the rectangular pine crate. Alaskan Airlines tape claimed what was inside was ‘fragile’ stuck about in bold blue-and-red lettering. Brett came with a long handled screwdriver and surgically passed it to Cole as the others gathered around. The pine cried as he pried. Laura stood back as the long slender top came free with a splintering pop, Rosa starting to bob up and down in place, hands softly clapping.

Cole peered downward, deep into the crate. He could not speak as he saw himself in a chrome gas cap that made it appear he was hanging on the rear wing of a jet fighter, when actually car horns were its uphill motivation. His square chin shook as he ripped free the side in a wash of squeaky packing spilling over his feet. On the neck of its skinny pink gas tank, Laura read *Meester and Meesis Caffy*, straddled by fancy stick-on racing stripes that curled away under the tie-dye seat of Numba seventeen.

Rosa was used to doing the eclipsing and only knew to throw her arms open as Cole wrapped around her as though she’d been lost at sea.

Numba seventeen’s BB gun tailpipe offered a small gray choke to the sunny Alaskan chill as Laura snorted and hiked a leg over, pressing herself against her biker hubby twisting the throttle. Cole’s thankful eyes roamed through his crowd of dear friends, stalling them on his mother with an ear-to-ear smile. She knew what he was telling her.

As he felt all 80cc’s rumbling under him, he looked to his friend and not foe standing with his famous curled grin. “Mr. Connery, what’s your next movie?”

“…This one.”

The guests parted down the middle as Cole eased out the clutch spitting snow from its knobby rear tire, Laura’s left hand waving. The crowd cheered as Numba seventeen slipped side-to-side with Cole’s legs fanning wide, cautious of his new bride.

Clara Tout, Donny and Coin Something, Philip and Caroline Norran, Rosa, her boy, and her bright futured daughter, Mr. and Mrs. Connery, Jenny and two fat tots, Bridget Poland and Holly Maple, Madelyn 'Mom' and Pilot, all watched the retired engineer and wife ride off over the knoll of Patch Road on a steel pink horse, where Rosa would later stand quietly trying to tickle the electric belly of the northern lights.

"Where are we going?" Cole shouted to the wind.

"Anywhere you *wish* my love…anywhere you *wish*!"

As Numba seventeen disappeared down a smooth gray stretch of road, Laura and Cole heard the color lightning white. The cold breeze freezing their hair back, thawed in a sudden rush of warm wind. Amazed, Laura watched their favorite little road burst to four lanes, and looked up to see the giant red steel pillars of the Golden Gate Bridge passing overhead as though they were supporting the cloudless Californian sky.

Lightning white, the sound of all good things colliding to create one stampeding destiny.

afterward

Time working on a canvas made of stars, painted eleven years over everything one could see, touch, hear, taste or smell with its invisible strokes. Storms came and went, buildings were erected, crops rose up and leapt in grain silos scared by the sound of diesel engines running all hours, over eight thousand tides tried to climb on land only to fail, a cancer research scientist finally shot up from his swiveling chrome stool far too stunned to cheer or scream, all Range Rovers from the twentieth century were declared collectors' items.

Lost over the years were Caroline Norran, auto accident; and Pilot, tuckered, lay down in a ball and slept like an angel. One was buried in a cemetery, the other near a stony edged waterfall. They both were greatly missed.

Anna said, "Oh, I'm sorry, excuse me," to a nice tall man named Gary while visiting her son Brett in Colorado Springs, Colorado, who now wears a badge with his name engraved across its silver banner. Anna married that nice tall man eight months later. They now live in Durango.

Cole and Laura Caffy went on to cross many bridges, some they stopped to dance on in slow circles, whispering things that brought a lovely shade of blush to Laura's cheeks, Cole and his silver mop had their ways. They cruised the Western Australian Basin in a glowing nineteen fifty-six cherry red pick-up that Donny Something still waxes each weekend, the license plate in capital letters, WISH 1. Clara Tout went on to, well, if I told you the mailman may well show up at your doorstep and pick it from your memory, so as not to waste your time, I'll go on.

The Caffy's sailed a Westsail 32 in bubbling tropical seas to quiet lagoons until one afternoon when Rosa's daughter strolled down the dock and proudly handed Cole another gift of paper tied with blue ribbon. She now works with a research team in the Americas developing water whistles that attach to commercial fishing nets only dolphins can hear.

Madelyn Caffy promptly moved into Laura Day's home six miles up river where she would call her son and tell him to be ready with his net to catch another message in a bottle she had just set free. Cole once freed a note that read, "Please disregard this message as I was lost, but my son, whom I love, has found me."

Five of the Sitka black tails had disappeared from the local herd that Cole and Laura had more or less adopted, others brought new life to the south thirty with soft spotted hides. Each of the newborns were named as they first balanced atop their spread legged hooves that soon sprouted to wobbling hops of courage. Spike, as he had permanently named the leader of the pack, went on to grow a beautiful six-pointed rack that Cole would grasp onto as they played on the banks of Spring Creek year after year. One biting winter night turned into a weeklong forty below blow and the entire herd was brought into the garage. Cole left the kitchen door ajar just long enough to fetch more spare blankets. He returned to find only a still unused red kayak overhead and an aging set of golf clubs in the far corner. He heard Laura's snorting giggle from behind as she immediately gave in and pushed aside the living room furniture so they each could see the frozen river below. Cole duct taped pillows to Spike's rack; he looked like, well, let's just say the does stared but those were the house rules. Another bedded down on the leather couch and huffed at Cole's nudging gestures to the uncomfortable glass floor.

Finding himself wishing for less and less as he continually discovered he had more and more, Cole took up the hobby of designing furniture in his retirement. He created wonderful high back sleeping benches and sold the plans to a Colorado ski resort. One was also donated to an engineering firm in Anchorage, now run by an extremely beautiful woman.

It was a bench of this design that Cole tugged to the deck he'd added to his home over the river. The leaves on the ground were dry as the October sky. From the waterfall down stream, beside a tiny cross, one could see Cole carefully sliding his latest bench in a way as not to scar the new maple deck. The wooden legs of the sleeping bench slipped from his hands as he jerked up straight, hearing a not so distant rifle shot echo from deep within the spruce. He spun and looked to the herd, feverishly counting under his breath. All were present and raised their noses to the bang, all except for Spike.

"No!" Cole pleaded, running through the kitchen past Laura, grabbing his brown jean jacket from the garage's hook. Hurrying to the deck with her arms to her side, Laura watched Cole claw wildly his way up the south bank and disappear in the thicket tree line.

He ran for all he was worth, waiting for that next horrifying shot to ring close. He stopped and put an ear to the breeze, just how Daniel had shown him to. He heard human voices, heard their bodies pushing aside brush in an excited blunder. Cole dodged over downed trees and through a muddy shallow. There, there he saw the six-pointed rack lying on the ground, shuddering just behind a bush that produced sweet blackberries in the spring. He hurried to the buck he'd known for more than a decade. He draped himself over its dying body and held him as the shaking kick began to fade with its soul.

Cole never heard the hunters side winding across the forest floor. He never heard the next round being chambered. Laura came running behind as the crosshairs were placed on Cole's light brown jacket, the color of the fatally wounded deer. The rifle kicked in the pocket of the hunter's shoulder as the trigger was pulled back. Laura fell to her knees and screamed her husband's name to the witnessing spruce, then rushed to his side. The black shine of warm gun barrel lowered, then fell to the earth beside fur-lined boots, realizing its mistaken prey.

Cole knew Laura was holding him, but couldn't respond, couldn't tell her to stop crying, couldn't tell her how much it hurt to see her do so, couldn't say simply, "I love you back," the sun's reflection the only glimmer in his blue-gray eyes, a small puncture hole in the back of his coat.

As the last breath eased from Cole's lips, he felt the white-hot pain through his middle subside. All was as still as it was quiet. The sound of Laura muted. Suddenly he was looking at himself, looking at Laura rocking with what one leaves behind. As he stood, a hand came to his shoulder and a dog with far too much skin to his feet. He turned to discover someone wonderful and struggled out, "…Daniel?"

"How could you have ever thought I'd be mad at you, Cole? You kept your promise to me. And who in their right mind could spend any time with her and not fall desperately in love? Thank you my friend…I've missed you."

Cole turned back toward Laura and Spike, finding only a small group of blood-stained autumn leaves strewn about the ground, hours had passed. Daniel brought his old friend's attention to a nearby gathering of blackberry bushes. In awe, Cole watched as a beautiful six-pointed rack raised in a salute, then pranced into the forest, his black tail waving good bye for the last time.

Cars filled the Montgomery Church parking lot as if Easter had fallen early on Anchorage, Alaska that year. Laura, front row, red hair just so, sat staring into the black square of onyx that once belonged to the ninety-five year old woman sitting at her side. The minister drew a deep breath before the quiet and grieving crowd, his half-moon belly trapped by an unforgiving belt, the tip of his black boots aglow. He exhaled and spoke through a warm grin with a clear and confident voice.

"How can we be sad today?" his question raising heads from the floor. "Oh, yes, I will miss Cole Caffy, too, but…I got to know Cole Caffy," he said, pointing to the ceiling. "And in my book that's reason for celebration. He didn't leave you behind, Laura. He didn't leave any of us behind. He just went ahead early. And if I know Cole, it was probably just to make certain the coast is clear. Well, I'm going to tell you all this once, one time, so listen up! The coast is clear! And the Crazy Man who once lived on a bridge, is there! Going on about being his same magical self…so maybe *that* will answer the smile on my face, on this sad day. I knew Cole Caffy."

Laura once bashfully told Cole her three wishes over lemon bars and Irish coffee. Two had come true. Then wonderfully the third as the mail-delivering minister glanced to her with an all-knowing glimmer.

"Laura Caffy…I think, no in fact I'm certain, Cole would have *wished* to hear you sing here today."

Laura's hands tightened into balls as her third wish crept out from her many memories like hearing a familiar note created by striking a precise key, a key that lingered in Laura's musical mind as she stood to her own, as well as the others, total amazement. The minister's eyes closed with Laura's as the church filled with a beautiful voice, a voice that could light up the dark winters.

Two days later, the one remaining Cessna of *All Day Airlines* was rolled from what it believed to be its own tin hanger tomb at Anchorage International. Laura's fear of the killing sky beat in her heart along with the pulse of the four cylinders pounding up and down behind the propeller that brought to mind Cole spinning Pilot high about the living room skies. Her hand shook as she released the ground brake, then pulling the plunger throttle from the dash she began a soothing song just behind her breath. A man in a blue jumpsuit said to another smoking a cigarette, "That's the lady that lost her husband. That plane's sat back there for better than fifteen years. Look at her go!"

She sang just that much louder as the little black wheels stopped spinning and left the earth. Seat belted beside her, an urn. One Cole would have liked, she thought.

A white Cessna broke the silence rolling downward at Light House Lake. The yoke was drawn back and the plane leveled out just off the ice. Whirling blades screamed at the sleeping snow, scaring it from the flat lake in streaming hoops just behind. The plastic window opened,

"Good bye, my friend."

The End

What ardently we wish we soon believe.

♦ *Young*

a note from Troy

Wishes, huh? To think what would become of our world if all had it their way. As Sigmund Freud once stated, "We all are great in our dreams." So would there be created a blissful Heaven on earth under a rainbow that did not shy away as enlightened you approached to touch? Or would the criminally ingenious have discovered their ultimate tool to seemingly fill their empty souls? Chaos my friends, that is certain. And to wish that away, I fear in fact the power of a wish itself would be the guilty party removed. When anger causes our fists to shake at the skies, we must remember, if there is a creator, total chaos would have been far too harsh and fleeting a lesson, leaving no room for character to be born and grow, grow damn you, grow! Because in the end, it is what we are, and what we have, that no one can steal. Deny this if you wish, but know it to be true in everything you do. This is life's game we play, willing or not.

Troy O'Neill
January 31, 2001

October 2007

The cast as seen in my imagination:

Cole Caffy .... Sean Connery
Sean Connery .... Sean Connery
Anna ....Megan Cavanaugh

Roommate from Hollywood California, who later appeared as Marla Hooch in the Penny Marshall movie *A League of Their Own,* also won roles in a number of sitcoms including *Home Improvement*.

Mailman .... Danny Devito
Holly Maple ....Gail Schramm

My cousin - not gay!

Laura May Day ....Annette Benning
Clara Tout...Fennie

My great Aunt, who was a great aunt.

Pilot..Bingo

My own childhood dog, and best friend.

Bridget Poland... Name unknown

A woman I only stood beside
for a breathtaking minute
nine years ago in Kennedy Airport.

All other characters' faces and limbs were painted strictly from imagination.

a note from Lori

I was lucky to be a part of Troy's life for almost fifteen years. He was brilliant, funny, thoughtful and caring. He had a special place in his heart for the underprivileged and for animals, as you can find from between the lines in this book.

Troy's life was tragically cut short due to an auto accident on December 2, 2007. It was his dream, shall I say, *wish*, that this book find it's way to publication and he worked very hard for that over many years. I'm honored to bring ***Wish*** to his family and friends now, and can only hope that each of you enjoy reading it as much as I do, and as much as Troy enjoyed writing it.

I would like to thank the following:

Gary & Sharon (Troy's parents), Wayne & Helen (Troy's grandparents), Garry & Marcia (Troy's step-parents), Patty (my mom) and Becky (my sister) – for their emotional support and encouragement.

Mike (my dad) – for his immense help with editing the final copy.

Numerous friends – for always believing in me.

I love you all!

www.lconeill.blogspot.com